CARRY TIGER TO MOUNTAIN

CARRY TIGER TO MOUNTAIN

An Elias McCann Mystery

Mark Zuehlke

A Castle Street Mystery

THE DUNDURN GROUP
TORONTO · OXFORD

Copy-editor: Jennifer Bergeron
Design: Jennifer Scott
Printer: Webcom

Canadian Cataloguing in Publication Data

Zuehlke, Mark
    Carry tiger to mountain / Mark Zuehlke.

(A Castle Street mystery)
ISBN 1-55002-417-5

I. Title. II. Series: Castle Street mystery.

PS8599.U33C37 2002   C813'.6   C2002-902278-9
PR9199.4.Z83C37 2002

1   2   3   4   5   06   05   04   03   02

 Canada

THE CANADA COUNCIL | LE CONSEIL DES ARTS
FOR THE ARTS | DU CANADA
SINCE 1957 | DEPUIS 1957

ONTARIO ARTS COUNCIL
CONSEIL DES ARTS DE L'ONTARIO

We acknowledge the support of the **Canada Council for the Arts** and the **Ontario Arts Council** for our publishing program. We also acknowledge the financial support of the **Government of Canada** through the **Book Publishing Industry Development Program** and **The Association for the Export of Canadian Books**, and the **Government of Ontario** through the **Ontario Book Publishers Tax Credit** program.

Care has been taken to trace the ownership of copyright material used in this book. The author and the publisher welcome any information enabling them to rectify any references or credit in subsequent editions.

J. Kirk Howard, President

Printed and bound in Canada. ♻
Printed on recycled paper.

Dundurn Press
8 Market Street
Suite 200
Toronto, Ontario, Canada
M5E 1M6

Dundurn Press
73 Lime Walk
Headington, Oxford,
England
OX3 7AD

Dundurn Press
2250 Military Road
Tonawanda NY
U.S.A. 14150

Special thanks to Frances Backhouse, whose red pen worked wonders, for believing in Elias and company and being so endlessly supportive. Thanks to the folks at Dundurn who also have shown such faith in this series. I am indebted to my agent, Carolyn Swayze, for making it possible for this writer to pursue his dreams.

Readers familiar with Tofino, Ucluelet, and Pacific Rim National Park may find some discrepancies between their world and that of Elias McCann. This is as it should be for Elias's world is as fictional as the people who populate it while such readers live in a world that is presumably more closely linked to reality.

Prologue

There was no warning. One moment the old freighter cruised on a gentle sea toward a narrow, rocky shoreline backed by towering green mountains whose summits were cloaked by silky bands of stratus cloud. The next, the temperature plummeted and the cloud rolled down, metamorphosing into a dense, impenetrable fog. For days only a gentle easterly had dusted across the bow, playfully riffling the crew's hair and carrying just enough of a chill that the men were grateful for the covering of their threadbare sweaters. Now a hard southerly shrilled across the deck and the ship yawed violently to port as the first rising wave struck the starboard flank. Though he was no sailor, Kim Hoai knew they were in trouble. His instinct was confirmed when the next wave slammed the 120-foot-long ship over so sharply that its portside gunnel was almost broached by the foaming white water.

Clutching the handle of the bridge's starboard door for support, Kim heard the fear in Captain Liou's voice as he snapped an order that set the man at the wheel spinning it sharply to bring the ship around to face the rushing waves. Even Cheng, wearing his trademark black leather jacket over a white shirt and stonewashed jeans, was pale faced, white knuckles locked on the edge of the map table. His wide eyes were fixed on Liou's back. *You brought us to this*, Kim thought. *Despite your guns and knives, you too are powerless.* The ship started to come about, engines roaring, throttle opened wide. The bang of a hard impact was followed by a violent shudder that coursed down the length of the ship, and then the rattling vibration caused by the straining engine abruptly ceased. The only noise remaining was the screaming wind and the hiss of water sloshing across the outside deck as the steep waves broke over the starboard side. In thirty-six days of sailing there had been three engine failures. Each had taken at least two hours to repair. They did not have two hours. There was a coastline and they surged toward it, carried by the current and the rising fury of the waves.

The captain yelled more orders, something about rudders. Kim wrenched the door open and dragged himself onto the catwalk, staggered downstairs to the door that led below decks. A wall of water cascaded across the lower deck and bitingly cold spray drenched him. Wearing only a white T-shirt, black denims, and sneakers, Kim was left shivering almost uncontrollably. The boat heaved perilously over on its port side. Kim grabbed the slippery rail and hung on grimly. Directly below him was nothing but the swirling madness of sea. With a shudder and a shriek of twisting steel the ship righted itself. Kim sensed it turning slightly, riding the waves so that its stern faced the next approaching wave. They were shooting forward with the waves, the rusty freighter transformed into a surfboard. Heading toward shore. Through the fog, Kim could dimly see the wildly *bucking outline of the bow. Anything could be out there directly ahead of them. If the stern bore up too high on a following wave the bow would cut so deeply into the sea that the old ship might flip. Or, given its dilapidated condition, just break into pieces.*

There was very little time. Kim made his way inside, lurching wildly from one side of the hallway to the other as he staggered toward the radio room. In the cargo hold, from which the stench of unwashed bodies, spilled urine, vomit, and fear had increased with each passing day, things must be far worse. No time to think of them now. The radio room was deserted. Kwan should have been there. Or one of the others. Someone should send a distress signal. Kim was only a cook. He knew nothing of radios. The satellite phone. A minute, not even that. A handful of words then, no more. His fingers fumbled with the controls. The slip of paper was in his pocket, as it had been since he had scribbled down the information that day in the square in Phnom Penh, but he knew the number by heart. Had looked at it so many times. He waited, prayed to a God that had betrayed them all long ago, this, His final joke.

A voice, surprisingly casual, foreign, yet familiar, speaking in the cadence of one talking to everyone and yet to no one in particular. English language. She must be saying to leave a message. Surprisingly, he had not prepared for this, never even considered it. All the words that had been in his mind to speak were Chinese, Khmer, or French and he had always imagined her listening attentively and joyously to his words, then answering in French. He knew only a few faltering, utterly inappropriate words of English. He could not speak to her in the language of America. "This is Cousin Kim," he was acutely aware of how timid he sounded as he resorted to Khmer, the language he had been forced to speak for so many years, instead of the French or Chinese which had come more naturally, the languages of the family home. "I tried to reach you. But, my cousin, it is not to be. Sorry. Live for us." What else was there to say? There was no time to explain the hope the little card found in the square that day had engendered. To describe the reason he was here, or even where here was. All that was meaningless now. Kim broke the connection. Let her live. She was the last one.

Behind him a noise. Kwan staggered from the head, pale faced, bile running putrid yellow down his shirt from a gasping mouth. "You should give a mayday signal," Kim said. The two of them were abruptly thrown the length of the corridor to crash with sickening force into the wall at the other end. The starboard door flew open way back up the tunnel of the corridor, which Kim realized was now almost directly above them, and a solid mass of water hammered down onto the two entwined men. Capsizing, Kim thought. Just as suddenly as the water suffocated them, however, it boiled away and the world turned mostly right side up.

Kwan rolled off of him, screaming. The man's right arm was pulled far back from his shoulder. He fled down the corridor, ignoring Kim's cries for him to send a mayday alert. Kim staggered after him, then, as the bow dug deep into the sea and suddenly chucked upward, hung onto a fire extinguisher bolted to the wall. Down the corridor, Kwan blasted up into the ceiling like a rag doll and there was a frightening crack. No time to check. Kim threw himself into the radio room and yanked at the handset. How to send? He had no idea. He squeezed the button on the handset like they did in war movies and shouted: "Mayday. Mayday." There was a knob on the set in front of him that looked like it could turn through channels and he remembered something about a distress channel. Perhaps he should turn the knob and try to find that channel. As his hand reached out for the knob, Kim sensed a presence behind him. Looking over his shoulder, Kim stared into Cheng's dull, flat eyes.

"Get away from it," Cheng snapped in Mandarin. He held a long, thin-bladed knife like those used by fishermen to gut their catch. Kim placed the handset gently on the table. The radio room was too small for him to move away. Cheng's breath was warm and bitterly scented by the endless cigarettes he smoked.

"We should call for help," Kim said. He loathed the quaver he heard in his own voice. It reminded him of past failures of courage, of bowing to other killers.

Then the ship clanged hard against something immovable, there was a terrific grinding and Kim slammed into Cheng, sending him sprawling across the corridor. Kim popped out of the radio room like a cork from a bottle and tumbled dizzyingly down the narrow hallway toward an open door that was swinging wildly back and forth. Another wrenching twist that bounced him up and down on the floor and the ship was at least momentarily right-side up. Kim groaned, found his feet. Cheng was there, the knife still in his hand. "The radio," Kim said, and moved toward the cabin. It was, he believed, their only hope.

"No," Cheng barked and the knife flashed. Kim felt a cold shock slice across his abdomen from just above his navel to the outside of his right ribcage. There was the grating sound of steel on bone as the knife scoured along one rib and then swiped out of him and rang against the wall of the corridor as the ship again heeled over. Kim was once more bowled down the corridor and this time he allowed the momentum to carry him all the way to the doorway, kicked the door back with one leg, and threw himself out on the deck. Water boiled around his waist and across the deck *before him as he managed to grasp a swinging line of rope with one hand.*

He could hear a terrible chorus of screaming voices coming from the bolted down hold. They would die in there. He hesitated, the thought of trying to cross the open deck terrifying. The fear, too, of Cheng catching up to him. Kim gauged the moment, waited until the deck rolled almost level and dashed across the twisting deck to fall gasping on top of the hold cover. It was large and heavy, requiring the shoulders of several men just to budge it. Kim's strength was fading, bleeding away through the wound in his stomach. There was only one thing he could do for them. Kim grasped the slick, wet bolt on one side of the hatch and undogged it. Crawled to the other end of the hatch and worked the bolt there loose. Then, although he was sure the wind and racket being made as the ship lunged over or up onto something must drown the sound out, he hammered a fist up and down on the hatch to draw their attention toward it. If enough of them pushed together, they could lift the hatch free. Then they would have some chance. As much as any of them had.

Kim imagined the noise coming from under the ship's hull was the shrieking sound of steel against unyielding rock. We are aground, he thought. Cousin, I tried to reach you. He cupped the little slip of paper with her name, address, and phone number in his hand. When the next wave broke across the deck and hammered against him, Kim let go, allowing the sea to carry him toward eternity.

chapter one

It was only because of the onset of the "fog wind" that I was home that afternoon to take Nicki's call. Earlier, when I had taken Fergus, my aging Brittany Spaniel, for his scheduled perambulation through the neighbouring woods that border the stretch of Duffin Passage lying to the east of my cabin, the day held the promise of clear skies and unseasonably warm summer temperatures. Meares Island rose from the water on the other side of the passage, swathed in its dark blanket of old-growth timber and backdropped by a vivid azure sky. Weather like this is as precious on Vancouver Island's west coast as gold in a prairie stream. Vowing not to let the day slip past in mediocre ways, I had invited Vhanna over for a leisurely brunch to be followed by a walk. Surprisingly, she accepted.

But minutes after Vhanna arrived to find me setting out brunch on the cedar-plank deck the wind struck, the fog rolled in, and the temperature plunged to a winter chill in mere seconds. The three of us, Fergus leading the way, retreated back into the cabin's shelter and I resorted to building a small fire in the stone fireplace to warm both hearth and soul. Satiated by maple-syrup-drizzled blueberry pancakes and crisp bacon well washed down with freshly ground dark roast coffee, and with no reason to venture out into such an inclement day, Vhanna and I found a welcome alternative activity. Fergus signalled his displeasure at this unscheduled development by shaking his head to create a jangle of tags, letting out a derisive snort, and then showing us the disdain of his turned back by hopping up on the couch next to the fire. As he stretched out and stared broodingly into the fading embers we climbed the stairs to the loft, careful not to chuckle at his prudish display of disapproval.

Now Vhanna slept and I was more than satisfied to lie there with her pressed alongside me beneath Merriam's blue loghouse-patterned quilt — safe, warm, and mostly at peace after the sweetness of early afternoon lovemaking — for as long as she liked. From the bed in the cabin's loft, I could see through the tall windows facing the inlet that fog still imposed a false twilight that rendered the old cedars next to the cabin deck invisible. Small shudders shivered through the cabin as the wind battered its walls with wintertime ferocity. But it was summer and such a storm was a seasonal rarity. "Fog wind," the fishermen call this: a sudden surge of fog and low cloud born off northern California, then sucked northward past Washington State into the lee trough off the western coast of Vancouver Island. Technically known as a stratus surge, these winds and the accompanying fog strike without warning and God looks over the fishermen, pleasure boaters, and mariners at sea who are caught in the storm's maw.

Vhanna's head was on my shoulder, her breath dusting against my throat, and the soft pressure of her small breasts against my side. Two months ago Vhanna had returned from a half-year away. Three months of that had been spent wandering a homeland whose desolation I could barely imagine. She returned from her quest there burdened by a new, darker sadness that I knew no way of lifting from her heart or mind. I had feared this would happen. For precisely this reason, I had quietly opposed her decision to go back to Cambodia. But there is no preventing Vhanna from following her decisions through to conclusion. This is, of course, one of the many things I love about this mercurial woman. And one of the things that also drives me to frustration and sometimes to an apprehension that our relationship is ultimately doomed. Vhanna is driven to always seek the attainment of some goal, the reaching of a destination, while I lack any reason or interest to do much beyond live in the moment. The refugee and the remittance man, playing out an unlikely, surely ill-fated love story.

Like most of my ilk, I contribute nothing of meaningful social or entrepreneurial value to our nation. I inherited the status and privileged position of remittance man from my father, Angus, second son of Hedric McCann. After his fall from social grace, Hedric banished Angus from Britain to Canada a year after the Great War ended. As long as he stayed away he would receive a regular cheque, known as a remittance. This was the common fate of many an upper-class man between the 1880s and early 1900s. When Angus died, I inherited his remittance rights and continue to prosper from their payment. It is hard to know what to do with all this lucre. I put it in the bank or invest it in various ventures that friends and acquaintances around Tofino set up or allow Vhanna, who takes an interest in such things, to sink it into select stocks and other financial investments. All of this vigorous manipulation of cash into investment, of course, only causes the money to spawn more money. This, Vhanna explains to me patiently on occasion, is a good and necessary thing for economies both personal and national. I know only that I am fortunate, blessed in a way most will never know.

But I fear for Vhanna and wish she would talk more of her experience in Cambodia. I know that she found no surviving family there, but she carefully guards against betraying any sense of how this has affected her. More was happening in Vhanna's mind, I believed, than the struggle to cope with a sorrow over the inability to find any living relatives in that tormented land. I noted also a deep weariness of soul not previously present. Vhanna's spirit is that of a survivor. Her experiences as a young girl fleeing alone for many days through the jungles and across the great sandstone escarpment of Chuor Phnum Dangrek to the dubious safety of a refugee camp in Thailand imbued her with an unsettling strength and determination of will. Before that horrific journey had come the murder of her father by the Khmer Rouge and then watching her mother waste away from a combination of grief and starvation during the great trek out of Phnom Penh into the wilderness. It is difficult for someone such as myself, who is inclined more toward the dedicated pursuit of idleness and leisure than any nobler, more socially involved, or worthy calling, to comprehend the ferocity of purposefulness with which Vhanna normally approaches life.

Now, however, that vital spark of determination that had given her life such meaning and brought about the fulfillment of many personal goals seemed badly dimmed, at risk of being snuffed out entirely. And I, who love her beyond reason, appeared powerless to breathe on that wispy little flame and nurture it, fluttering and hesitant as it is, back to a bright, vital fire.

So I brooded, worried, and tried to spread pleasure into her life however I might in ways not too painfully obvious. Not that I effectively fooled Vhanna, for her perceptiveness far outreached my limited talents at deception. My purpose in inviting her for brunch and a later walk with Fergus into the woods on a workday that she should be spending organizing treks and other adventure trips for women into the back of beyond was undoubtedly rather transparent. Quite lamely, I had argued that Artemis Adventures, Inc. could prosper well enough on its own for an afternoon without its chief executive officer, president, and most other entitlements of responsibility being present, and that such a fine day called out for bold escapes from the confines of sterile offices. Considering the office of Artemis Adventures, occupying the lower floor of Vhanna's large house, overlooked Templar Channel, my argument was rendered feeble at best. A wide sweeping beach fronted her cliffside house, across the channel lay the rocky shoreline of Wickanninish Island, and beyond that stretched the endless expanse of the Pacific Ocean. So her acceptance without a moment's hesitation was all the more surprising and welcome. That — when the weather changed so dramatically — she further easily agreed to set aside the walk for making love was even more welcome.

Yet afterwards, propped up on an elbow beside me, Vhanna had cried. Just a slight dampness around the eyes, which I easily brushed away. She shook her head and offered only a small smile when I asked what was the matter. Then Vhanna pressed against me tightly until, under the caress of my hand on her back, she found the seeming peace of an untroubled sleep. Was it, though? Or did visions of a wartorn land surface even now in her dreams?

The excited electronic chirp of the phone downstairs jerked my mind away from these thoughts. I hesitated, not wanting to move, hoping not to disturb Vhanna's slumber, content to let the phone ring itself out. But Vhanna's body twitched and her head came up, eyes blinking sleepily, dreamily. I smiled at her. "You should answer it," Vhanna whispered, returning my smile with a wry one of her own. She believes I am exceedingly irresponsible and in this judgement is completely correct. Vhanna does not normally allow a phone to go unanswered. There is a duty to be accountable and present when others come looking. I sighed and twisted out of bed. Grabbing my tattered green terry cloth robe, I hurried downstairs. Across the room, Fergus cast a bleary glance over his shoulder, ears twitching against the assault of each persistent ring. An edge of unease descended upon me. This was the sixth ring and I knew only one person who would wait through more than four before deciding that there would be no answer and giving up in annoyance because I had yet again deliberately neglected to turn on my answering machine. Such calls made by this persistently patient person always spell ill for somebody. I cut the eighth ring off mid-course by lifting the handset. As I feared, the caller was Nicki and she spoke of death.

chapter two

It has been almost two years since I succumbed in a moment of lunacy to the entreaties of Mayor Reginald Tully, who is also my doctor and friend, that I should become Tofino's community coroner. At first the idea seemed entirely absurd. Triumphantly I waved before him the advertisement he had clipped from *The Westerly News*, Pacific Rim's community newspaper. "Listen to this, Reginald: 'On-Call Coroner will act as independent medico-legal investigator who will co-ordinate investigations to clarify facts surrounding unexplained and unnatural deaths. Applicants should be community-minded, possess strong interpersonal and written skills, and have the ability to communicate effectively with a variety of medical and legal professionals.' You know as well as I do that I am not community-minded, have few interpersonal skills, and wouldn't know how to deal with medico-legal professionals even if I knew who they were or what they did."

I didn't mention at the time my reluctance to even consider the other qualifications sought, specifically the "sensitivity necessary to work with grieving families and a 24-hour availability to attend death scenes and co-ordinate aspects of the investigation, including examination of the scene and body." That seemed entirely too emotionally burdensome and grisly for my taste.

Due to a variety of reasons, however, Tully's continued pleading that I give the position a try wore me down to the point that I foolishly agreed. Since then it seems to have become impossible to cast off this mantle of grim responsibility and civic duty. Although I regularly offer to resign, Tully will not hear of it. And ever since I haphazardly managed to unravel the secret behind a murder disguised as a suicide in the woods of Clayoquot Sound last year, the regional coroner, who formerly would have happily accepted my resignation, has become one of my staunchest advocates. Dr. Carl Harris, like Tully, routinely defends my rank and status as a duly sworn-in official against criticism from my personal nemesis — Sergeant Gary Danchuk of the Royal Canadian Mounted Police. Head of the Tofino RCMP detachment, Danchuk is Nicki's boss. For her part, she is the dispatcher-cum-switchboard-operator-cum-administrative-assistant-cum-general-office-troubleshooter for the detachment. Which is why when there is a death in or around Tofino it is usually Nicki who has to track me down with the news and call me forth to my unwanted duty. Although the task of finding me is often frustrating, Nicki is always of irrepressible good cheer. I find this even more surprising considering that she has to spend an unhealthy number of hours rubbing shoulders with the neither-royal-nor-mounted Sergeant Danchuk.

"Sugar," Nicki was saying, "when are you going to get with the times and carry a cell phone or at least a pager?"

"When world peace is declared," I parried grumpily.

Through the windows I noticed a small hole had opened in the fog. A thin shaft of light reached down through the gap to glitter on the water in front of the cabin. "Everything is going to melt down, total communication blackout, the demise of all computers, and a general collapse of the stock market and the hideous dot-com companies. Haven't you heard? Apocalypse. The horsemen let loose."

Nicki laughed throatily. "Don't have the vaguest idea what you're talking about, dear." There was an unnatural pause and the sound of somebody shifting position. I sensed Nicki straightening her nearly six-foot frame and donning her formal employee's mask. No doubt Danchuk had just bustled into proximity.

"What's happened, Nicki?"

An audible sigh. "I don't know, Elias. There's apparently a ship up the coast in trouble. A freighter, sounds like. Coast guard has a Sikorsky on the way to pick up some members and they said it would probably be a good idea if a coroner came too." There was none of Nicki's trademark sassy levity now. "It sounds bad, Elias. There's traffic on the radio indicating there are people in the water and the ship's up on rocks."

A freighter? People in the water? This summer? The summer of the illegal Chinese migrants? "Nicki, has Harris been alerted? This may be too big for them to want me to take it. You know I don't have any qualifications for this job."

"His nibs already called him," she said with a chuckle. Obviously Danchuk had ranged out of earshot again. "He said much the same thing. Much bafflegab about forensic this and thats. Harris told him there's nobody else available who is also close enough to get out there pronto. And pronto is the word here. Get somebody on-site and the experts and what all will follow. You're to marry up with the rest of the not-so-happy gang at the helipad by the hospital. The chopper is en route and due in thirty minutes or less. Dress warm, sugar, but get moving." She rang off abruptly.

There was nothing for it but to do exactly as Nicki commanded. Hurrying upstairs I tossed the robe on the bed and quickly explained what little I knew to Vhanna, while pulling on jeans and a denim shirt. As Vhanna wrapped herself in my robe, I led the way downstairs and over to the boot room next to the kitchen door. I jerked an old blue wool sweater pocked with moth holes over my head, hitched a pair of yellow rubber bib overalls off a peg and shrugged into them, then dragged on a pair of black gum boots. After pulling the pant legs of the overalls over the boots, I added a black oilskin jacket as a final layer and tucked a mariner's wool watch cap into one of its pockets. Although such outfits are standard dress for many Tofinoites, I normally eschew such garb as being uncomfortably hot and airless. On storm-tossed coastlines, however, I could think of nothing more practical to wear.

Vhanna ran her fingers through my close-cropped beard and met my eyes gravely. "Be careful," she said, while slipping a light pair of neoprene gloves into the oilskin's other pocket with a pickpocket's deftness. I kissed her lips and for a moment she clung hard to my neck with both arms while I circled my hands gently around the small of her back. Breaking the embrace sooner than I would have liked, but knowing the clock was ticking away, I bent over and ruffled Fergus behind the ears, reassured him that I would be back soon. Then I headed out the door, slapping on my battered hard-canvas Filson hat as I went.

A high wind still moaned through the tops of the cedar and spruce trees that surround my property as I walked over to the Land Rover, which I keep parked under the protective expanse of the branches of an ancient, massive Sitka spruce. Seldom do even a few drops of rain manage to filter down through its canopy to dampen the chipped, green-painted aluminum body of my 1960s-era relic, which is blessed with a cantankerous, unpredictable personality. Alongside the Rover stood Vhanna's sleek, shiny, and all-too-new Mazda Miata two-seater sports roadster. I describe its colour as dark green. Vhanna assures me, however, that it is actually Emerald Mica. Vhanna opens the door to her car with some form of magical electrical device while she is still about fifty yards away. I normally spend several seconds and sometimes more than a minute jiggling delicately away at the Rover's lock with its tiny little key until the latch decides to unhook itself. When in a hurry, as was the case today, I resort to pushing the sliding driver's side window open, reaching in, and fumbling about until I find the inside lock button and release it by hand. This is the advantage of having a broken window latch.

Clambering into the driver's seat, I turned the ignition key on and pushed the starter button. The Rover's starter wound, the engine coughed, spasmed, choked, and gave a throaty roar before settling into a shuddering idle. All to the good so far, co-operation 100 percent today, perhaps. Gentling the gearshift into reverse, I backed out from under the Sitka and drove down the narrow dirt lane that leads from my house out to the road into town. Rover and I were soon rattling through the downtown core of Tofino en route to the hospital. The downtown amounts, of course, to a few small blocks of businesses interrupted here and there by houses in various states of disrepair. The businesses tally up to a couple of grocery stores, a smattering of small hotels and bed and break-fasts, a drug store, a bakery, a government liquor store, and other odds and sods that include whale watching and fishing charters, and even a bookstore.

During the summer months, Tofino's population bal-loons unnaturally from its normal population of just over one thousand souls to as much as ten thousand. This means that in summer the narrow, mostly uncurbed streets are choked with gaggles of improbably dressed tourists, many of whom march in orderly lines behind their tour bus guides' brightly fluttering flags, like so many geriatric soldiers on a forced campaign. Germans drape themselves in cowboy garb complete with Stetsons, leather vests, and even the odd Davey Crockett coonskin. Japanese drape themselves in the latest in digital cameras or throwaway Kodak and Fuji cardboard box cameras and designer leisurewear. North American seniors don nylon jackets with tour company logos on the back so they won't become hopelessly lost amid the swarms of other identical-looking groups. Mixed in with these regimented tourist battalions are the usual visiting flotsam of tired and stressed-out families in rented motorhomes or SUVs tow-ing trailers, teenaged kids with rusty Volkswagen vans car-rying surf- and sailboards, hitchhikers burdened by back-packs, and yacht owners sporting blue blazers, white pants, and white-peaked captain's caps. Today, however, I had virtually clear running through the heart of town, for the storm had apparently swept it clean of all who did not call Tofino home.

Only the occasional Tofinoite stirred. A group of women wearing plastic rain pants tucked into rubber boots walked up from the fish plant on the waterfront toward the bakery for an afternoon coffee and scone. Outside the Crab Pot Café, James Scarborough, its owner and one of my business partners, unloaded the morning's catch of crabs — still in their traps — from the back of his pickup truck and shoved the wire containers through the kitchen door. I beeped my horn and he grinned my way, miming the action of downing a cold pint with his free hand and gesturing me inside. Would there were time. I shrugged an apology and carried on, deciding to see if Vhanna might like to join me for a feed of Dungeness and some cold brew that evening. Most likely I would dine alone, for Vhanna had spent an entire morning with me and that was probably a stretch for our relationship. But still an invitation seemed worth the attempt.

Cutting up the hill and turning into the hospital parking lot, I saw the RCMP Blazer already parked near the circular hardstand of the helipad. Thankfully the helicopter had not yet arrived. The last thing I needed was for Danchuk to have an excuse to set into me about being late, or being impossible to contact, or in any other myriad number of ways being entirely unsuitable for my duties. Not that I disagree with his assessment that I am unsuitable. He is entirely right in this. It is purely an idiosyncrasy of British Columbia's provincial law that has enabled me to rise to this unlofty perch in community status that presumably nobody else of sane mind and disposition desired. Only this province and the northern territories fail to require their coroners to be medical doctors. This oddity arises out of a historical sparsity of population in relation to the sheer vastness of landscape that rendered many communities so isolated that people had to impose orderliness and civility by drawing on available internal resources rather than looking outside for social supports. Somebody had to be

able to ascertain and record for posterity, and the offi-
cialdom of record-keeping that is so dear to the
Canadian heart, the causes of deaths of their fellows,
particularly those who became deceased through unex-
pected and violent means. Hence the need for community coroners when the presence of a medical doctor
could not be assured. Hence the decision to write into
the Coroner's Act a provision that a coroner need only
be a member of the community in good standing.

As I told Mayor Tully at the time of my enlistment,
and as Danchuk so often reminds him, that should have
excluded me from the running. But Tully was having
none of my argument that a remittance man, who lives
off the interest earned by a British inheritance and serves
no useful community purpose, could not possibly qual-
ify for the status of respectability. I had little better to
do, he argued, except mope around in the wake of my
wife's death. For some reason I acceded to his uncon-
vincing arguments and became the coroner. So now I am
gainfully employed in the business of death. It is a
strange pursuit. I remain perplexed by the fact that I
have so far found it one that rests upon my shoulders
somewhat comfortably and seems an increasingly natural fit. If I were to believe in such things, I might even be
led to declare that I have perhaps at last found a calling.
The mere thought of this, however, renders me rather
queasy. There is no need for those Protestant work ethic
callings. Like my father before me, I wish only to live
quietly and to do so without responsibility.

Climbing out of the Rover, I tossed the Filson
grumpily onto the seat and despite the pointlessness of
the act locked the door with a jiggle of the keys. This
had not been a productive train of thought and I
remained concerned about my role in the forthcoming
events that must be played out against a backdrop for

which I was ill prepared. No doubt my presence here would prove as pointless as the ludicrous effort to secure the Rover with a key in the lock. Mere inches above the lock was the window with a broken latch for which the replacement part had been ridiculously over-priced. Besides the Filson, there was precious little I valued inside the Rover and nothing at all worth a thief's time or expertise. I have found that the best security from theft is having nothing worth stealing. So while Vhanna protects her possessions with an ever-growing array of security devices, alarms, and the rapid-response ability of a professional security service, I maintain a material aestheticism that enables a life free of protective systems and the consequent worry over potential loss of things that ultimately matter little.

Forcing my thoughts to the business at hand, I opened the Rover's back door and reached into the rear compartment to grab a small khaki canvas daypack off one of the hooks mounted on the cab's sides for such purposes as racking up hunting rifles or fishing poles. The pack was an emergency kit consisting of a litre of water, some hard rations, a couple of space blankets, a first-aid kit, a clasp knife, a change of socks, a pair of gloves, and a toque. Permanently stowed in the Rover, it held sufficient supplies to enable a person to probably stave off hypothermia, treat minor injuries, and live through a cold, wet night in the bush. Slinging the pack over one shoulder, I walked across the tarmac toward the police Blazer.

Danchuk stood by the hood with his head tipped back to allow face-to-face discussion with a female Mountie. His short, stout body was wrapped in a yellow rain jacket that had POLICE emblazoned in large letters across the back. Covering his baldpate was a tightly pulled down ball cap, the bill turned backward so that he looked like a chubby adolescent skateboarder with an attitude problem.

When he turned to face me, I was surprised to see that underneath the jacket a Kevlar bulletproof vest stretched across his bulging belly and sunken chest. From his left hand dangled a short-barrelled shotgun by its pistol grip so that the barrel almost scuffed the ground. Behind his shoulder, Corporal Anne Monaghan flashed the kind of wry smirk my way that one reserves for co-conspirators. Her blonde curly hair was pushed up inside a ball cap, too, and otherwise her outfit matched Danchuk's. Except that she was apparently armed with only her service pistol.

"Expecting trouble?" I asked Danchuk.

Blessing me with a blue-eyed glare, he rested one hand on the butt of his holstered pistol and snapped the shotgun up so that it was propped against his shoulder. "No way to know who or what we're going to find out there, McCann," he grunted. "Best be prepared."

I silently noted that preparedness didn't extend to any footwear other than some heavy black lace-up boots that looked like standard issue Mountie stuff. Both officers also wore only a light pair of black rain pants over their normal uniform trousers. Instinct told me this could be a mistake but I also knew the futility of pointing this out to Sergeant Danchuk. Undoubtedly he had told Monaghan, in a full spate of official Danchukness, what they would wear and he would certainly brook no interference from me in such matters as the appropriate equipping of police officers.

From southeast of the heliport came the hard thumping sound of a big helicopter's blades cutting air and the telltale whine of a Sikorsky engine. The wind had torn several large gaps in the fog now, but there were still lots of pockets around and the directional windsock next to the pad was snapping hard out to the northwest. It would not be an easy landing. I said as much. Danchuk responded with a derisive snort as if dismissing that I might have any knowledge of helicopters or their flight. Then he glared at me. Obviously struggling to keep a civil tongue in his head when addressing me was grating roughly upon his nerves, for he said through clenched jaw, "Let's understand the lines of authority here, McCann. I'm in charge of this party. We get out there, you go where I tell you and you do what I tell you. Clear?"

I shrugged and forced a smile. "Sure, Gary." Danchuk hates it when I address him by his given name. Doing so implies friendship or acquaintanceship, the possible existence of a level playing field between us. Sergeant Danchuk despises me, a feeling that is entirely mutual. This state of acrimony has existed between us since the night he responded to my report of having found Merriam at home, my Remington 16-gauge over-and-under shotgun by her side, a dreadful hole torn in her chest by one of its slugs, and her life having flown. Danchuk will never accept that Merriam died a suicide. He harbours the suspicion, or more surely the certain belief, that Merriam died by my hands. This is one Mountie who is convinced he will eventually get his man. He makes this clear at all times in his dealings with me and he also ensures that I understand that his having to work alongside a murderer is a duty he abhors.

Oddly his attempts to poison my dealings with the rest of his detachment are largely for naught. Nicki has known me more years than she has had to serve under Danchuk. The other Mounties, who come to Tofino and mostly soon go on to more career-enhancing postings, are generally polite. Some, like Monaghan, who came to Tofino only last year, demonstrate a cheerful and friendly attitude to just about everyone they currently are not having to lock up. Sometimes she is even friendly with these unfortunates. It helps my status among these officers, I imagine, that Danchuk has a personality that little inclines others toward friendship or respect, no matter how grudging. This encourages most of them to maintain a professional distance from their superior. Three years ago Danchuk became the detachment commander, rising to the exalted rank of sergeant. Scuttlebutt says he is unlikely — due both to ability and attitude — to rise above this rank. He fears being permanently exiled to service in rain-drenched Tofino and many of us here share this grim apprehension that a stalled career will leave him beached here until retirement. For me the thought is grimmer than for most others.

Danchuk now glared at the fog and tipped his head, like Fergus trying to figure out what kind of bird was rustling the brush nearby, as the sound of the approaching chopper grew in volume. "He'll be a few minutes yet," Danchuk announced with a knowing nod. With that he headed toward the hospital. "Brief him," he snapped at Monaghan.

"Yes sir," she said with a needless formality that Danchuk either didn't notice or didn't care to acknowledge as he scurried across the lot and into the entrance door. "Time for a last quick nervous pee," Monaghan smirked.

I smiled, but uncharacteristically held my tongue. She was young and new. Danchuk was her immediate superior. I remembered that. Remembered army sergeants who had spent more time yelling orders while on duty and in their off hours falling down drunk than they spent providing leadership and the kind of professional knowledge that would help us all stay alive in the clinch. Danchuk might be no better or worse than those men. But, like them, he had the authority and Monaghan would have to march to his orders. Best not to contribute too overtly to inciting dissatisfaction in the ranks. No matter how tempting that might be. It was a resolve I felt sure I could honour for at least a few minutes.

"Tell me what you know about it."

Monaghan jerked a wrinkled map of the coastline from a hip pocket and folded it out awkwardly onto the hood of the Blazer, unmindful of the beads of water that it immediately soaked up. Head cocked awkwardly to one side she peered at the map while running a long slender finger across islands and headlands well to the northwest of Tofino. The nail was a little too long, I thought, to adhere to regulations. It was also highly burnished as if she spent an hour a week being pampered by a manicurist. Finally Monaghan found the spot she was looking for and jabbed the tip of her finger on it. I leaned over and saw her nail indicated a spot on the east coast of Nootka Sound, not too far from the sound's mouth. There was a little pimple-like protrusion called Escalante Point, and south of that, a tiny island. Further into the sound, where it narrowed dramatically in front of Bligh Island, was a symbol of a three-masted ship going down at the stern. The island drew its name in tribute to one William Bligh, who sailed as an ensign into these waters aboard *Discovery* in the company of Captain James Cook in March 1778. On April 28, 1789, Bligh gained eternal notoriety as the sadistic captain who sparked a mutiny on a 215-ton ship named *Bounty* that was hauling breadfruit trees from Tahiti to the West Indies. Many three-masted sinking schooner symbols were scattered with careless abandon all along the length of the map in front of various sounds, rocky points, inlets, and stretches of sandstone shelf and cobble beaches. Since the first Spanish explorers and adventurers who preceded the British started plying the waters off Vancouver Island, its shoreline has claimed countless vessels and justly earned a reputation as the Graveyard of the Pacific.

Monaghan looked over at me and grimaced. "We don't know much other than the location. A Polish trawler picked up a mayday signal. Just one broadcast and that not on the distress channel. They put a report on it through to the coast guard who issued a general call for all ships to keep a lookout. A fishing boat named *Dignity 5* spotted a ship on the rocks near Escalante Point about three hours ago and he's been standing off the shoreline since. Can't get in there because of the surf, even with his Zodiac. Storm's still tearing up the seas. Hell, they just about got swamped and are fighting to stay afloat themselves. They're our radio and locational link. Looks like a small freighter, badly rusted, is breaking up on the rocks. No idea of its name or nation of origin. Attempts by *Dignity 5*'s captain to make radio contact have been unsuccessful and he's getting no response to flashlight signals. Last report said the fisher thought the ship had cracked its back and snapped in two. He thought he saw bodies or people in the water that were being thrown up against the rocks. It sounds damned bad."

I had a desire to put a comforting hand on her shoulder, but decided that would be unprofessional. She was trained for this stuff. "What have we got headed there?" The throbbing roar of the helicopter was almost overhead now.

"We'll be first on scene. The *Cape St. James* left almost an hour ago but it's heavy seas so progress is slow. They've a full crew with Chuck and Josinder aboard."

The *Cape St. James* was a brand new motor launch deployed to Tofino by the Canadian Coast Guard just this year. It was capable of twenty-five knots, had a crew of four, and had only five spare berths in which to cram survivors. "With your two Mounties aboard there's not much room left," I said softly.

Monaghan snorted. "The sergeant's determined that there be enough police present for full containment."

I stared up at the sky. The fog had drifted back to form a thin veil over the landing site. It seemed the chopper was circling, looking for a hole. My face was damp from the moisture carried by the fog. Monaghan's hair sticking out from under her cap was slick and darkened by the mist. "Anyone else close?" I asked.

"*Dixie 4* is trying to get there, but it's going to be hard going for her, and *Cape Calvert* is en route from Bamfield. Be a long time before she gets up there."

Calvert was just about the same class of boat as the *St. James*. *Dixie 4* was a small converted fishing boat operated by the coast guard's local auxiliary unit 38. Summed up the rescue force was good, but too spread out and moving up the coast in vessels that had little or no speed in storm seas like this. And God only knew what kind of shoreline we were talking about.

"It's going to depend on the air support," I said. "Besides the Sikorsky?"

"Yeah, there's a DND Search-and-Rescue Labrador coming from 442 Squadron in Comox with an Emergency Response Team and Immigration officials aboard. And there might be some U.S. Coast Guard choppers coming, too. The trouble the Americans face is another storm bank is rolling right up over top of them."

A second fog wind. Nothing I had even considered possible. "That happens?"

Monaghan shrugged. "I'm from North Battleford. Ask me about a prairie wind or even a tornado, not about this coastal shit." She yanked off the ball cap, ran fingers through her hair to yank away a spray of water. "Sometimes I think I'll just wrinkle up into a prune." Her eyes widened fractionally and she set her cap back squarely on her head. "Returneth our lord and master," she muttered. "And none too soon, either."

She was right, for suddenly from out of a large wall of fog the helicopter emerged, its white and red paint job flaring in the watery sunlight that was leaking through the thin gap between that fogbank and another one hanging off to the north. The wash thrown by the Sikorsky's sixty-two-foot-wide span of blades sent leaves and rubbish swirling up and away. The force of the blade-generated wind hit like I was standing on a rocky point facing directly toward an ocean battered by a winter northwester. Danchuk and Monaghan each had a hand clamped hard on top of their heads to keep the ball caps from joining the other debris sailing off into the nearby brush. After pivoting once, the big machine settled its wheels down onto the helipad. The side door snapped back and the engineer leaned out — bug-headed helmet rendering him alien and fierce looking — and waved for us to start coming at double time. Obviously the crew was afraid the fog was going to close back in and stop their extraction.

Monaghan reached into the Blazer, dragged out a little pack, and shrugged it onto her back before running toward the Sikorsky. I ran after her, hunching instinctively below the still churning rotor blades. We dived through the doorway and I flashed the engineer a thumbs-up to get going. To my disappointment, he ignored the gesture, waiting instead for Danchuk to arrive, place the shotgun on the deck floor, and awkwardly attempt to lever his short body up into the cabin. Impatiently, the engineer bent over, grabbed Danchuk by an elbow and dragged him inside. Already we were moving, rolling across the helipad for a moment on the wheels before rising in a hard rotation up through the narrowing gap in the fog.

chapter three

Inoticed a headset with earphones and mouthpiece lying on the bench I sat in across from the exit door, which the engineer was still slamming shut even as we lifted off. Slipping the headset on, I plugged it into a jack that linked it into the helicopter's internal communication system. From his jumpseat, Danchuk shot me a puzzled look. I ignored him, trying above the racket of the engines and the buffeting that the airframe was taking from the wind to hear what the crew was saying. The pilot and co-pilot were discussing the wind and visibility problems, but unsurprisingly they sounded calm and professional. They would be used to flying in weather far worse than this.

There was a time in my life when I was more at home in the back of a large helicopter than in the passenger seat of a car. These were the first years of adulthood when, to my father's everlasting disdain and embarrassment, I joined the army and served first with the Princess Patricia's Canadian Light Infantry and then transferred into the

Canadian Airborne Regiment, which was more chopper mobile than other regiments.

After about forty minutes of hard jolting flying, the headphones crackled.

"Okay, I've got it," a voice said over the headphones.

"Roger that, I see it," another replied.

Peering out one of the side windows, I saw only cloud streaming past the water-streaked Perspex and occasional glimpses of grey, storm-tossed water below. Then the fog swept away and we flew under a heavy ceiling of dirty cloud no more than two hundred feet above the white-capped ocean. Nothing out my side of the chopper but ocean and, farther off, some rugged mountains edged by a sea-bashed rocky shoreline. Recalling Monaghan's map, I figured we must be heading north into the centre of the mouth of Nootka Sound. That put Escalante Point off to the east and meant my side of the chopper faced west. The wind was buffeting the Sikorsky about, so I resisted the urge to try going over to the other side of the helicopter for a better view of things. Danchuk was on my side of the helicopter, too, and wasn't making any move to improve his vantage point either. He looked so green around the gills that I had a fleeting moment of pity for him. He sat hunched over, his eyes fixed on the chopper's vibrating floor. Monaghan was on the opposite side, next to the engineer, with her eyes glued to the window.

The pilot and co-pilot were discussing options, with the engineer tossing in an occasional consideration. "Get these people down on that flat-rock bench," he said. "Then get those ones off that rock with the sling."

Not liking the sound of that, I waited a moment until the helicopter steadied and then quickly pulled my headset jack free, unbuckled myself, and dodged across the Sikorsky to plop onto the bench next to Monaghan. By the time the engineer turned to rebuke me for moving, I was buckled in and had the headset hooked up to another outlet. "It's okay, chief. All set now." He glared, then shrugged, and went back to his business, obviously deciding I wasn't going to be around his world long enough to become a nuisance that needed addressing.

Turning my attention to the window, I looked down upon the worst human tragedy I had seen since Cyprus. The sea was frothing and rolling up onto and, in many places, over great slabs of grey sandstone. Cast up against the rocks, like some toy model thrown down in a child's tantrum, the hull of a freighter turned hard over on one side seethed back and forth. The stern was rolling free of the bow and both sections rose and fell with each surge of wave that lifted them up and then dropped them back hard upon the rocks as the wave withdrew. I could see right into the guts of the stern section and made out a shattered engine room, a cargo hold sloshing with water and an odd assortment of boxes and what I feared were people inside. The superstructure above the main deck was torn and rent with jagged holes apparently created by its being repeatedly pounded against outcroppings. The bow was completely upside down, so that a rusty section of keel pointed up at the sky. The bow section looked to have been upended onto a flat bench of sandstone around which the surf boiled to crash against some rocks further inshore.

A thick oil slick had pooled around both sections of the ship, choking the sea in a gooey, black scum. Inside that scummy mix, I saw oil-covered forms that could only be bodies. There were other figures lying unmoving, except when the surf cast the ones still caught in its maw about or when those that had been tossed up on the rocks were pushed about by the edges of the surf brushing against them. A few lay completely clear of the water or floated in isolated tide pools.

Almost directly below us a small fishing boat wallowed about in the rough sea. A couple of people wearing garish orange survival suits waved their arms frantically and pointed toward various points on the shoreline where they obviously thought survivors from the wrecked freighter might have found shelter.

Pushing the mouthpiece of the headset close to my lips, I said, "Where are we at in the tide cycle?"

There was a pause, probably caused as much by the crew wondering who was speaking as by anything else, and then the voice I had identified earlier as the pilot's responded. "It's almost at low slack. Then it's going to start rising. You have about six hours before it hits low tide and starts to turn again."

That was good news because I could see there were some people moving around on rocks that were cut off from the shore by the sea. Some were desperately staring up at the hovering helicopter with arms raised imploringly. Others lay with arms akimbo and seemed oblivious to the Sikorsky's presence, either because they were exhausted from escaping the sea or injured or both.

There was another problem. "How long before that second storm gets up here?" I asked.

The pilot's response was instantaneous this time. "The estimate is that it'll be here in five hours at the most, possibly in four. So you have to get in and get everyone rounded up fast so that we can start evacuations. The plan is to shift everyone who is in good shape to Yuquot and the Red Cross Hospital there. The more badly injured we'll try to evacuate up the sound to Gold River. There's a police boat coming down from there right now that should be able to take some of them. We've got a Labrador inbound as well.

"Okay people," the pilot said. "We are going to set down on that big shelf just inshore and you are going to extract with haste. Then we're going to get those seven people off that furthest out rock and bring them in to you. That's going to take us two trips and, depending on how easy it is for us to work with them and how panicked they are, who knows how long." Looking about, I saw there were four people clinging to a large pyramid-shaped rock well out to sea beyond the wreckage of the freighter. Presumably the pilot had spotted another three on some other part of the massive rock. No way the tide was going to recede far enough for any of them to be rescued except by the helicopter.

There was a harsh wheezing sound in the headset followed by Danchuk saying, "You bring them in and we'll secure them."

I stared at him. His mouth was set in a hard line and his eyes were bright with what looked like a kind of rage. He was gripping the shotgun lying across his lap with both hands.

"Are there extra first-aid kits on board?" Monaghan said. "We're going to need them."

The engineer quickly unlocked two large metal boxes marked with first-aid symbols and handed one to Monaghan and the other to me. Despite the way the chopper was tossing this way and that in the wind, he moved about without any effort, trailing behind him the long communication cord attached to his headset. "They're ready," he said. "Let's get them in there."

A moment later the chopper banked sharply to the right and moved over the shoreline. Then the pilot brought it back into a hover and started descending toward a large flat shelf of rock that stood between the water and the edge of the treeline. When he was almost at ground level the engineer opened the side door and, as the wheels touched the stone, signalled for us to get out. Monaghan went first, jumping down lightly, then turn-

ing back to hoist the heavy first-aid kit down and stag-
gering off to escape the prop wash. She carried it one-
handed, like a small suitcase, and lurched along tipped
badly to one side as she struggled with the weight. I followed with my pack strapped on my back and the other
first-aid kit held in both arms across my chest, so I would
have better control over my movements than Monaghan
had managed with the suitcase-carrying approach. The
kits felt like they weighed a good fifty pounds. Danchuk
exited right beside me, shotgun held at port arms so he
looked like a soldier getting ready to fight for control of
a hot landing zone. As soon as we cleared the immediate
area of the chopper's prop wash, the pilot started lifting
off, already banking toward the rock where the people
were stranded.

Monaghan had stopped just beyond the span of the
propellers and dropped her first-aid kit next to her feet.
She was opening and closing her hand fitfully. There
was a sharp red indentation left by the thin steel handle.
I passed her and carried on with my burden until I
reached a solid chunk of granite tossed down on the
sandstone bench like some ancient Celtic altar. After setting the case down on the bench and dropping my pack
alongside it, I ran back and grabbed Monaghan's kit
and added it to my collection of gear. Having followed
me over, Monaghan shrugged her pack off and set it
alongside the rest of the things.

"If we need to give anyone first aid this should be as
good a station as any," I shouted to her. Because the
Sikorsky was still close the whine of its turbine engines
and the thumping of props made it hard to hear or be
heard. The Sikorsky's propeller wash was lifting up
spray so that it appeared to be flying on top of a thousand beads of water as it approached the little group of
people collected on the pyramid-shaped rock.

Danchuk came up and jabbed a stubby finger toward a cluster of people standing near the treeline — all small, thin Asians, their clothes soaked through with saltwater and their skin blackened by oil. There were three adult males, one woman, and a young boy who looked to be no more than ten but might have been in his early teens. One of the men wore a winter parka, designer jeans, and a sturdy pair of hiking boots. Another had on a light black sports coat, matching slacks, and pointy-toed street shoes that had probably once been nicely polished but were now stained with salt and oil and badly scuffed. The other man, the woman, and the young boy wore only T-shirts and tattered, faded jeans. Each person had wrapped their arms around themselves and stood shivering in the wind, looking desolate and scared. I noticed that the police boots worn by Danchuk and Monaghan were rapidly becoming as badly beaten up by the rocks and the saltwater as the well-dressed migrant's.

"Monaghan," Danchuk snapped, "you round those people up. I don't want any of them running off." He dug in the pocket of his jacket, extracted a plastic bag, and tossed it onto the stone. "Plastic restrainers in there. Cuff them if they make any move to resist."

Somewhat reluctantly, I thought, Monaghan gathered a fistful of the handcuffs and stuffed them into her jacket pocket. Then she walked toward the group. They seemed to huddle more closely together as she approached, even though Monaghan was keeping her hands at her sides and, as far as I could tell from my position behind her, trying to look friendly and unthreatening. But a cop is a cop and there was no hiding her identity. When she gestured to them to follow her, they all looked anxiously one to the other and back again as if hoping someone would assume a leadership role. There was no obvious taker and finally the young woman stepped cautiously forward. As she went past Monaghan, the woman's eyes darted nervously in the direction of the blonde Mountie, then she walked toward where Danchuk and I stood by the big altar-like stone. The other four trudged after her, heads down, hands clasped in front of them as if they were already cuffed. Stone-faced, Monaghan followed them.

Once this group was in place, Danchuk gestured with the shotgun for them to close up with their backs to the stone and to sit down. The latter he indicated by lowering his butt and the palm of his hand at the same time and shouting, "Sit. I want you all sitting down in a line." They obviously got the message, and lowered themselves down on the slippery, wet rock to sit cross-legged. Seated, they looked even smaller and sadder than they had standing near the treeline. "Monaghan, you round up the rest of the ones that are wandering around and corral them here. Watch the treeline for signs of any who might be trying to escape."

"Yes sir," she said stiffly and set off on her assignment, while Danchuk stood in his soggy shoes with the gun cradled in his arms and guarded his catch.

Seeing that the forces of law and order had this group of illegal migrants duly under control, I scooped up my rucksack, shouldered it, and headed down toward the rocky shoreline. There might still be people in the water down there that we hadn't seen. And, of course, there were those who had obviously died in the water. I hoped some of the search-and-rescue, coast guard, and other police showed up soon so we could properly comb the area. Going as close to the water's edge as possible without being at risk of getting caught by a rogue wave, I scanned the shoreline for signs of survivors not being gathered up by Monaghan's one-person dragnet. Besides the few scattered people trapped on rocks out in the water and a couple who were clinging to the upturned keel of the freighter's bow, I couldn't see anyone. And there was nothing I could do for those people. They would have to wait for the helicopter.

Out at the pyramid-shaped rock, the Sikorsky crew was apparently having a difficult time getting the obviously terrified migrants to strap on the harness and allow themselves to be winched up one at a time to safety. Although each seemed to take a turn clutching the harness as it swayed back and forth among them, they each quickly released it, ignoring the signals and gestures of the engineer leaning out of the Sikorsky's doorway indicating they should put it on. Nobody seemed willing to risk the ride. I figured the engineer was going to have to lower himself down and take control of the situation and have the co-pilot operate the winch. Otherwise the situation out there would remain stalemated. Obviously he reached the same conclusion, as the harness was winched back up to the helicopter and a minute or two later one of the crew swung out of the hatch and started a descent. That took a lot of courage because there was no telling what people could do who were panicked and clinging for dear life to the false security of a rock that at high tide would be completely submerged.

As there was nothing to be done to help that situation, I started walking along the shoreline, continuing to patrol for other survivors. Coming to a narrow surge channel that cut through the sandstone like a miniature canyon from the shore back to the treeline, I spotted something washing back and forth in the water that ran in and out of the crack with each incoming wave. "Oh Christ," I hissed through clenched teeth. The something resolved itself into a person lying face down in the water. There were a lot of jagged handholds on either face of the crevice but they were greasy from the water and

growths of seaweed and sharp with barnacles. The oil
that had leaked out of the ship when the tide had been
higher also coated the rock. Rooting in my pack, I
extracted a coil of bright red line. Meant for hanging the
bag up in trees to keep my provisions out of the range of
bears, cougars, mice, and other natural freebooters, it
was really too thin for what I intended. I looped one end
of the line around a sturdy sandstone outcrop with fairly rounded edges that would probably not cut the line
and tied the end off with a knot. Then I tugged on the
neoprene gloves that Vhanna had put into my coat.
Wrapping the free end of the line around my right hand,
I paid the line out across my palm and started working
my way carefully down into the crevice.

Messing around in surge channels is a hazardous,
foolhardy undertaking. Each time a wave rolls in its
power is channeled up the length of the narrow crevice
resulting in dramatic and unpredictable changes in
water depth. One wave might barely raise the water up
above your ankles, while the next one may just as easily pluck you up and drag you right out to sea or knock
you silly against the rock walls. The best approach to
surge channels is to avoid them entirely or at least cross
them quickly and carefully. This channel was a bad one.
It had a classic U-shape with steep ragged walls leading
down to a bottom filled with a chaotic jumble of boul-
ders, sucking sand, and deep pools of water. That was
when the surf rolled out. When it returned, the channel
swelled with a hissing, frothing surge of saltwater. Each
wave plucked the body in the channel up and rolled it
higher up the landwash before sucking it back to roughly the same spot where it had previously rested. This
was in a deep pool of water protected on the seaward
side by a big slab of granite wedged into the channel like
a plug. Probably the body would have been swept out to

sea had it not been for the boulder being in the way and the tide being low.

The thick rubber soles of my gumboots provided fairly good traction and I could also get good tight holds because of the glove on my left hand, while the line helped maintain balance whenever I started to slip. In a few seconds I had half climbed, half slithered down to the waterline and was able to find a couple notches of rock that provided good footholds that seemed to be higher than the inflow of the waves. I perched there, waiting and watching the waves as they swept in and out, following a remorseless, timeless rhythm. I figured the channel was filling with each new wave on an average of every ninety seconds. If I moved quickly that should leave enough time.

As a wave sucked back with a low hiss and crackle of gravel rattling across the hard stone, I lowered one foot into the pool next to the body, reaching down for a bottom I could not see. I found it at the same time that the water level came up to my knee. I figured the next incoming wave would probably raise the water level up to my crotch but hoped to be gone before it arrived. The force of a wave in this narrow space could well pull me off my feet. Switching the line from my right hand to the left, I steadied myself and reached down to grasp the shifting form of the person by one shoulder and rolled it over. It was the body of a man clearly beyond any need of help. His widely gaped mouth was full of oily water and there was a deep, bloody wound on his forehead through which some blackened bone and what looked to be brain tissue showed.

Looking furtively down the channel to see if a wave was inbound, I managed at the same time to wrap the line around his chest and tie a knot that might hold if the rope didn't break. Then I clambered up out of the

crevice just before a wave that was larger than the pre-
ceding ones swept in. It rose up the wall alongside me to
almost knee depth and I could feel its drag, pulling me
away from my handholds as it rolled back out to sea. I
clung on tightly and when it receded quickly pulled
myself out of the crevice and rolled onto my back on the
sandstone shelf. I lay there for a few minutes, allowing
my nerves to steady and the trembling of my body to
still. Then I started hauling the line up. Although the
nylon cord stretched so badly that every yard of line
pulled up seemed to grow a good foot in length as I
reeled it in, the line held and soon the body came scuff-
ing up over the rim. I've never been very good with
knots and had tied this one so that it had become so
badly cinched up by the body's weight that I couldn't
begin to loosen it. I sawed it apart with one of the blades
of my Swiss Army knife, returned the line to the pack,
and shouldered it. Then grabbing the body under both
arms, I dragged it up the rocks to a point that appeared
to be above the high tide line.

On the rock out at sea the engineer was just finishing rigging up one of the Asians. Soon what looked to
be a man was kicking and flailing about hysterically as
the sling lifted him up toward the Sikorsky's cabin. By
the time he was alongside the compartment, the man
had either calmed down considerably or fainted from
fright, so he didn't resist the process of being swung
inside, unhooked, and strapped into a seat. The sling
dropped again to the engineer, who started hooking
another person to the harness.

Meanwhile, Danchuk and Monaghan had rounded
up and secured the last of the people who had been scattered along the shoreline, although none appeared to
have been handcuffed. Monaghan had one of the large
first-aid kits open and was tending to various cuts,

scrapes, and bruises that the migrants had suffered in getting to shore. It looked like she had also put a splint on one person's leg below the knee.

Generally everything seemed under control, so I went back to my search. In a few minutes, I had pulled two more bodies from where they had been half tossed up on the rocks and dragged them up above the high water mark. While moving the third corpse, it struck me how unsqueamish I had become about touching dead people or moving corpses about. Only two years in the coroner's job and a mere dozen or so death investigations had seemingly left me inured to the worst effects of being engaged in the business of death. It is hard to believe sometimes how adaptable we are, how quickly the abnormal becomes normal if that is what we are regularly exposed to. Perhaps when I was done with being a coroner, I could become a mortician. Tofino could probably use one and it would be an honest vocation.

I entered an area of rocky shoreline that was rife with tide pools. Most were clogged with various species of seaweed, mussels, starfish, sea urchins, and other tidal life. As yet, only a few of the pools had been polluted by oil from the freighter, but I knew that this would quickly change. A few hours after the next high tide, much of what lived here would perish as the oil suffocated the various organisms that lived in each pool. While the amount of oil spilling from the freighter's fuel tanks was probably insufficient to cause major marine damage, it was still going to be hellishly devastating to the life in the immediate vicinity.

Even as this thought passed through my head, I found myself looking down upon the body of a young girl floating face up in the crystalline water of a small tide pool. Her arms were stretched out on either side of her body and her legs spread so that she looked as if she were just relaxing, like somebody doing a gentle back-stroke in a swimming pool might. Long hair drifted out in a wide fan about her head. A few coal-black strands lay softly across her small, dark face, which was suspended just under the surface. Unlike the other bodies, which had all suffered varying forms of fatal physical trauma, hers was unmarked by any physical injury.

I plunged into the water, sinking up to my waist so that icy water ran into my boots and down inside my overalls with such force that the breath blasted out of me in a hoarse gasp. Cradling her in my arms, I lifted her out of the water, being careful to hold her body so it remained horizontal. She weighed nothing at all. Water showered out of her hair and off her thin white T-shirt and frayed black jeans. Setting her down on the bare rocks edging the pool, I dragged myself up alongside her and jerked off my neoprene gloves. I felt her throat, searching for some sign of a pulse. There was nothing, so I yanked the T-shirt up and pressed my ear to her thin little chest and listened hard. With the sounds of the waves striking the rocks, the overhead calls of circling gulls and ravens, and the incessant throbbing of the helicopter offshore, it was difficult to tell, but I sensed the tiniest little thrum of a heartbeat.

In the dim reaches of my memory I recalled a principle hammered into us during one of several Princess Patricia's west coast training exercises involving amphibious operations. There had been a life-sized dummy in ocean water, an eight-man section of green soldiers in wet suits, and a sergeant with grey hair razored right down to his scalp and a nose that looked to have been flattened by the repeated bashing of a bar stool. In a voice so soft and raspy you had to lean in to hear him, he said, "Cold water drowning." Treating the dummy just as if it was a real person, he had shown us what to do. He kept us working over the dummy and then each other repeatedly until he was satisfied that we had all got it right.

All these years since that exercise I had never put what I learned to use and was thankful not to have had to. The girl, I realized now, *had* drowned. If this had been a warm lake she would be dead. But the ocean off Vancouver Island remains cold year round. Even in summer the water temperature on the north Pacific Coast seldom rises above ten degrees Celsius. So the girl had drowned in cold, almost frigid water. Such water chills the skin and induces hypothermia. It drives the blood away from the outer parts of the body and back toward the heart in a desperate attempt to sustain life by retaining heat around the vital organs, particularly the heart. The need for oxygen is greatly reduced as a result and it becomes possible for someone who drowns in cold water to survive long periods of being submerged. "Never assume a cold, lifeless person is beyond hope," the sergeant had warned. "Get busy. Just do your A, B, C, and D."

His words ringing in my memory, I got busy. First, I ensured the girl's airway was open by pulling her jaw forward while applying pressure to her forehead with my other hand to keep it stationary. This got her tongue lifted away from where it had probably lolled to block her throat. I waited a few seconds to see if this might prove sufficient to get her breathing again, putting my cheek and ear directly over her mouth and nose, so close that we were almost touching. I sensed no light breath of air against my skin. So much for "A." Time for "B." I started rescue breathing, blowing into her mouth and then repeating the procedure a few seconds later. This failed to restore her breathing, but did suddenly bring forth a thin flow of fluid out of her mouth. Quickly, I rolled her over on her side into a drainage position. The flow of fluid, which looked to be mostly water, continued.

Hunching over behind her, I bent across her thin shoulder and with difficulty managed to get my upside down mouth over hers for a couple more rescue breaths. I kept this procedure going for several minutes until suddenly she let out a little cough and the fluid stopped flowing. Turning her onto her back again, I tried another couple rescue breaths. This time when I felt for it there was a faint pulse in her throat. I went back to rescue breathing, turning her over onto her side again when another trickle of fluid dribbled from her mouth. Then I gave her a breath every five seconds while holding her on her side in the drainage position.

"Come on," I whispered between breaths. "You can do it, girl, you can do it." Her pulse seemed stronger with each check. Then I felt the softest flutter of air against my ear when I brushed it down against her lips. I waited, hand resting lightly on her shoulder, ear close to her mouth. Another soft brush of air, followed by a little, almost politely shy cough. I straightened up and saw Monaghan walking toward us. "Anne," I yelled, "she's alive." The girl's body jerked, as if she were trying to fight her way out of danger. I held her, keeping her in the drainage position. Monaghan came running. "In my pack. There's a couple space blankets," I said. She grabbed the pack lying on the rocks and started pawing around in it. Came up with the blankets and ripped off the plastic cases, spread the thin aluminum-foil-like material out.

Slowly, gently we sat the girl up and Monaghan helped me tug her T-shirt off. Then we worked the jeans off. She offered no resistance. In fact, she seemed only semi-conscious. The girl lolled around in our arms like a rag doll. In my bag was a polypropylene sweater and long johns. Monaghan got these out and with a great deal of effort we managed to pull them on the girl, pushing up the ridiculously overlong sleeves and legs but leaving her feet and hands wrapped up inside the fabric. Then we wrapped her in the blankets. "I'll hold her here," I said, "but we have to get her evacuated quickly. She's in shock and there could be all sorts of internal damage. There's a watch cap in there, can you get it?" Monaghan scrounged around in the pack and came up with a black wool watch cap and passed it over.

"I'll see if we can get some idea of when the first evacuation flight will be ready. We should be able to get all the injured out on the first flight," Monaghan said. "Most of them seem to be either okay or beyond help, not many in between. Jesus."

"Are they migrants?" I asked.

"Looks like it. At least that's how we're treating it." She stood up and glanced furtively over towards the approaching helicopters. "I'll make sure she's slotted onto the first one out," Monaghan said and jogged off toward where Danchuk was continuing his sentinel duties. Far down Nootka Sound the shadowy shape of a big tandem-rotored Labrador chugged rapidly toward our position. That was good since it could take up to eighteen passengers at a time. Buzzing along in its wake, like gulls chasing a bald eagle, were a couple of smaller helicopters. As this flock closed in, I saw that the smaller ones were dressed up in white paint adorned with the RCMP stripes and logo. The Labrador bore the yellow paint and red maple leaf insignia of the Canadian Forces' search-and-rescue arm.

I shook the watch cap out of the ball it was wadded into and tugged it onto the little girl's head. The wool cap was huge on her small head and flopped down well past her ears to ride so low on her forehead that it threatened to cover her eyes. I tried to keep up a steady stream of reassuring words. Not that she was likely to understand anything I said. Perhaps if I knew Mandarin or whatever Chinese dialect people might speak in Fujian Province, from which the migrants had been coming all summer long in one ship after another, she would understand and be reassured. But I knew no words of Chinese. Nor have I any particular talent with children. I suspected the girl was probably about ten or eleven. She might be older, but I doubted that she could be any younger.

Children and young teenagers are an unknown quantity to me. I seldom spend time around them and so find it generally somewhat alarming when one does cross my path. Fergus and I are alike in this. Unlike most dogs, Fergus doesn't adore children. They, however, are usually much excited and very anxious to make his acquaintance. While they become wide-eyed and given to much hugging and petting, Fergus adopts a wild-eyed look that betrays the fact that he is on the edge of panic and wants no more than to flee to some refuge far from their fawning attention. Then, like the old campaigner he is, Fergus stalwartly endures their patting of his head and friendly scratching behind his ears. He flatly ignores the thrown balls or sticks, leaving it instead to the children to fetch such items if they so desire and return them to him. I admire Fergus's manner with children and have learned that I can usually cope in a like manner.

The girl stirred in my arms, shivered hard, and let out a little whimper. For want of anything better to say, I told her about Fergus and described a walk we had taken in the woods recently. She seemed to relax under the spell of these incomprehensible words. When I took her little hand in mine it was still icy cold and blue. The Labrador rolled overhead and started setting down on the rocks, followed by the two police choppers. The doors of these two flew open and a squad of police in emergency response team garb piled out, their shotguns and automatic weapons at the ready. A gaggle of men and women clambered out of the Labrador. These all wore blue pants and jackets with IMMIGRATION emblazoned in large yellow letters across the back and CIC in yellow set below a matching Canadian flag with yellow bands and a maple leaf rather than the normal red image on the front. They wore matching blue ball caps bearing the initials CIC on the front. All the cops and immigration officers wore white medical masks strapped over their mouths and noses. "Just a little longer, girl. A little longer and you're home free," I said and prayed this would prove true.

chapter four

It took a few minutes for the newcomers to organize their ranks, but finally two of the police officers came running over with a stretcher for the girl. Without so much as a glance my way, a female officer started checking her vital signs. "She was unconscious in the water when I found her," I said. "No idea how long, but she still had a heartbeat. I gave her resuscitation and her lungs seem to have drained. I think she's in shock and hypothermic. There could be internal damage to some organs."

The woman nodded brusquely. She had dark eyes and red hair cut so short it was pretty well contained inside her cap. Like everyone else, she was wearing a facemask. "We'll get her out on the Labrador," she said. "The first one is going right through to Gold River and we can get her in the hospital there. Does she speak English?"

"No." I hesitated. Whispered in the girl's ear, "You don't, do you?" She shifted a little in my grasp, but didn't seem to register the meaning of the words. It was more like she wanted to turn her head to see who was speaking. To the policewoman, I said, "Why the masks?"

"Threat of diseases. Tuberculosis particularly. You should have one on, too." I noticed then that the woman also wore plastic surgical gloves. Seeing the direction I was staring, she said, "AIDS. Some of the injured are bleeding."

Such threats had never occurred to me, although I guessed there was sense in such caution. Somehow, though, I was unable to imagine this girl infected with TB or other contagion. I wondered how much of her saliva I had got in my mouth during the resuscitation process and shrugged. Nothing I intended to worry about. I really didn't believe in the hazardous scenario that the policewoman was spinning. "Danchuk must be going ballistic," I muttered, as I helped the woman lay the girl out on the stretcher.

A short guffaw from the policewoman. "He the short one?" I nodded. "He was making a lot of noise about not being warned and other yadda yadda. He and Monaghan are all masked and gloved proper now."

The woman and the male officer who had come over with her started toting the stretcher back toward the helicopter. I walked alongside, pack tossed onto one shoulder, holding the girl's hand in mine. "You know Monaghan?"

"Went through training together. She's real stand up. Bright, too." The woman gave me a sideways glance. "By the way, who are you?"

"Elias McCann." She continued looking at me inquiringly as she carried the back of the stretcher along. "Oh," I said, realizing. "Coroner. Tofino coroner. Somebody thought I should be here."

She nodded grimly and looked back over her shoulder toward the wreckage of the broken freighter. "Looks like you'll have more business than anyone else here."

When we got back to the sandstone bench where the survivors were mostly gathered and those who were injured were receiving basic on-the-spot first aid preparatory to their evacuation, I let the girl's hand go and started to walk away. I got no more than about ten feet before she let out a terrified cry and started wriggling around on the stretcher. "You better come back here," the woman said sharply. After I took the girl's hand again and knelt down next to her, she settled down and lay still, brown eyes staring up blankly at my face. Her hand was locked tight inside my own. "Think you should stay with her now. We don't want her doing anything to hurt herself or make the shock worse." I nodded and sat down cross-legged next to the girl, keeping her hand in mine. It seemed a more useful task than the one I was supposed to be attending to. The dead would wait. Monaghan had said that most of the migrants were in relatively good shape, but, examining them, I thought she had been speaking in relative terms. Since the police reinforcements and immigration officials had arrived, they had managed to collect several dozen migrants. Most looked pretty hypothermic to me.

Looking out to sea, I saw the *Cape St. James* was now on station. The cutter had launched its Zodiac and a couple of crew members in bulky survival suits were braving the choppy surf to probe in close to the wrecked freighter. They were dragging bodies out of the water and into the inflatable, then running them back to the cutter where they were laid out on the open deck. The deck was filling up fast. I wondered how many migrants had been aboard the old freighter.

A few of the police, I noticed, were now probing about inside the woods. They seemed to be searching along any tracks that deer or other animals had opened in the heavy undergrowth as routes from the forest down to the shoreline. Off to their right I caught a glimmer of something black that stood out briefly against the lush green background, but the image was gone so quickly I wondered if I had not imagined it. Suddenly one of the Mounties snapped a shotgun up to his shoulder and pointed it toward the woods well to the left of whatever I may or may not have seen. "Halt," the man shouted. Then he crouched as another officer, also carrying a raised shotgun, came up on his flank. "That one's got a knife," the first man yelled. He started moving toward a figure that I could see moving dimly in the shadows. "Drop it. Drop it, right now," the officer yelled. "That's right. Lie down. Get right down. Down on your face." The two officers were closing in, another two running to their assistance. One of these was Danchuk, his shotgun already shouldered and pointing out in front of him.

After much scuffling about in the bush, the police officers returned with four men in wet, oil-sodden clothing. All had their wrists cuffed behind their backs with plastic bands and were being pushed along roughly by the four officers. When one of the migrants stumbled, a cop smacked him hard across the back of the head with an open hand. "Get moving," he barked. The man staggered forward. The four of them looked terribly small and scrawny in the midst of the heavily outfitted, armour-vest-padded, and generally large and broad-shouldered police. Even Danchuk looked oversized by comparison. The lower half of one of the men's T-shirts was drenched in blood, as was the front of his jeans. He seemed to have suffered some kind of dreadful wound to his stomach. I noticed that while the other three men were generally dragging their feet, forcing the officers to pull them along by their elbows, the wounded one walked quickly out just ahead of the entire group. It was as if he wanted to keep his distance from those around him, cops and fellow migrants both.

The wounded man seemed different from the others. He was Asian, of course, with classic oriental eyes, straight black hair, and a wiry body. In this he looked like the others that Danchuk and party had corralled so far or, for that matter, like any of the five hundred or so already locked up at my old alma mater in Princess Patricia's days of the Work Point military barracks near Victoria. There they awaited Canada's semblance of due process before inevitably most would be shipped back to China to face whatever official and unofficial retribution awaited them there. If not for the many hours spent studying Vhanna's features at great length, I doubt that I would have noticed any dissimilarity between the wounded man and the three others being dragged along behind him. Though their body builds were more alike than not, his was more finely tuned. He was pronouncedly leaner, both in body and face. Whereas the others had somewhat flat, rounded faces with prominent cheekbones, his was shaped more like a narrow upside down teardrop. He had the daintier build and facial structure that Vhanna had once said during a wander through Vancouver's Chinatown were more common to the Cambodian, Laotian, or Vietnamese peoples than to the Chinese. The other three shared characteristics that I assumed were common to the Fujian-region Chinese.

Yet here he was in the midst of their summer — a summer that in past weeks had set British Columbia's historical racist pot boiling. Thinking of what had brought these people in a rustbucket freighter to Canada's shores, I found myself gripping the girl's hand more tightly. *What*

chance do you have? If you survive the shock and live,
what happens? A swift hearing and deportation back to
somewhere you sought to escape from? Being taken into
government care and shuffled through an endless series of
foster homes until you are likely returned to China any-
way or else manage to slip away one night and end up in
the grips of those who brought you here in the first place?
A deportee or a slave to evil men, that was her likely
future. Without any official papers, without a sponsor,
without education, and, most importantly, without great
amounts of money to buy legal entrance, she had no
future in Canada. If she lived through the shock and
physical trauma of her drowning, the government would
try to dump her back into China so fast that I wondered
if she would even see anything of Golden Mountain, as
the migrants were said to call North America.

While my mind chewed over these grim thoughts, I
watched the police and the captured migrants. The four
of them, including the wounded one, had been
sequestered away from the others. A first-aid man from
the Labrador had torn open the man's shirt and proceeded to clean and bandage the long, deep gash running across his hard, brown stomach. He had sat and
watched this treatment with a curious detachment,
showing no sign of experiencing either pain or queasi-
ness or horror at the gruesome sight of the deep wound
carved into his own flesh. His chest and stomach were
covered in a network of small, jagged scars. I had seen
scars like that before — the telltale sign of wounds produced by the shrapnel cast out from an exploding mine
or grenade. How would a young man from Fujian come
to suffer such a wound? Vietnam, Cambodia, or Laos
seemed more likely places to encounter such violence.

"Change of plans, McCann." I looked over my shoulder at Danchuk, who glared down at me. "The first Labrador load is going to Tofino. You and the girl will be on it. That way, she and the other more badly injured can be shifted by ambulance to Port Alberni if necessary. Closer and quicker than if we stage the evacuation through Gold River."

Made sense to me. Also meant that I wouldn't end up being stranded in a logging town in the middle of nowhere until a ride by helicopter or car could be arranged. "The boy with the knife wound going to be okay?"

"That guy ain't any boy." Danchuk pulled his cap off and ran the flat of his hand over his pate. "We figure him for one of the Snake Heads, maybe even the top one." Maybe I was wrong about the scars, maybe they were the result of some other violence — the sort experienced by someone engaged in a life of crime. Something like the scatter of pellets from a shotgun fired at close range. I eyed his chest and stomach again and thought this conclusion improbable. Had the old wounds been inflicted by gunshot, he would most likely have been killed.

"I don't think he's Chinese at all," I said, and immediately regretted voicing my suspicion. Talking to Danchuk is rarely useful and more often than not it just stirs up his animosity toward me. Which proved immediately the case.

He sneered. "And you're, of course, an expert on Asians, aren't you?"

"Gary," I said, but he didn't let me continue.

"Listen to me, McCann. You aren't here to have opinions about anything living. You saved this girl and that's great. Good for you. You saw the corpses out there in the water and you can write in your report that they were killed in a shipwreck. When the bodies are all recovered you can go to the morgue and take a look at each one and write up whether they were killed by drowning or by injuries suffered when the boat broke up out there or by having their bodies bashed to pieces on the rocks. What you don't do, McCann, is meddle in a police and immigration investigation of how this smuggling scam was to have been carried out." He grinned. "I'm going back to Tofino with your flight, too. We found a good clue that might lead us to whoever is setting up reception committees for these migrant ships coming in." He grinned again, the same puzzling flash of menacing teeth.

I stared at him flatly. "You think there's anyone but the Snake Heads setting up the transportation for the migrants once they get off the ship?"

This time Danchuk's smile was indulgent, that of a teacher sharing deep insight with a dim pupil. "The Snake Heads over here operate out of Vancouver and Toronto. They don't know much about logging roads or beach landing sites. Got to be locals who are providing that kind of information. Probably locals providing the transportation and contact links between a place like this and the Snake Head headquarters in Vancouver." He nodded. "Seems logical. That's how we're seeing it. And now we've got some evidence to back this up."

"Somebody in Tofino?" I thought of the people and the town, and could hardly picture it. This was organized crime Danchuk was talking about. A penchant for organization, planning, and secrecy was not commonplace among Tofinoites. Unless you were a Mountie, it was hard not to know who grew marijuana and where. And growing pot or harvesting hallucinogenic mushrooms were about the sum of Tofino's crime wave. That and break-ins of tourist cars and summer homes by teenagers.

"Someone, McCann," Danchuk said with a triumphant tone. "Someone all right. Got some interesting questions to ask someone." The emphasis he put on the word "someone" grated my nerves. As he turned away, Danchuk said over his shoulder, "But you don't need to know who that someone is. This is police work. You stick to coroner work." With a chuckle he sauntered off. I shrugged, bewildered by his bizarre attitude and equally bizarre behaviour. Presumably the suspect, if there was one, was somebody I knew. But that was crazy, because I knew nobody who would be involved in smuggling aliens into Canada. Nobody at all.

chapter five

By the time the first load of passengers boarded the Labrador the second fog wind had started to roll in. Mercifully, it seemed content to follow a route that left the immediate shoreline and a narrow band of sea fronting it out to about five hundred yards or so sufficiently clear of fog. This permitted the rescue operation to proceed unimpeded. A number of the bodies recovered by the coast guard crew aboard the Zodiac had been transferred over to the fishing boat, *Destiny 5*, and it was now steaming down Zuciarte Channel en route to sanctuary at Gold River. The Sikorsky was airlifting bodies off the deck of the *Cape St. James* and the chopper crew and some of the Mounties then laid these out above the high tide line next to the ones I had earlier retrieved. The Mounties on shore had also fished a few more corpses out of the water and brought them into the collection point. There had been no more survivors beyond those that had been lifted off a few of the offshore rocks, several clusters that had managed somehow to reach the sandstone shelf, and the four men that the police had rounded up in the woods. In all, the living numbered just fifty-two. Most were cold, wet, and mildly hypothermic, but otherwise unharmed. A few, like the girl, the young man with the knife wound, and an older man who had suffered multiple fractures of his right leg, were in worse shape. There were fifteen slated for immediate evacuation by the Labrador. The three of us who had come up from Tofino on the Sikorsky would join them.

"Any tally on the dead yet?" I asked Monaghan as she crouched down to check the girl's vital signs one more time. The child was breathing normally now and her lips were no longer blue, although her skin still had a deathly white pallor. Monaghan's long-nailed fingers gently stroked her cheek as she looked over at me.

"Best guestimate we have right now is seventy-eight."

I pointed at the wreckage of the ship. "They had 130 people aboard that thing?"

"They cram them into the cargo holds as tight as they can fit them in and still leave room for people to lie down to sleep. A couple slop pails for toilets, some pre-packaged food in boxes for them to eat. A thin mat or blanket to lie on and another couple buckets of water a day for drinking. Takes between thirty and forty days at sea to make the crossing, depending on the weather and the speed these rust buckets are able to maintain. Everybody's in pretty rough condition by the time they arrive."

I shook my head. "But they just get caught. How many ships have been intercepted already this summer?"

"Three." Another officer came up and crouched to take hold of the front of the girl's stretcher. Monaghan grabbed the back end and I continued my duty of standing alongside the stretcher holding its occupant's hand. "But there are probably others that aren't getting caught," she said. I looked at her, surprised. "Not that anybody's telling the media that, of course. Enough trouble from them and the politicians already."

That made sense. The media, particularly Vancouver Island newspapers and radio talk shows, made it sound as if we faced a Chinese amphibious invasion force that threatened the very survival of the nation and the Canadian way of life. Even someone who ignored the newspapers as assiduously as I did could not escape the headlines that blazed out of the news boxes or leapt up from where the paper lay on the counter at the bakery's coffee stand. "MIGRANT INVASION." "HUNDREDS MORE ON THE WAY!" "CRACKDOWN NEEDED!" Scant effort at genuine objective reportage, stories laced with editorial opinion about how the migrants must be immediately shipped back to China and the smuggling rings broken up at all costs.

I wondered if, when this shipwreck story broke, as it probably already had, there would be much pity for those who had died here today. When this fog wind cleared and flying conditions improved, the officials involved in the rescue would be faced with a swarm of airborne media landing by the dozens all along the shoreline to get their images of the dead and of the ship's wreckage. Perfect fodder for the nightly news.

Eventually, after one of the roughest rides I had ever endured in a helicopter, the Labrador dropped down through a rapidly thickening fog and pinned the Tofino landing pad in the glare of its underslung spotlight. Although it was early evening, it was almost nighttime dark. Standing outside the landing circle, I could see a group of medical staff from the hospital waiting with wheeled stretchers. The moment we set down, the door was thrown back and the stretcher with the little girl was lined up alongside the doorway. She was quickly slipped from that stretcher onto one with wheels and a couple of nurses or orderlies started rolling her toward the emergency room doors. There was no television show panic with people running frantically this way and that, just a purposeful distance-eating stride. Still holding her hand, I followed alongside across the tarmac and through a pale-green reception area to the emergency room.

Doctor Tully, robed in his white coat, was standing next to a mobile tray loaded down with probes and various electronic equipment that were so much meaningless technology to me. Nodding a greeting to me, he bent over the little girl and went to work.

"Okay, honey," a middle-aged nurse said softly to the girl, "time to let his hand go. You're going to be alright now." I was surprised to feel the girl's hand tighten in what seemed almost a reflexive move.

"Sometimes it's almost like she understands what we're saying, Janet," I said.

The nurse shrugged. "Doubt it. But we've got a lot of work to do here with her. And you're in the way."

Slowly, firmly, I started unwinding the girl's fingers from around my own. She resisted but was too tiny and frail to prevent my disengaging her grip. "I can wait outside if that might help."

Janet nodded. "Good idea, Elias," Tully said. "You can check on her again when we move her out of here."

As I started to turn away a small, soft voice said, "Please. No go." The tone was less pleading than quietly despairing.

I bent down to her, feeling awkward and completely out of my depth, but also profoundly moved to try to ease away her fear. "Don't worry, honey. I'll be nearby and the nurses and doctors will make you feel better." I paused, looking for some signal that she comprehended. "What's your name?" I said when she offered no response.

After a long pause, the girl whispered, "Hui. Me, Hui. Hui Hua Huang." She smiled shyly. "You Elias." She pronounced it something like Eee-rye-ess.

I took her hand in mine and shook it gently, but formally. "I'm pleased to meet you, Miss Huang." She giggled weakly at that and didn't offer any further resistance to my leaving the ward while Tully, Janet, and the others tended to her.

The reception room was empty except for a nurse at a desk scribbling away on various charts and schedules. I walked over to her and got directions to a payphone. It was down the hallway, fixed to a wall in a small alcove that also featured a couple vending machines and some battered chairs and couches. Same sickly green walls guaranteed to make a person feel deathly ill even if they were of robust health.

Digging in the canvas rucksack, I found my small stash of emergency cash and was relieved to discover it contained precisely the necessary three quarters. Feeding one into the slot overrode the automated message telling me to insert a credit card or calling card and replaced it with the steady hum of a dial tone. A few seconds later, Vhanna's cell phone was ringing. She answered on the second ring. "It's me," I said. Quickly I gave her a run-down of what had happened, ending with how I was at the hospital waiting to see Hui again.

"I'll come," she said. "Fergus is here with me. When I called Nicki earlier to see if she had any news she thought you would be overnighting in Gold River. So I brought him to my place for dinner and the night. I'll bring him, too." Although I told her that she didn't need to come, Vhanna insisted. She sounded a little shaky.

"You okay?"

There was a long pause. "Yes." I could almost feel her thinking, weighing whether to tell me something or not. "Can't be leaving you helplessly trying to figure out what to do with a kid," she said with a forced laugh. "Be there in about fifteen minutes." She hung up. What was that all about? I wondered. But there was no time now to think about it.

The second quarter yielded up Lars Janson. Lars and his wife Frieda were Vhanna's adoptive parents. A Swedish merchantman who eventually became a professional forester and ended up in Thailand to teach modern forestry practices, Lars had become disillusioned watching the ancient teak and yang trees of the tropical rainforest going the way of those in North America's Pacific Northwest. Deeply affected by the plight of the thousands of refugees streaming out of Cambodia, Lars and Frieda had joined the Red Cross and gone to work in the prison-like refugee camps on the Thai border. Eventually Lars had discovered a ten-year-old girl hiding in a lair, like that a tiny mammal might have built, among some rice sacks in a storage locker. The girl had the bloated belly and large eyes and head of the near starved. For some reason Lars never could determine, Vhanna had fled the dormitory to which she was assigned shortly after her arrival in the camp six weeks earlier to live alone in hiding. He had picked the near-dead girl up and Lars and Frieda carefully nursed her back from the edge of death.

The two became so attached to this one refugee that they undertook the long and difficult bureaucratic task of adopting Vhanna and bringing her home to Canada. In this process they had a distinct advantage over those attempting to arrange the immigration of other Cambodian refugees to other nations. Most had been stripped by the Khmer Rouge of any documents of identification, but Vhanna's mother had managed to secret away her passport and papers proving Vhanna's identity. When she died, Vhanna had the presence of mind to take the documents with her. She also carried in her memory a series of numbers and an address in Hong Kong that her mother had forced Vhanna to memorize. In time, Lars learned that the address was a bank and the numbers were those of an account into which Vhanna's father had transferred most of the family's wealth out of Cambodia mere weeks before the Khmer Rouge captured Phnom Penh. Vhanna may have been an orphaned refugee, but she was also the sole inheritor of a small fortune.

Vhanna does not speak of her experiences in the refugee camp or the ordeal of her flight from Cambodia after witnessing the deaths of her parents and so many others. She sometimes speaks of the times before the Khmer Rouge came to her home, but only rarely and with a guarded tone, as if doing so jeopardizes the sanctity of those cherished memories.

I thought of these things from Vhanna's past as I told Lars what I hoped he would be able to undertake. It was no surprise when he left the phone for only a moment to discuss the matter with Frieda and then returned to say that they would be happy to do what they could. Lars and Frieda have a huge collective heart, especially when it comes to those in need. "None of this is right, Elias. There must be sympathy." I told him that I would call again as soon as I learned anything more and Lars said that he would stay by the phone until midnight.

I plugged the last quarter into the phone and dialed Father Allan Welch. He answered with a thickly growled hello on the fourth ring, just as I was about to hang up. "Am I disturbing anything, Father? Or have you just had too many glasses of the good Irish?"

"Reprobate," the Catholic priest said with a deep laugh, "what do you mean disturbing a man of the cloth at so late an hour and interrupting his spiritual meditations and deep ponderings? There is much of God's work to do in the morning."

"You mean shaking off the hangover from this evening's drink and then going to the gym for a marathon workout," I countered. Father Welch is a weightlifting junkie with a build akin to a World Wrestling Federation bully, shoulder-length grey hair he usually wears in a ponytail, and a penchant for black T-shirts and nylon jogging pants as opposed to clerical collars. He is also a dear friend. "Allan, I may need some help here." I quickly briefed him on the events of the day, focusing particularly on Hui.

When I finished there was a long pause as he thought everything over. "Hell of a thing, Elias. Those poor people. God pity the refugee."

"God might, but sure as hell not Immigration or the Mounties."

"You're right there. There's way too much of a public hue and cry for the government on this one. None of my parishioners are coming forward this time, as they did with the Vietnamese boat people." He sighed. "Different times, different story. But only in the details really, isn't it so? And look at my own people all those years ago. Was not their plight similar?"

"Love to discuss the philosophy of this with you sometime, Allan, but not tonight," I said a bit edgily. It was late and the clock was running on whether he could find the answers tonight. Tomorrow might just be too late.

"Let me make some calls, see what or who I can scare up, and then I'll pop over to the hospital to see what might be worked in the way of divine intervention."

I laughed. "Just remember to dress appropriately, Father."

"Scoundrel," he said and was about to go on at greater length when I gently placed the handset back into the cradle to end the call and focus his attention on the task at hand.

There was nothing else I could do at that point so I walked out into the night and strolled across the hospital grounds to a small opening in the trees that lined the embankment looking down on Duffin Cove. The fog swirled about me, rolled into coils by the wind that raked through the branches of the trees overhead with a low soughing sound. A fine drizzle danced coldly against my face. I tipped my head back and let the chill air and rain-water wash over me, taking with it the worst effects of the fatigue that was starting to clog my thoughts and make my movements feel sluggish and uncoordinated.

The sound of a vehicle pulling into the hospital parking lot drew my attention and I saw the flash of headlights turning into a visitor stall. In the dim glow of the yard lights, I recognized Vhanna's silhouette behind the wheel. She was driving her red Jeep Cherokee rather than the Miata sports car and had slotted it in next to the Rover. I walked across the pavement toward her. She must have leaned over and opened the passenger door because Fergus suddenly came around from that side. His head was down against the drizzle and the wind so that he seemed to be surveying the world from under a furrowed brow, like an old seafaring merchantman who has seen too many high seas and bitter winter winds. Seeing me, he came across the parking lot with a slow, purposeful stride, stub of tail wagging happily. He brushed against the rubber leg of my overalls and I reached down to give him the obligatory deep scratch behind his ears and across the top of his neck. Then we set off with common purpose toward where Vhanna stood at the back of the Jeep.

Vhanna carried a small black leather daypack over one shoulder. She wore a green Gore-Tex rain jacket and had her hair pulled back in a ponytail. As I came up she unshouldered the pack and tossed it my way. I snagged it out of the air, catching one of the shoulder straps one-handed. "I brought you a change of clothes," she said. "And a sandwich."

"Thank you, oh sister of mercy." I dug in the pack. There was a denim shirt, a pair of jeans, even clean socks and underwear. A Tupperware container held two thick slices of multi-grain bread from the local bakery enclosing equally thick slabs of white cheddar and smoked ham topped with a small hill of romaine lettuce. I bit into it happily. We stood facing each other as I munched away contentedly. Vhanna's teeth were catching the ghostly light filtering down through the fog from the parking lot security lamps and I could see she was grinning. I swallowed. "What?"

She smiled. "You." She came over and leaned against my side, put an arm around my waist. I took another mouthful of sandwich, chewed, waited, tried not to laugh. "You're such an in-the-moment guy." Her voice dropped several octaves. "Me hungry, me eat."

I grunted agreement. Took another bite. "This is delicious. Right amount of Dijon. If I had a bottle of ale." It was almost gone and I wished there were another. "When I called earlier," I said softly, "you seemed a little upset."

She leaned a little harder against me and hugged me a bit tighter. Again that pause, a reluctance or hesitation there. Finally she said, "There was a strange message on my answering machine when I got home this afternoon." She broke off suddenly, her body tensing slightly as two shadowy figures materialized out of the fog. Monaghan and Danchuk. In the ghostly light cast by the security lights, Monaghan looked washed out and drawn, like she was on the brink of exhaustion. Danchuk just looked round, bitter, and hard. "Sorry to break up the little homecoming, McCann, but this is really a fortunate coincidence." As he had on the beach at Nootka Sound, he sounded both angry and triumphant. My hackles rose.

"What coincidence?" I said flatly.

"The coincidence that I was just about to go looking for Ms. Chan and then," he snapped his fingers, like a magician doing a conjuring act, "Presto, here she is." Suddenly he was all business. "Ms. Chan, we would like to ask you some questions in regards to our investigation of today's events at Nootka Sound. If you would come back to the station with us, there is an inspector there who is waiting to conduct the interview. Are you agreeable to that?"

"Wait a minute, Gary," I said, but Vhanna squeezed my arm hard. She stepped away from me and looked directly at Danchuk, hands shoved deep into her pockets.

"It's okay, Elias." To Danchuk she said, "Am I charged with anything or is this just a case of answering some questions?"

It was Monaghan who answered, despite the dirty look Danchuk threw her way. "No charges, Ms. Chan. We're just hoping right now that you can clear up some concerns we have."

Vhanna nodded, her features giving away nothing of her feelings or thoughts. This is an ability she has. The talent of a survivor to shut down her emotions and don a protective mask that denies all insight into her state of mind. "I'll drive over to the station and meet you there, then," she said.

Danchuk hesitated, obviously unwilling to let his quarry have an opportunity to escape. His pause, however, opened the way for Monaghan to quickly agree.

"I'll come too," I told Vhanna.

She shook her head sharply. "No, you need to stay here for when they finish treating Hui. She will be looking for you." She placed a hand on my arm reassuringly. "It'll be alright. You better put Fergus in the Rover." With everything now organized to her satisfaction, Vhanna stood quickly on tiptoe and brushed her lips against mine and then was gone, climbing into the Jeep and banging the driver's door shut. Monaghan walked off toward the police Blazer and, after a last angry glare my way, Danchuk strutted along behind her. I noticed that there were three figures in the back of the police cruiser. I guessed that these were the other three men who had been arrested along with the young man who had been knifed and who the police suspected of being Snake Heads.

Why would Danchuk or any other Mountie want to interview Vhanna about the Nootka Sound migrants and the shipwreck? Danchuk had insinuated that he had found evidence linking the Snake Heads rounded up there to someone in Tofino. That he could possibly suspect Vhanna was that person was beyond understanding.

Fergus and I stood there alone in the parking lot and watched the two vehicles roll off into the dense fog. I fished the Tupperware container out of my jacket pocket, retrieved the scrap of remaining sandwich and bent down to offer it to Fergus. He sniffed it, ran a tongue across the cheese and ham appraisingly, looked up at me with sad eyes and then sat back and shook his head with a rattle of dog tags and a flapping of his ears. It was a reluctant shake but the message was clear. He was worried and had no taste for food right now. Feeling the same way, I tossed the scrap into a trash can beside the hospital door, coaxed Fergus into the back of the Rover, then shouldered Vhanna's little pack and walked back into the building to see how Hui was doing.

They had tended his wound and given him an injection of something so that he now drifted in and out of a vague, troubled sleep that never quite drew him down into its depths. Asleep, it was like he lay just under the surface of a body of water, able to see the shimmering, unfocused images of people standing along the shore and to hear their conversation — as if from the opposite end of a long, echoing tunnel. Awake, he kept settling back down under the water's surface, so that his conscious thoughts became confused and intermixed with the images, dreams, and murmuring voices that so disrupted his sleep. The fact that the knife wound was no longer a fiery pain in his belly must be due to the drugs they had given him, Kim thought. All he felt now was a dull, throbbing ache that formed a constricting band across his stomach where the bandage followed the precise line of the slit Cheng had slashed in his flesh.

He was amazed to be alive. When he had let the sea sweep him from the ship into the surf, Kim had been mentally prepared to die in its embrace. But it held him for only a terrifying moment before hurling him like a speared fish thrown over a fisherman's shoulder up onto shore. He had flopped against hard stone, landing painfully on his wounded belly so that the little air remaining in his lungs whooshed out on the edge of a shrill scream. As the wave that had borne him into shore rolled back to sea with a loud clatter he had been dragged along by its powerful suction, bouncing and scraping painfully across the slippery, ragged rocks. Then the wave was gone and he lay on the wet stone at the sea's edge, gasping for air. Another wave pounded in and he was lifted up off the stone as it swirled beneath him and washed his body further up onto the stony shoreline. But as it withdrew, Kim was once again dragged back in its hold to the point where he had been when it caught him up. He realized then that he must do something to save himself or the sea would soon claim him.

Another wave, bigger and rougher than the last two swept him up the shoreline again and dashed him down hard on the rock so that he cried out, feeling as if his stomach were being ripped wide open along the knife wound. He clawed frantically at the stone, ignoring the sharp edges that flayed the skin of his hands and managed to drag himself a few inches closer to a high tide line that he could not see but knew must be up there somewhere ahead of him. Then he was sucked back in the wave's retreat, but this time he fought its pull and sensed that it dragged him less distance. Kim used the seconds before the next wave's arrival to crawl painfully up the stone incline. Then that wave was on him, bearing him up. When he bottomed out again, Kim kept crawling, gauged his moment and as the wave started to withdraw pushed himself unsteadily to his feet. He stood there fighting for balance, refusing to let the wave sweep him off his feet and drag him outward. When the water receded past him, Kim staggered up the shelf. The next wave merely swirled about his ankles. It was nothing; the sea had lost its claim to his life. Kim walked free of it, passed the high tide mark, kept going to the edge of the dark woods. Only then did he turn to look back at the ocean and the heaving wreckage of the ship, the struggle of the others in the surf. He was too tired to help. Kim flopped down, sat cross-legged, and let his head drop down onto his chest.

Eventually he heard voices and looked up wearily to see some of the refugees milling nearby at the treeline. There was a mix of men, women, and a few children. It had not occurred to him that children might be among those kept in the cargo hold. Not that it would have mattered. He had had no influence regarding how the people were treated. Captain Liou had hired him only as a cook. Each crew member had been hired for a specific assignment that was necessary to the running of the ship. They had sailed from the port at Kompong Som, rounded Vietnam to enter Chinese waters, and steamed into the channel between Fujian Province and Taiwan. All that time the crew had no idea of the purpose of their passage. Shortly after midnight on the night they sailed into the channel several small fishing vessels had slipped alongside the ship. Minutes later, four men had swarmed up the ladder onto the deck and roughly ordered the small Cambodian crew into their sleeping quarters. Kim caught only a glimpse of people crammed stern to bow on the fishing boats below before he was hustled through a door and it banged shut behind him.

That was when the crew discovered the nature of the cargo they were to carry. Up until that moment Kim and Kwan, the radioman, had speculated that it would be drugs — opium or heroin. Or maybe guns.

After that he had seen no more of the migrants until he was sitting on the stone shelf looking at the little group standing nearby. He had heard them, though, especially their moans and cries of fear during the typhoon that the ship had sailed through two days to the east of Taiwan. Then there had been the pleas for water and more food. But Cheng, the Snake Head leader, had flatly refused Captain Liou's offer that the crew might share some of their own rations with those in the holds. "They have congee," he said with a dismissive laugh. Kim had learned that congee was a thin gruel that the poor in China ate and which provided scant sustenance.

Kim understood Cheng and the other three men who were his subordinates. He had seen many like him. The Khmer Rouge had been little more than a criminal gang that was just perhaps a little more deadly than Cheng or his cohorts could even imagine. Kim had been a Khmer Rouge soldier from the age of six. He had worn the checkered scarf and carried the AK-47 with pride at a time when the gun was taller than he was. He and the other warrior children in his squad had sung songs praising Pol Pot and had fought ferociously against the Vietnamese invaders and their massive Soviet-made tanks. One misty morning, when he was fourteen and a seasoned veteran, the squad had been patrolling through a marsh toward a macadam road where they were to secure a narrow wooden bridge. The twelve-year-old boy ahead of Kim tripped a Bouncing Betty mine that shredded him. Some of the shrapnel that had passed clean through his thin body pierced Kim's chest and stomach. The blast had stunned him. When he regained consciousness, Kim found himself on a stretcher. The men carrying him to an aide post wore the green uniforms and pith helmets of the Vietnamese army. He had been told that the Vietnamese were cannibals who would roast his brain and then dish it up using his skull as their bowl. Instead they had tended his wounds and later, after several months in a re-education camp, had released him from captivity to live as he wished in the occupied zone that they called the People's Republic of Kampuchea. He had been living hand to mouth ever since.

With a start, Kim realized he had been dreaming again. Or had he been thinking? It was hard to tell. He brushed memories of the war and his childhood aside, focused on the recent past. The shipwreck. Cheng had been there on the shore with the other three Snake Heads. It seemed incredible to him they had all survived, but he remembered the ability of the best Khmer Rouge killers to surface unscathed from the smoke and carnage of battle. Kim had seen the chubby corpse of

Captain Liou floating in the surf and thought he recognized Kwan lying dead on a rock that stuck up out of the sea. The number of dead did not shock Kim. As a child he had seen corpses stacked as high as houses, waiting to be thrown into huge quarries that would be blasted down to cover them. Kim had stood shoulder to shoulder with the other children in his squad and raked young and old alike with bullets as ordered by the commanders. After each slaughter, he had marched onward and sung the songs praising Pol Pot, celebrating the new utopia they were building, and had never once given a thought to those that he had killed. That his mother had died at the hands of others like him, that they had murdered his father, and that his two older brothers and four younger sisters were lost to him was something he did not think of. They might have been in one of the groups that they exterminated for the good of the utopia they were building. It had not mattered. The leaders said the killing was necessary. They said that the people eliminated were like lice that fed on the bodies of the healthy and so must be plucked off and crushed to pulp.

Later, the Vietnamese and Cambodian lecturers at the camp had taught him that Pol Pot and the Khmer Rouge were nothing but a hideous lie that had used young children like himself as executioners. He had searched then for his siblings but found only graves that might have been theirs or picked up rumours that might have told how they had died. Died from starvation, or been executed, or contracted one of the contagious diseases rampant in the country, or survived only to become a prostitute and perish from AIDS. He could not validate the stories and eventually he stopped looking, decided he must only seek to survive. Until he had seen the notice on the board in Phnom Penh.

It was one of the many boards where people tacked up notes reporting that they lived and searched for this or that family member or sometimes, as had been the case with this note, any family member. Vhanna Chan, daughter of Yuan and Lin Chan. Yes, Kim had known her. He remembered the house and the lovely melodies that Lin had played on the grand piano beside the open French doors that led out onto a garden rich in yellow and gold flowers. It was the piano music and the memory of a girl older than him who had held him on her lap as they listened to the music that stuck with him through all the years of madness. A memory that burst into his consciousness so evocatively that he wept openly and without the slightest sense of shame. Vhanna Chan. An address, a phone number, a hope of reconciliation.

He had not taken the notice. Instead he had scrawled the information with a stub of pencil onto the back of a cigarette package and stuffed it into his pocket. There might be other family who would see the note and also look for Vhanna Chan, so he had left the note there for them. And he had headed for Kompong Som, Cambodia's main port. He had rejected trying to phone Vhanna Chan. He wanted to see her face, to be sure that his memory was true. To do that he must go to her land. Kim did not consider the difficulty he faced in doing this. He did not think in terms like that. Perhaps this was because it was already as if he were dead and just a spirit that walked the land. A spirit should not be held back by earthly obstacles. And, in truth, the obstacles had proved to be very few. It had not been long before Captain Liou materialized in a noodle house. Kim overheard the sea captain discussing with another his need to gather a crew that was made up of suitably desperate men who would be willing to risk a dangerous, illegal voyage across the Pacific to the Golden Mountain for meagre profit. He sensed the shifty way of the men, their distrust of everyone, and was reassured that Liou was the man who could make it possible for Kim to reach Vhanna. Kim had followed Liou, shadowed him for days until he was sure of the man's purpose. Then he had approached him and offered his services. As they talked, Kim had allowed a certain look to come onto his face — an expression he had learned to hide away in recent years, but one he had worn often during his time as a Khmer Rouge killer. Liou had gone pale when Kim had turned his eyes blank so that he appeared as nothing more than a death's skull. Liou had looked into those eyes and saw what he feared to see. He had tried to be grudging, rather than desperate with fear as he agreed that Kim would be his cook on the forthcoming venture with the old freighter. Kim had nodded and then set about learning how to cook.

Again he shook himself, struggled to keep focused on the present. There had been the helicopter and the fishing boat standing offshore. There had been Cheng coming down the beach toward him with his knife in hand. There had been the other three men moving up on Cheng's flank. Kim had run for the forest then, plunged into its dense, dark depths and struggled through the brush that snagged his legs and arms, tried to push him back or to hold him captive. They had come after him. For a long time he had hidden in undergrowth while they searched with determined purpose. Finally they had spotted him and he had run again, knowing he was too weak from the blood loss to escape. But then there had been the other men, the ones in uniforms who had carried guns. He had willingly surrendered to them, let them handcuff him with the plastic strips. It did not matter when they took the cigarette package with Vhanna's name and address. He had long ago memorized its details. The small man with the angry voice had puzzled

Kim. It was the way the man had laughed as he read the information on the package. He had heard Khmer leaders laugh like that many times. He had thought such people would not exist in this land, or at least not wear uniforms. Of course, Kim realized that such a thought was based on nothing. He knew nothing at all of America.

The men in uniforms had captured Cheng's three subordinates, but Kim had seen no sign of Cheng himself. He had known then that the Snake Head had escaped. But where would he go? Perhaps he would die there in the bush, starve to death or perish from thirst. Kim wished it so, but he suspected Cheng was too evil to die that way. Still, for now Kim felt safe. As safe as he had been in the Vietnamese hospital when they had tended the shrapnel wounds to his chest. His task now was to rest and to heal. And to consider how he would go about finding his cousin, Vhanna Chan, now that he was at last in her land.

chapter six

Feeling somewhat refreshed after changing out of the rubber overalls and other sodden clothing into the denim shirt and jeans Vhanna had brought, I had no sooner returned to the ratty little waiting room than Doc Tully entered. He plunked a couple loonies into the machine and watched some oily black liquid dribble into the paper cup that dropped out of a chute. The black liquid stopped running and some slightly steaming water drizzled in and raised the fluid level to the brim. Tully took the cup and I looked down at its contents dubiously.

"Looks like it could eat up your stomach walls, Reginald."

"After enough of this your gut builds up a special hardened lining that the strongest acid can't penetrate." He took a sip that seemed overly tentative for someone professing a habit of consumption from the machine and then grimaced. "Usually we keep some pots of decent stuff going in the staff room, but someone forgot to put any on. This stuff is only fit for visitors and patients."

"How is she?"

Tully shrugged. "She'll be fine. Needs rest and rehydration. And some tests in the morning. It's too early to tell if there was any damage to organs or any adverse effects to her brain. I'm optimistic. Think you got to her in time." He patted my shoulder paternally and looked at me solemnly through his thick glasses. Meeting his gaze was hard as the depth of the glasses distorted his blue, watery eyes. I wondered how he could possibly carry out surgery with vision so poor. "You did something really good there, Elias. The sort of thing they give out heroism awards for."

That was an awful thought and I quickly cautioned Tully to constrain his penchant for exploiting every opportunity that might serve the cause of community boosting. As the long-standing Tofino mayor, Tully is fond of old-fashioned community values and all excuses to host ceremonies in the village hall to honour anyone who has done anything from maintaining the showiest rose garden to recycling and thus diverting the most waste away from the landfill in a year. I could see ghastly images of some kind of Medal of Bravery, or whatever it's called, being pinned to my chest by the Governor General while Tully stood by regally adorned in his mayor's sash. "Forget it. I wouldn't come. I'd be sure to be out of town."

He sighed regretfully. "You would, too. I don't see why, though."

"God sakes, Reginald. There was nothing heroic about it. Those awards are hardly ever given out for truly heroic acts. Usually it's just somebody doing something that had to be done anyway. It's not like anybody thinks about whether they should do what they do or even that they are putting their life at risk. It's not like there's a war on. Every time you turn around now someone is being called a hero for just doing what's right or necessary. Or for simply surviving by enduring something dangerous." I waved a dismissive hand. "Enough of that. Should I go in and see Hui now or wait until morning?"

"Morning will be fine. She's fast asleep and I don't expect her to wake up any time soon. One of the nurses will keep a close watch through the night." Tully looked at me curiously. "You're certainly being protective of her, Elias."

"I just want her to be okay," I said flatly. "I'll leave my number with the nurse. In case she wakes up and asks for me. Once she's feeling better, she'll be fine on her own." I allowed a small chuckle. "Besides, isn't there an old Chinese proverb that holds that the person who saves the life of another is forever responsible for their welfare?"

Tully smiled ruefully and then studied me somewhat gravely through the great bottles of his glasses. "I think you might believe that more than you are letting on, my friend." Before I could deny this notion he swallowed the last dregs of his caffeine and hot water mixture, frowned sourly, crumpled the paper cup, and tossed it into the garbage can. "I'm going to do one more round to check on the others and then head home. They all came through surprisingly well, really. Just some broken bones here and there, a bunch of abrasions, and, of course, hypothermia symptoms. Nothing life threatening. Even the fellow with the knife wound just needed bandaging up and a mess of stitches. He'll have a hell of a scar to add to his old collection. Somebody sure wanted him dead, though."

"So it was a knife cut?"

"Without doubt. Nothing else could have made such a clean incision. Some of the others had bad cuts, but they were all the result of something jagged and rough-edged. Like you would expect if a person's hand was dragged across crustacean-covered rocks or banged into a piece of torn steel on a ship that was breaking up. This was straight and narrow, a precise depth from the entry point near the navel over to where it struck a rib and followed that along right across the body to the exit point near his hip. Classic knife fight wound. Whoever had the knife was right-handed and was probably trying to stab him directly in the stomach, but the victim twisted to one side and fell backward so that the wound was only glancing."

"Strange that anyone would be trying to kill somebody else on a ship that was breaking up. Or even on the shore after such a wreck. Seems just trying to stay alive would keep everyone occupied."

Tully nodded. "I'd think that, too. But then I'm not a criminal. Who knows what they think or what they will or won't do? My experience is that violent people don't think or act like the rest of us. That's why so many of them end up here in emergency or on the autopsy table downstairs." Tully knew of what he spoke, for he was Tofino's leading surgeon and also pinch hit when necessary as the pathologist. Tully knew nothing more about the wounded man, other than the fact that Danchuk and his cohorts in the war on crime had taken a distinct interest in him. Obviously they continued to suspect him of being one of the Snake Heads, a supposition that still seemed implausible to me. If he were one of the gang members, why would they have been trying to kill him? I could imagine nobody else on board the freighter being armed and engaged in trying to commit murder in the middle of a shipwreck other than the Snake Heads.

However, as Danchuk had earlier reminded me, the puzzle of the wounded man was not any concern of mine. My only official task with regard to the migrants was to write a report stating the number deceased and the general nature of the causes of their deaths. I saw no reason to consider holding an inquest into the circumstances of the shipwreck. There was precious little that could be done here in Canada to prevent such a tragedy reoccurring. What could I recommend? That the ships bearing migrants be allowed to enter Vancouver harbour and legally unload their human cargo? So long as the migrants were willing to risk their lives to come to this country, then ships would ply dangerous waters in search of isolated landing spots. When such ships succeeded in making a safe landing, the migrants aboard could be unloaded and spirited away by buses or trucks to a city where they could become lost in the crowds and enter a pipeline that apparently ran from Vancouver to Toronto and on to New York City. It was a pipeline that many experts with far more knowledge of such things than I possessed seemed incapable of cutting. Nothing a coroner in Tofino wrote about the deaths inflicted by a freak storm on this particular migrant shipment could prove worthwhile.

There was, however, the chance to influence matters in one small way, and the moment Father Welch's old Volvo rolled into the parking lot outside the hospital I set about exploring that possibility. As I walked toward his car I was pleased to see the diminutive form of Bethanie Hollinger, Tofino's social service caseworker for the Ministry of Children and Families, climb out of the passenger side of Welch's car. Bethanie has shoulder-length blonde hair so straight that it looks ironed and a slender hipless and seemingly breastless body. Standing no more than five-foot-two, it is not surprising that Bethanie is often mistaken for a child or an early pubescent teen. A penchant for black miniskirts, heels, and shrink sweaters gives her a distinctly flirtatious appearance that stands at odds with the serious nature of her job and the authority she wields. Bethanie is, in fact, not at all like the visual image she projects. She is thirty years old and in her spare time is a passionate philatelist who rarely strays from her little house up the street from the bakery.

Bethanie came to Tofino three years ago. According to the usually reliable gossip mill, she had fled to Tofino from the mean, hard streets of Vancouver's East Side. There she had seen one too many of the children taken into government custody and placed in group foster homes end up dead from an overdose of heroin taken between turning tricks for men cruising the district's kiddy stroll. Not that Tofino and the native community of Opitsat on Meares Island have no social ills that threaten the lives of children. It seems that nowhere on earth is without its share of incestuous or abusive parents, pedophiles, rapists, pimps, pushers, or others who prey on the vulnerabilities of children. So Bethanie's days remain long and grim, but perhaps not to the same extent as they were in Vancouver. Little wonder that she finds both refuge and sanity in studying the minute details of stamps from foreign lands through a magnifying glass and meticulously gluing them into little books according to some undoubtedly incomprehensible indexing and cataloguing protocol.

I came to know Bethanie during an inquest into the death of a young teenage native boy who had been put in social services care. Drunk on stolen vodka and on the lam from his group home he had fallen off the government dock on a stormy night and drowned. My first impression of Bethanie had been based entirely on her clothes and her California Valley girl blonde looks so I expected to deal with someone suitably lacking in intelligence. But I soon came to realize that underneath the Twiggie facade was a thoughtful woman who cared deeply about the well-being of children. Bethanie and I had worked back from the time of the boy's death through the hours that had led up to it in the hope of developing some recommendations or new procedures that would prevent such a tragedy reoccurring. We had come up empty. Short of locking the boy in chains, there was little the foster home parents could have done to prevent his running away. And it is as easy for a determined youth to find, buy, or steal booze as it is impossible to secure docks and wharves against their use as refuges by drunks.

Approaching Bethanie and Father Welch, I saw that she wore a long black leather trench coat tied at the waist with a belt. "Thanks for coming, Bethanie," I said. "You too, Allan." Father Welch shrugged inside a thick lumberman's jacket that was starting to bead with raindrops. His beard was dripping. As was Bethanie's hair. In one hand she carried a bulging brown leather attaché case.

"I don't know that there's anything I can do, Elias," she said in a voice that was always surprisingly gravelly. Looking at Bethanie, one expected her to speak in a sweet, even lilting voice. Instead, she sounded like a chain-smoking bartender.

Suggesting we go inside the hospital to get dry, I led the way. After we settled on the battered furniture in the waiting room, Bethanie dragged a notebook out of her big attaché case and took notes while I described the situation with Hui and her general medical condition. Bethanie scribbled away with a skinny hand as if every word I uttered had some kind of significance, although what I knew of Hui's situation could easily fit in a shot glass. When I finished, she made a few more notes and then sat with her eyes fixed for several minutes on the two pages of jottings.

"She'll be under the jurisdiction of the Immigration Department. They wouldn't have to agree to anything we proposed." She shrugged. "I'd be surprised if they agreed to leaving her up here where she's isolated from the rest of the people on the boat and not easily brought to hearings. She might even have parents who were on board and survived, or some other relatives."

"Lars and I can make sure she attends any hearings that are required. We could sign a guarantee or something if that would help. And obviously if she does have relatives who survived they would have to be involved."

"Okay," she said. Bethanie pulled out a business card, scribbled on the back, and then handed it to me. "That's my home number. If you or Lars need to reach me outside office hours, try me at home." I thanked her and tucked the card in my back pocket, silently reminding myself to remember to take it out of there before next doing laundry. "I'd like to see her if that's possible," Bethanie said.

I led her and Father Welch over to the duty nurse's desk and she in turn put down her romance paperback and slipped off to check on Hui. "She's still sound asleep. If you're all quiet it should be okay," she reported.

We followed her down dully lit hallways and into a little windowless room that contained a single narrow bed. Hui lay on her back with her head propped up on a pillow. Her eyes were closed and lanky dark hair billowed out around her face. One balled up hand rested outside the covers next to her head and every few seconds her body twitched as if responding to a bad dream. An intravenous drip of some kind ran from a bag suspended on a rack through a tube that entered her other arm. Bethanie reached out and lightly brushed thin fingers across the girl's brow as if trying to smooth away her fears.

Including the nurse there were four of us crowded shoulder to shoulder into the little room. Compared to the tiny form lying under the covers we all looked monstrously large and well fed, even Bethanie.

After a few minutes Bethanie indicated she was ready to leave and the rest of us withdrew one by one to make room for her exit. We trudged back to the duty nurse's desk, left her to her romance, and made our way outside where we stood under the covered entrance to keep out of the increasingly heavy rain. "Well, what do you think?" I asked.

Bethanie pursed her lips and offered another non-committal shrug. "I made some calls. The children from the earlier boats are being put into foster care until their status is decided. There've been some problems already with a few of them disappearing from the group homes they were assigned to in Victoria. The suspicion is that the Snake Heads either lured them away or snatched them outright. Either way they're probably never going to be seen again. Maybe it'd be safer up here, maybe not. I'll find out tomorrow who to talk to at Immigration and see what I can work out. It's a long shot, though. You understand that?"

I nodded. We left it like that, Father Welch and Bethanie driving off in his Volvo. There was nothing more I could do at the hospital for Hui, so I climbed into the Rover. Fergus was curled up asleep and snoring softly on the passenger's seat. It was well past the hour when Fergus normally would have climbed the stairs into the loft and stretched out with a great sigh of pleasure in his big wicker basket for the night. When I fired up the Rover he didn't so much as stir. I yawned mightily, slipped the transmission into gear and drove off on the next mission of a night that showed no prospect of an early end.

chapter seven

Vhanna's Jeep was still in the police department
parking lot when I drove past a few minutes after
midnight. A full two hours had passed since she had
accompanied Danchuk and Monaghan back to the station. Seemed an awful long time for just a few questions.
I slowed, backed up, and pulled in behind the Jeep,
switched off the lights, the wipers, and the engine, then
sat there in the darkness listening to the rain rattling
noisily on the roof above my head. The station was typical of the kinds of functional RCMP buildings that are
common to the nation's small towns — a one-storey
wood-sided square box with a small porch facing a narrow three-stalled parking lot around which ran a concrete sidewalk leading from the street to the building. A
thin strip of clover-infested grass and a forlorn little
poplar tree stood on the frontage between the building
and the street. On one side of the building a Canadian
flag hung wet and limp from a short white pole. On the

other side the top of a tall radio-antennae mast was lost to view in the rainy night sky. Three halogen spotlights mounted on the building were largely futile in attempting to brighten the grounds. A bank of three long windows mounted side by side faced the front of the building and another matching window stood next to the porch and looked out on the parking stalls. Tightly closed blinds through which the glow of fluorescent lights shone covered all the windows. The building was bleak, institutional.

One of the parking stalls held Danchuk's police Blazer, the other Vhanna's Jeep with the Rover parked behind it, and the third, which was closest to the building, contained the type of grey American model sedan that Mounties favour for unmarked vehicles. As is normally the case, the true identity of this one was betrayed by the presence of a telltale small radio antenna mounted next to the trunk. Presumably this car belonged to the inspector who, according to Danchuk, had expressed an interest in speaking to Vhanna.

I sat there in the dark, lightly drumming my fingers on the steering wheel, and listening to Fergus's rhythmic snoring. There was no cause for concern here, I cautioned myself. Vhanna had nothing to do with migrant smuggling. Some questions would be asked and duly answered, then Vhanna would walk out of the station, climb into the Jeep and drive home. Something she could not do right now because I was blocking her exit with the Rover. Therefore I really should do the sensible thing of just going home and then checking in with her in the morning.

Reaching behind me I snagged my Filson hat off one of the gun rack hooks and put it on, opened the door, and stepped out into the rain, closing the door gently behind me so as not to disturb Fergus. I followed the little sidewalk along the square it cut around the parked vehicles to the doorway and tried the door. Not surprisingly it was locked. A yellow light illuminated a doorbell switch. Above the door stood the kind of camera used for surveillance. It was directed downward so as to monitor anyone who might come up to the door. There seemed two options here. I could fall back to the Rover and retreat homeward or possibly cause a disturbance. My finger pressed the doorbell, which buzzed loudly within.

I waited. A minute passed, then another. I pressed the button again, holding it longer this time to create the desired extended sound inside the station. As I was considering yet another stab at the button the sound of locks being unlatched emanated from the opposite side of the door, which then opened wide. I looked down at a bareheaded Danchuk who had one hand on the handle and was scowling up at me. "What do you want?" he snapped.

Looking over his head, I could see only the reception area where Nicki holds court during the day. Behind that a door with a window in it that was covered by a closed blind led into the guts of the building. I knew from past official coroner visits that behind the door were two cubicles that passed for offices and a small interview room. Further back were a couple of cells normally occupied by nothing more dangerous than a few drunks locked up for the night out of concern for both their own and the public's safety. There was no sign of Vhanna. "I thought I'd check on Vhanna."

Danchuk grunted something like a black bear sow might upon discovering an inviting blueberry bush. There was an odd tone of sympathy or almost camaraderie indicated by the sound. "Sorry, McCann, you can't wait in here. There's nobody to supervise the front section." He shrugged. "Don't think it'll be much longer. Ray seems to think it's just some kind of coincidence." He shook his head, baldpate glowing yellow in the light. Because we were so close together, I couldn't see his expression. Stepping back would put me outside the scant protective covering that the little porch provided from the rain, so I held my position and waited. Finally Danchuk moved back a bit and looked up at me with a surprisingly thoughtful and unbelligerent expression. "Sometimes you think you have someone all figured out and then you realize how little you actually know about them," he said softly. "She'll be along in a few minutes probably, McCann. I'll let her know you're waiting." He shut the door gently in my face.

With absolutely no idea what Danchuk had been talking about, I walked thoughtfully back to the Rover and leaned against it. The rain pattered noisily on my hat and dribbled off the brim onto the oilskin jacket, but the night was warm and I felt no inclination to retreat into the Rover's steamy confines. Fergus's heavy breathing and steaming fur coat had caused the windows to mist up so that it would be like sitting in a boat shrouded in a fog bank. Too much of the day had already been plagued by fog for me to willingly submit myself to an artificial front.

Had Danchuk been talking about somebody else or about me? Vhanna, perhaps? What had Danchuk believed he knew about whoever the person was that was now nullified in some way? I realized the self-reflective and introspective Danchuk I had encountered in the doorway was probably as contradictory to my normal perception of him as was the realization he professed to have reached about the unnamed someone.

The sound of the station door opening drew my attention away from further speculation on the world of Danchukness. Two figures came out together. One was tall, the other short and obviously recognizable as

Vhanna. The tall one wore the kind of long trench coat that can be worn over a business suit, which made him an outlander of some sort. Probably this was the inspector who had wanted to ask Vhanna questions because of something recovered from the shipwreck site.

As the two of them emerged from under the porch the tall one unfurled a broad umbrella. Vhanna and he walked under its protection to where I stood by the Rover. "Hello, Elias," the man beneath the umbrella said.

"How are you, Ray?" I asked as we shook hands.

Ray Bellows answered that he was fine and, present circumstances not withstanding, it was always a pleasure to come back to Tofino. At the time Merriam took her life Bellows had been the sergeant in command of the local RCMP detachment. It had been Bellows with the then Corporal Danchuk who had attended my house on the night of her death. While Danchuk immediately set about constructing delusional scenarios whereby Vhanna and I had conspired to kill Merriam, Bellows immediately saw the truth. He extended to me the same southern gentleman courtliness with which he greeted felon and victim alike, putting me immediately at ease. I was also deeply touched by the gentleness with which he had leaned over Merriam's body and delicately closed her staring eyes with his fingers. It was a kindness that returned to her some of the personal dignity that the gaping wound and the carelessly tossed pose in which she had landed seemed to have stolen from her. Ray Bellows was a policeman whom Tofino had respected and missed when he was promoted away.

"I have already apologized to Ms. Chan for taking up so much of her time and keeping her so late," Bellows said. "I regret if this has caused you any distress as well. At the time, given the information we had, it seemed some appropriate questions were justified." As he talked,

Bellows made sure that the sweep of his umbrella protected both himself and Vhanna from the rain. I didn't mind that there wasn't room under it for the three of us, as my hat and jacket provided sufficient protection. "I'll let Ms. Chan explain what transpired to you."

"You're an inspector now?"

He smiled. "Yes. I'm attached to the anti-gang unit in Vancouver. Particularly the Asian gangs."

"The Snake Heads?"

"More properly known as the Big Circle Boys," he said. "That's the gang behind this. They're tough, dangerous, tightly organized, and nearly impossible to get an edge on. A very highly developed operation with headquarters over here in Vancouver and New York and strong links to Hong Kong and mainland China. They're also responsible for most of the thousand or so human smuggling cases we've investigated in the last year. This incident and the other boats this summer constitute just the tip of the iceberg in a racket that rakes in millions for the gang. They bring people in on planes, stuffed into container shipments aboard freighters, transferred from passing freighters into the holds of fishing vessels, you name it. With these freighters they're just trying to get more ashore in one go and as cheaply as possible. If they succeed, fine, and if they don't, I suspect they really don't much care."

"Works well for them perhaps, but not so well for the seventy-eight that died today," I said.

Vhanna interrupted. "People like that don't care about the lives of others. They would only care about the product that they lost. That's how they would perceive these people. As a product to be rented out or sold."

Bellows agreed. I asked if he thought there was much chance that the smugglers involved in this freighter operation would be caught. "I think we've got all the ones who were actually aboard, barring any that might have been among those killed. There's a remote chance that one or two might have escaped into the bush but if they did they'll either die in there or end up having to come out and give themselves up. But the ones on the ship are nothing. Just soldiers. There isn't much chance that we'll break the cell in the gang that was organizing the operation. We'll do what we can, of course, but there isn't anything really to go on and the ones who were on the ship won't talk. If they did they'd be signing a death warrant for themselves and their families." Turning to Vhanna, Bellows thanked her formally for her cooperation, bid me adieu, and went to his car.

I rested my hand on Vhanna's arm and she looked up at me. "I need to go home, Elias. I need to clear my head of all of this."

"Can I ask what happened in there?"

She shook her head, releasing a small spray of rainwater beads from her long hair. Her face was already damp with rain. I noticed her cheeks seemed tauter than normal, as if from tension or anger or both. "Tomorrow maybe. Okay?"

I nodded reluctantly. "Tomorrow then."

By morning the rain had stopped and patches of sunlight shone through gaps in clouds that were rolled up like great balls of cotton. They rode on a strong westerly that shoved them up the inlet into Clayoquot Sound toward the mountains. Summer was back, with the temperature already up to around fifteen degrees Celsius and the promise that it might break twenty before the day was through. A heat wave on the Pacific Rim, if not anywhere else.

Fergus and I went for a long morning stroll in the woods that lead from my cabin along the inlet shore. Dog was fully rested and energetic, man weary and sluggish. Sleep had been elusive and I had spent much of the night brooding before a fire with a glass of Bowmore single malt from the Islay islands in my hand. I pondered the rightness of the course of action decided upon regarding Hui, worried about Vhanna and the still unexplained connection between her and the migrants, puzzled over what I was supposed to do as a coroner in relation to the shipwreck and the seventy-eight resulting deaths.

The same questions plagued my mind while trudging behind Fergus down muddy trails that wound past soaring firs under which stands of thick-leafed salal intermixed densely with tropical-looking ferns. In every life there are defining moments that leave an indelible impression upon your soul and ever after affect your behaviour. Such a moment was mine on a sun-washed day patrolling the Green Line in Nicosia in 1974 when a terrorist bomb engulfed a square in fire and the spray of shrapnel. Among the wounded was a little Greek girl who died in my arms and who undoubtedly never understood any of my words of reassurance as I desperately and futilely tried to stem the blood gushing from a gaping hole in her small chest.

From then on, my time in Cyprus was a descent into nightmare. The Turkish army invaded and the Greek-Cypriot militia tried to fight it off even as the United Nations peacekeepers, among whom we Canadian paratroops numbered, were caught in the middle. We could do little but dodge the bullets and shells while attempting to protect the thousands of Turkish and Greek Cypriots trying to get across the firing lines to the perceived safety of territory held by their respective ethnic groups. When the crisis eased I had seen enough of death and personal suffering inflicted for the sake of national prejudices and perceived pride. Still in my twenties, I quit the army and began to take up a lifestyle that more with the passing of each year seems to mirror that of my remittance-man father.

I am aware that the misery and despair caused by war, famine, and poverty appears to be growing throughout our troubled world, but I do not dwell on this. I have learned that the best way to deal with world news is to remain largely unaware of it. So I subscribe to no newspaper or magazine, own no television, seldom turn on the radio, and resist all Vhanna's urgings to acquire a computer of this or that speed and megabyte capacity in order to become adept at searching the Internet. No doubt there are some, Vhanna among them, who would say that I am increasingly becoming a hermit, locked away with my books, my music, my single malt whiskey, and only a loyal, aging dog for companionship. That may be so, but there it is. I see no reason to change, nor do I have the inclination to do so.

Back at the cabin, I spent a good fifteen minutes cleaning the worst of the collected mud off Fergus's thick coat and out of his paws and ears. For his part, Fergus tolerated my ministrations but made it plain that he really didn't appreciate the problem or see why he should be excluded from the inside of the cabin in his present condition. I banished him to the enclosed and covered kennel run that stands next to one wall of the cabin anyway and ignored his soft, plaintive whine as I went inside.

Given the current course of affairs I had ensured the answering machine was both on and operational. Its light, however, was not blinking. Apparently Bethanie Hollinger had nothing yet to report and Vhanna was either not up or was disinclined to discuss matters. As Vhanna is a perpetually early riser given to often greeting the dawn from a position on the beach that fronts her home, the second possibility seemed the more likely.

It occurred to me that I had a job to do and should turn my attention to contacting the regional coroner for some direction on what course to follow in the shipwreck investigation. I certainly had no idea where to go with such a dire tragedy in terms of preparing a correct and bureaucratically acceptable report or conducting a further investigation into the causes of either the shipwreck or the migrants' deaths. The former seemed out of the purview of a community coroner and the latter too pathologically direct to be left to someone with no forensic qualifications.

Instead of phoning Dr. Carl Harris, the regional coroner in Nanaimo, however, I grabbed my Filson hat off its hook and walked toward the Rover. Fergus's sharp bark of protest caught me up short at the Rover's door. After a moment's thought I relented and freed him from the kennel. He made a beeline to the passenger door and sat on his haunches until I opened it to let him jump up on the seat, which was covered in an old blanket precisely to keep Fergus's collected mud and dirt from rendering the seat incapable of occupation by others. Fergus and I then chugged off toward Vhanna's.

Vhanna's grey cedar-sided modernistic house hangs on the edge of a cliff overlooking the ocean. It is a monstrous three-level place that is simply, but expensively, furnished. Decks wrap around its girth on all levels and a long cedar stairwell switchbacks down to the rocks and brilliant white sand of the beach below. An eight-foot-high rugged stone wall encircles the front of the house and a high-security system provides the best protection against break-ins that money can buy. On occasion I have climbed over this wall at great personal peril when Vhanna has unduly ignored my attempts to get her attention by ringing the bell mounted on the steel-barred gate cut into the wall. Doing so triggers some kind of invisible motion alarm and brings an immediate response from Stan Jabronski, Tofino's security system czar and also the chief of the local volunteer fire brigade. Jabronski is an old friend and one of the Tofinoites in which I have invested entrepreneurial capital, so he is normally more amused by my skullduggery than motivated to carry out a citizen's arrest. But he would undoubtedly do so if Vhanna insisted that she did not want me coming onto her property. Luckily she has not yet briefed Jabronski to that effect. I hope she never will.

Today, however, it was unnecessary for me to scale the wall because she triggered the release on the outside gate and the main door to her house when I announced my presence into the little speaker box mounted alongside the gate. Fergus and I sashayed in happily and soon found Vhanna out on one of the decks watching the surf roll in off the ocean. Most of the clouds that had been hanging about earlier had by now blown away so that the sea sparkled in sunlight and it reflected brightly off the large panels of glass behind the padded resin chaise lounge in which Vhanna was reclined. She wore a tan-coloured sleeveless button-up shirt and green canvas shorts. The shirt was some kind of state-of-the-art material capable of going from soaking wet to full dry in under an hour. A narrow pair of sunglasses with brownish unframed lenses covered her eyes. She had once informed me that a company that designed optics for NASA made them. I believe a price tag of about $600 was mentioned. On a matching table next to her elbow stood a slender water-beaded glass that looked like it contained gin and soda with a twist of orange. Scattered next to the glass were sheets of paper containing various printouts of charts and schedules, above which Artemis Adventures, Inc. letterhead was imprinted.

"There's beer in the fridge," she said with a smile.

I went into her sprawling kitchen that was floored with black slate and had matching countertops. When I opened her gargantuan aluminum refrigerator, a 650-millilitre bottle of Spinnaker's Witbier Belgian-style wheat beer beckoned. I fished out a frosted glass stein from the freezer and poured most of the bottle into it. Spinnaker's is a brewpub in Victoria that has been turning out quality beers at its site alongside the city's inner harbour for more than a decade. Vhanna has a standing order for deliveries once a month up to Tofino as fragile cargo on the bus line. As she seldom drinks beer, I am left with the surprising realization that this indulgence can only be explained as being aimed at pleasing me.

Back on the deck, I plunked down in a matching chair on the other side of the table from Vhanna. Fergus had taken up residence at Vhanna's feet and was lying contentedly with his head on paws surveying the scenery. Particular interest was being given to the shorebirds scurrying around where the surf met the sand. I knew he pondered the prospect of giving them chase, but was also not at all anxious to leave Vhanna's company in order to attend to such a mission. This was a sentiment I understood, knowing that, like me, he would undoubtedly choose to put off most tasks in order to while away time here.

"Cheers," I said. Glasses clinked and Vhanna and I each took a good swig. "How are the books looking?" I asked, although I had no real interest in the undoubtedly growing profitability of Artemis Adventures.

Vhanna pursed her lips thoughtfully, as if giving my query serious concentration that it didn't deserve. "I think it's time to get out of the whale-watching operations locally. There are too many players, too many boats, and too few whales being increasingly harassed by it all. So I'm going to sell that side and concentrate on the trips into the real wild."

I thought on that, realizing this would likely mean more trips led personally by Vhanna and more time spent away from Tofino. When I commented to that effect, she looked at me and smiled softly as if pleased that I should be concerned. Having expected her to dismiss such concerns out of hand, a wave of tenderness all out of keeping to the moment washed over me. This was only partially a response to how absolutely stunning and desirable she looked in the shirt and shorts. I think, of course, that Vhanna is the most beautiful woman on the planet, present, past, or future. Her active outdoor lifestyle has given her a hard, thin covering of muscle that wraps tightly over a lean frame and thin, delicate bones. Today, as normal, her hair hung black, thick, and straight to the base of her spine, glowing with a high-gloss sheen that again results from an overly healthy way of living.

Vhanna's mother was half-French colonial and half-Cambodian Chinese; her father was pure Cambodian Chinese. From the European gene pool she inherited a lithe tallness and angular facial features. Her cheekbones are high and her nose thin in memory of the French tobacco planter who bedded and married her mother's mother.

Her hand traced up my bare arm from wrist to elbow then dropped back down so she held my hand loosely in her own. "I'm away about as much as I care for already," she said. "If anything, this will mean less day-to-day distraction." She laughed. "The Zodiacs are a pain in the ass to maintain and keep operational anyway. And I was having to mix in undesirable clientele to get a full load."

"Meaning men?"

She nodded and grinned again. "Artemis is supposed to be about all-women outdoor, ecologically benign adventurism. I should never have got into the whale-watching enterprise in the first place," she added more seriously.

"But you couldn't resist the profit potential."

"Is that a rebuke?"

I laughed. "Greed has been the downfall of many an entrepreneur. Think of all those guys who go public to raise expansion capital and find the new shareholders elect a board of directors that turns said entrepreneur out on his ear."

"Artemis is never going public," she said sternly.

I shrugged, took a long swallow of beer. It was tempting to stick to business banter and even see — given her seemingly light mood — where else events might lead. I looked out at the point where the ocean waves were gently spilling up onto the beach and thought briefly of the wisdom of crossing lines. "Are you going to tell me about last night?"

She leaned back in her chair, took a slow sip from her glass, and licked her lips. The sunglasses kept me from seeing her eyes or the emotions that might be visible there. Then Vhanna sat up straight, looked at me flatly through the blank brown lenses of her sunglasses. "We need to go to the hospital," she said as she swivelled around on the chair and put her feet firmly on the ground. "I'll go change."

As she walked toward the French doors leading into the house, I ran my eyes down the length of her long back. Doing so I thought of the slight twist in her spine — the result of a brutally wielded AK-47 rifle butt on the road from Phnom Penh to nowhere. Every time I saw it or brushed my hand, fingers, or tongue down its length, following the unnatural curve, the lasting nature of this injury caused an ache of sadness to pass through my heart. "He probably had no idea what he was doing," she said once when I started grumbling about the injustice of the injury caused. "He was only about twelve years old and looked more scared and confused than even I was." Then she changed the subject and that was the last time we ever discussed the slight deformation she had suffered in a calamitous war.

She emerged from the house as a Vhanna I had never previously seen. She wore a silky purple dress that danced with grey and white little birds, was slit up the leg to the thigh, and shaped to form a tight collar at her throat. With her hair plaited down her back, Vhanna looked like an image from a timeless war movie about the Asian woman who would come to love and ultimately be betrayed by the lusty, but irresponsible, American GI. White, black, red, yellow, such soldiers had left their mark upon the Asian landscape in terms of illegitimate children fathered by women who thought that love meant duty, obligation, and a heart's desire forever. But the Freedom Bird home to hamburger heaven beckoned and the young men fled with likely little more than a glance over their shoulder, leaving the women and the children to sort out a life amid a culture and populace that would never forgive their perceived racial or ethnic betrayal. I had thought about this over the years. Had I done something similar in Cyprus? All that sexual adolescent drive and the presence of exotic women, who probably didn't appear exotic to their own men but were profoundly so to impressionable, naïve, and very young Canadian soldiers. I had sowed seed hither and thither without regard for whether the recipients were married, single, or inclined toward the use of contraceptives. I had been young, running with the stallions, lacking a care in the world.

"We'll leave Fergus here," Vhanna said flatly. Then, offering no explanation as to why we had to press on immediately to the hospital or why she was wearing this outfit, she strode on sandal-wrapped feet through the house and outside toward where the Miata and Jeep were parked in the double garage.

chapter eight

The hospital was as grimly sterile in smell and appearance as always — as if antiseptic had been splashed on every surface of its pale green walls and battleship linoleum floors. I generally avoid these places where I suspect more people come to die than to emerge hale and hearty with renewed good health. In recent time, my visits to hospitals have been generally confined to descents into the cloying hell of an autopsy room. This occurs when Doc Tully insists I need to actually view some incision or external injury suffered upon a corpse in order to understand fully the manner in which the poor soul came to life's end. Although I always attempt to wriggle out of such invitations, Tully is a skilled fisherman. He is adept at lining me in with bait that both whets my appetite for knowledge and plays on my sense of responsibility to ensure the truth of the cause of death of each person is known.

Today, however, I learned the reason for my coming to the hospital in Vhanna's wake was not to delve into death but rather to explore life. Without pausing at the front desk, Vhanna walked down a hallway past rooms shared by patients accorded only scant privacy by a paper-thin curtain surround to a room at the far end. Outside the open door, Constable Josinder Singh perched awkwardly on a small whitewashed wooden chair. Singh was young and dark, and sported a black turban on his head rather than the traditional Mountie cap. "Good morning, Ms. Chan," he said with a flash of white teeth as he drew his lanky frame up from the chair to face us. "Mr. McCann," he added with another smile.

We exchanged similar pleasantries with Constable Singh, who then informed Vhanna that she was expected and that Inspector Bellows had notified him that she was to be allowed to see the man he guarded. On the way to the hospital Vhanna had not divulged who or what was at the hospital that we needed to see for me to understand why the RCMP might think she was involved with the smuggling of illegal migrants into the country. Although I had been burning with curiosity, I also knew from Vhanna's body language that she was in no mood for explanations, so had held my tongue throughout the ride. That we had come to see somebody under police guard had never occurred to me.

"How is he?" Vhanna asked.

"The injury apparently is not life threatening. He neither speaks nor, it seems, sleeps. So far today he has not eaten the food brought to him. But he drinks the water and juice, which the nurses say is what matters the most." Singh shrugged and then said with greater formality. "I understand that Inspector Bellows has briefed you on the procedure. I must be in the room at all times. Mr. McCann can also be present if you wish."

Vhanna agreed that she understood. Then Singh opened the door and preceded Vhanna inside. Having not been told by Vhanna that I could not tag along, I stepped inside and stood back against the wall on one side of the door. Singh closed the door softly and assumed a position on the opposite side of the door from me so that we looked like sentries. Vhanna crossed the room to stand alongside the bed in which the thin man with the knife wound lay under a white sheet covered by a pale green blanket. The back of the bed had been raised slightly so he was in a semi-upright position, and he wore a standard-issue white dressing gown that seemed far too large for his wiry frame. His eyes focused on Vhanna for a long moment and then a smile touched his face as she steepled her hands in front of her small chest and bowed deeply toward him. The man positioned his hands similarly and, as best as he was able while seated, bowed in the same manner toward her. He then spoke softly in a language I didn't know and Vhanna replied, her voice slipping into a delicate singsong rhythm. I glanced over at Singh who raised his eyes and shoulders toward the ceiling to show he had no idea what words were passing between them.

For several minutes the flow of voices moved back and forth, at the pace two people might assume during a lazy tennis warm-up. Then suddenly the man stopped smiling and his cheeks tautened with an emotion that could either be anger or dismay. Vhanna's voice became sharper than before, her tones harder and more demanding. His own voice was tight, the words delivered with an almost desperate quickness while his tone dropped to a seemingly shame-wracked whisper. The emotional pain each word evoked in him was evident in his tone and expression. Suddenly Vhanna swivelled on one heel and strode to the door, yanked it open, and stormed off down the hallway. The man looked from me to Singh with eyes that shone with tears before turning his head to face the wall.

I found Vhanna outside, standing on the edge of the parking lot and staring down through the trees toward the water below. Her arms were crossed tightly so that she gripped each elbow in an opposing hand, head lowered in such a way that her face was hidden. I stood beside her, uncertain whether to place a hand on her arm or to put my arms around her. Finally I did neither. "I don't understand what just happened," I said softly.

When Vhanna looked at me her eyes also glistened with tears. "Not here, Elias." She led the way to the car.

We descended the long stairway that zigzagged down from her home to the beach with Fergus thumping down the steps in the lead. Once we were on the sand, Vhanna kicked off the sandals and left them lying at the bottom of the stairs. Side by side we walked toward the water. Vhanna shook her hair out of its plait and let it stream behind her, lifted gently by the breeze. She offered her hand and I took it. When we reached the high point where the receding tide had wet the sand, we followed the line of the beach. Before us Fergus ran right along the edge of the waves, playfully scattering small tan and white shorebirds that flew off in tightly packed flocks, the white on their wings sparking brightly against the blue sky and water.

"When I went back to Cambodia this year, I spent a good part of my time in Phnom Penh, particularly in Chamcar Dang where my family lived. Everything is different now and I found nobody who even remembered us." She shuddered. "Before, when I was young, Phnom Penh was so trim and well cared for. There was beauty and order at every turn. The image is still there but it is like trying to see it through a soot-covered lens, everything is filthy and in decay." She turned to face me, took my other hand in hers, and gazed up at me sadly. "But it's the faces, Elias. They were no longer the same people who had lived there when I was a child." Before the Khmer Rouge came, she said, six hundred thousand people had made the city home. Roughly equal numbers of Cambodians, Chinese, and Vietnamese. The city had a strong cosmopolitan flavour derived as much from its French-colonial past as from the mixture of ethnic groups. "All that was lost under Pol Pot when the city was emptied. It is as if every last city person was killed or forced to become a refugee." She paused, said ever more softly, "Like me."

Today, Vhanna said, Phnom Penh is a shambles populated by country folk who came to the city to escape the blighted, wartorn and land mine strewn countryside and a wealthier collection of rogues and exploiters who live inside armed camps on the city's outskirts. There is little sanitation, the housing of the poor consists of shanties, and the larger houses such as that in which Vhanna grew up have been broken into multiple dwellings or are occupied communally by as many as several dozen people. Work is scarce, prices high, and the availability of basic necessities poor. "Family was everything before," she said. "You knew all your family. Aunts, uncles, cousins, nieces, nephews. You lived near them and saw many of them every day. You were in and out of each other's houses. None of that exists anymore. There is a vacuum and nothing to fill it. People just exist in isolation from each other." She leaned her face against my shoulder and I put my arms around her lightly, pulled her into me. "We lost everyone," she whispered. "In losing our families, we lost ourselves."

I stroked her hair from the top of her head to her waist, trying to reassure her. I wanted to tell her that what she said was not true. That she was not alone and not lost to herself. But I could form no such words, could offer no illusory assurances. I had no idea whether Vhanna was lost to herself or not.

She pushed away from me gently and offered a sad smile, brushed a tear from her eye. "People try to connect. Those who are literate put up notices on boards around the city that tell how and where family can find them. You talk to someone and they'll ask if you have met anyone by this or that name. I did the same. For one week I wore the clothes that the peasants wear in the streets. I visited my home and spoke to the families crowded into there. Nobody had heard of any of them. I put the notices up and waited at the hotel, hoping for word. But the days passed and there was nothing. Finally I came back here, reconciled to having to just forget." She shook her head. "And then Kim comes. But he comes this way." Vhanna's eyes were now dark like hard stones when she looked at me and her mouth formed a thin line. "He is not family. Not anymore." She shuddered. "My God, he was one of them."

I started to reach out for her but she stepped back and shook her head, held one hand up. "Please, Elias. Go now." She smiled weakly. "I'll call you soon."

"You'll be okay?"

She nodded, smiled again. "I just need to think."

Rather than asking the questions I wanted, I said, "There's some things I should do." *My god, he was one of them.* I suspected I knew her meaning, and if so knew there was no comfort to be offered. Looking down the beach, I saw that Fergus was far down at the other end, a small dot trotting along in the surf line. He was well beyond the range where he would hear my whistle.

"It's okay," Vhanna said, "I'll look after him. I was going to go down the beach a way and do a Tai Chi set anyway. I'll walk down and bring him back after I finish if he hasn't returned by then. He'll be fine."

I knew this was true and that the moment Vhanna started working her way through the 108 moves of the Taoist Tai Chi set that Fergus would come bounding back from his wanderings to studiously watch her movements. He is endlessly fascinated by the duality of the exercise's graceful fluidity and restrained violence that holds the yin and yang of the set in balance. Having been a Tai Chi practitioner for most of her adult life, Vhanna is highly skilled. She also practises Tai Chi combat, which predates the more pacific, meditational forms commonly followed today. At the end of each Taoist set, Vhanna regresses to this older form, blasting through a dizzying series of rapidly executed kicks, sweeps, and punches that one is grateful not to have to try to stave off. Vhanna tells me that the combat form was derived from Tai Chi Chuan. Here the yang, normally concealed and dominated by the yin in other Tai Chi forms, is fully revealed. Vhanna says that the concealment of the yang form within the yin form of Tai Chi has given rise to the saying: "Looks like a woman, fights like a tiger." Regarding Vhanna this is most apt. Particularly as I have seen her use Tai Chi combat in a fight and she was every bit the tiger.

chapter nine

I drove back into town and without really thinking about it headed over to Lars and Frieda Janson's. I wondered at what Vhanna had said on the beach. Her voice had been filled with something akin to revulsion when she had said that Kim was one of them. If anyone might have any insight to shed on matters it would be Lars and Frieda. The Janson's home was a rough-and-tumble two-storey with washed out unpainted cedar siding, unframed windows, and a cedar roof heavily overgrown with a thick blanket of moss. The living room and kitchen faced the water and were fronted by an old-fashioned covered deck that had an uncovered extension off one side on which a large hot tub was positioned. About fifty feet from the house was a low-roofed cedar sauna that looked liked a little hut. A path bedded with cedar mulch extended from the hot tub to the sauna and from there down to the water's edge next to a small wharf that tilted to the right because the wooden posts supporting it were rotting away more quickly on that side than the other. This was the home in which Vhanna had grown up after Lars and Frieda brought her to Canada.

Her adoptive parents lived a simple life that reflected their aesthetic tastes and natures. To make ends meet Lars ran a water taxi operation between Tofino and the numerous islands offshore on which people lived or which tourists wanted to visit. For a few bucks Lars gave people lifts and ran supplies out to those who didn't own a boat of their own. Lars's boat was currently tied up to the little dock. It had a fourteen-foot steel hull with a square back running up to a snub nose bow, a wide flat bottom, big inboard engine and a control stand near the front fitted with a steering wheel, gauges, and a low windshield. A narrow metal bench was mounted to the stern and another one across the front. Otherwise the boat was just deck and control stand.

I found Lars down at the boat. The engine hatch was open, his head and shoulders were deep inside and his rear was up high in the air so that he looked like he was diving right in on top of the engine. His faded blue, tattered overalls were stained with grease that was both new and old.

When I stepped down into the boat and sat on the stern bench the vessel rocked enough to let Lars know somebody was on board, but he didn't look up. I could hear pliers working a coupling. "There's a little fuel leak," he said, "that I just can't seem to ever cut off. Hate to think it, but I believe I am going to have to buy a new hose." Slowly he withdrew from the inside of the engine compartment and looked over his shoulder at me. "Oh, it's you, Elias," he said with a smile. "I thought it was Frieda. Although I didn't know why she rocked the boat so much. You really are clumsy around boats. But my daughter likes you anyway, and so there it is." Lars and

Frieda have always called Vhanna their daughter and have treated her as such. He laughed, wiped an oily hand clean on a rag and stuck out a hard and cracked hand that I shook with a grin. "Good to see you, Elias. Any news about the girl yet?"

I shook my head. "Bethanie is looking into things. She'll call. If I'm not in, she knows to call you directly."

"It'd be good to give the little tyke a home. At least for awhile. Until all this is sorted out." He shook his head. "Frieda and I went over this morning and had a peek at her. She was asleep." Lars dropped the engine cover closed, sat on it, and looked out toward Meares Island. The boat rocked gently with the rise and fall of the waves. "Reminded me of Vhanna. About the same age she was when we took her in."

"I think there's a good chance that Bethanie can convince whoever it is that she has to convince that the best place for Hui is here until the issue of her refugee status is resolved."

He shrugged. "Frieda and I are getting a bit long in the tooth for being parents, Elias." From a pocket he pulled his curved pipe and a packet of tobacco. After tamping the bowl full he lit it with an old silver-plated Ronson lighter and took a few short puffs to get it going and then a long, satisfying one. He looked at me seriously with his grey eyes as he blew a trail of smoke from his nostrils. "What does Vhanna think about the girl?"

It was my turn to shrug. "I've told her, but we haven't really discussed the matter." I hesitated and then plunged ahead. "She's got matters of her own on her mind that are related though to Hui." Quickly I explained the little I knew about the young man in the hospital and the puzzling things that Vhanna had said. "Do you have any idea what that would all be about?"

Lars puffed on his pipe and stared at the hills for a long time before answering. "You say that she said he was one of them." I nodded. Lars took a final pull on the pipe and then tapped the spent ash overboard to clear the bowl. He looked sad and tired. "If you say the man is a little younger than Vhanna I can think of only one thing she could mean. He must have told her that he had been Khmer Rouge."

"I was afraid of that," I said.

Lars tucked the pipe back into the pocket of his overalls, stood up, and turned to face me. "Not that he probably had much say in the matter, you see. The cadres came and rounded up children at will. Some were sent to camps where they were supposed to farm the land free of the corruptive influence of adults. Others were left with their families. Others were simply murdered or left to die. And some, many in fact, were taken into the ranks of the Khmer Rouge itself. They were trained to be fighters and for many that meant becoming the very people that had killed so many of their family. Kim may have become one of those that murdered Vhanna's family." He sighed. "As much as she has sought to find some survivors in her family, Elias, I don't know that she could or would welcome one of those. And I can't say that I blame her. Whether willingly or not, if this Kim was Khmer Rouge, he as likely as not was a murderer. There is also the issue of why and how he came to be here among Chinese migrants. I do not understand that and I certainly don't like it. I think Vhanna would be best to wash her hands of him." He gestured toward the house. "Come up and have some tea. Frieda would like to see you, I'm sure."

"Another time, Lars," I said quickly. "I've still some things that need doing with regard to the coroner's report I have to do on the shipwreck."

We walked up the path toward the house together and paused at the steps leading onto the porch. Lars gestured to the hot tub. "I remember when we introduced Vhanna to the hot tub, sauna, and cold dive into the sea. At first she was so shy of her body." He laughed softly. "And shocked that these two old people would do all this soaking and sweating, naked if you please. She would sit in the house and refuse to come out until we were what she considered decently covered up again. Finally I talked her into trying it alone and after a few times she decided she didn't mind if we were there and that the whole activity really did do the body good. Vhanna is not a person who comes to changes or decisions quickly and easily. She considers everything, makes a thorough plan, and only then acts."

"That's for sure, Lars." I tapped a finger to the brow of my hat in salute and took my leave. As was Lars's way, a small story was told and the meaning was left to the hearer to interpret. I was not sure, however, what to make of this story in terms of what it meant for Vhanna and her dealings with Kim.

Tofino's RCMP four-wheel-drive Blazer was parked outside the hospital when I pulled into the parking lot. As Gary Danchuk usually treats the Blazer as his personal property, I could only assume he was lurking somewhere inside. After due consideration, I decided against withdrawing to return later when Danchuk would likely be elsewhere.

Walking toward the hospital, I passed an old paint-faded but immaculate blue Cadillac shoehorned into a small-car-only stall close to the entrance doors. A scrawny fellow in his early thirties was sitting behind the wheel. He had long, stringy blond hair, wore a ball cap pulled low down on his brow, and was tapping the fingers of both hands with nervous energy on the top of the steering wheel. There was something vaguely familiar about the car that the man behind the wheel didn't go with, but at the moment I was unable to think of where I might have seen it before.

In the foyer I met Constable Josinder Singh on his way out. "Inspector Bellows, Corporal Lee, and Sergeant Danchuk are with him," Singh said, "so I'm off for lunch." I nodded and then checked on Hui's condition with the duty nurse. A hefty woman with badly dyed red hair and plump arms, the nurse soon informed me that Hui was awake and her condition had been downgraded off the critical list. And, yes, I was cleared to see her. Hui's room was in the same ward as the one in which Kim was being kept under guard and as I approached her room I saw that the door of Kim's room was open. Curious, I passed by Hui's and poked my head into Kim's. "Afternoon Ray, Gary," I said cordially, and nodded to the other man in uniform who looked over his shoulder as I entered the room.

Bellows smiled and offered a friendly greeting; Danchuk nodded gravely and kept his silence. Kim was sitting in the bed in a pose identical to the one he had maintained when Vhanna had come to see him earlier. Not a trace of emotion touched his eyes or face as he looked over and I wondered if he recognized me as being the man who had accompanied Vhanna or if we Caucasians all looked the same to him. "I'm here to see Hui," I said.

"Been meaning to talk to you about that, McCann," Danchuk said. "This Hua Hui Hang girl, or whatever her name is, is to be moved this evening to Victoria. She'll go in the same ambulance that's taking him," he gestured at Kim, "down there."

I felt a hard lump form in the pit of my stomach and forced myself to say evenly, "Her name's Hui Hua Huang, Gary. Have you talked to Bethanie Hollinger about any of this?"

Danchuk shrugged. "Don't see what Hollinger's got to do with anything. This is just procedure. We're concentrating all the Chinese in Victoria for processing by Immigration court. Most of the others off the ship are already either at the Work Point base or are being transferred to there from Gold River by bus." He smiled nastily. "Good riddance to these two, as far as I'm concerned."

Beside Danchuk, Bellows shifted uncomfortably and stepped forward so that the sergeant was partially obscured from my view. "I know you're concerned about Ms. Huang," he said, "but you can be sure she will be properly taken care of."

"Bethanie is looking into whether she can be placed in Lars and Frieda Janson's care, Ray. She may not be able to arrange things before the ambulance is ready to leave. Why such a hurry?"

"More like to ask why you have such an interest?" Danchuk growled. "Since when did you start worrying about the welfare of little girls from foreign countries?" His tone made it sound like I was a suspected child molester now, as well as a wife murderer.

Bellows spun on Danchuk, his lips pursed in a thin, irritated-looking line. "Gary, there's no call for being discourteous." He ran a hand through his fair hair and slightly loosened the knot in his tie. "If you give me Ms. Hollinger's number, Elias, I'll call her and see what might be arranged. We are certainly going to move Mr. Hoai to Victoria today, however, and it makes sense to move Ms. Huang at the same time. So there may be little that we can do to delay matters. I will call, though."

Somewhat mollified and knowing that there was really nothing I could do to prevent Hui being transferred out of Tofino if that was what the authorities decided, I pulled the card Bethanie had given me the night before from my jeans pocket and read the number off. Bellows duly jotted it into a thin notepad. He then gestured with an open hand toward the uniformed corporal who had remained standing beside Kim's bedside during the course of this discussion watching us all impassively. "Corporal Lee, I'd like to introduce Elias McCann, Tofino's community coroner. Mr. McCann participated in the migrant rescue operations and is overseeing the coroner's report on the shipwreck." To me, he said, "Robert is a member of the Vancouver anti-gang unit and an expert on the Asian gangs in particular."

I shook his offered hand. He was a short blocky man with wide sloping shoulders from which a thick bull neck extended to support a square-slabbed head. Corporal Lee was also Asian, I assumed most likely Chinese.

"Corporal Lee and I have been trying to interview Mr. Hoai," Bellows said, with an ironic smile. "But it seems that he doesn't speak English, French, or Mandarin."

"Or a Fujian dialect either," Lee added, "which, as my parents emigrated from there, I speak fluently." He directed a flat, no longer friendly glare toward Kim. "Personally I think he's playing us for fools on the Mandarin, but the rest appears genuine. Although possibly he understands French. Which would make sense if he is indeed Cambodian, as Ms. Chan attests." His eyes drifted around to fix on mine. "I still find it bizarre in the extreme that her cousin should end up crewing on a Chinese migrant ship that comes to these waters and that there is no prior connection between them that brings this event about." We met each other's eyes and I sensed Lee probing behind mine for some sign of complicity or illicit knowledge that would add to his enlightenment on this matter.

"I should check on Hui," I said. As I bid adieu to Bellows, Danchuk, and the suspicious Corporal Lee, Bellows advised Danchuk that he would make the call to Bethanie Hollinger from outside. "Not much I can do here right now," Lee said. "Might as well go out with you and catch a few rays." He appeared to have returned to the sunnier side of his disposition.

The two officers left and for an awkward moment I found myself alone in the room with Danchuk and the silent Kim. Danchuk scowled, his eyes seemingly focused on a space somewhere between us, while Kim gazed at us both impassively from the bed. "See you later, Gary," I muttered and turned my back on him.

As I went into Hui's room two Asian men with heads lowered and wearing white lab coats over brown khaki pants walked past us in the opposite direction. One carried a plain clipboard, while the other had his hands shoved into the pockets of his coat.

When I stepped through the doorway Hui looked up from her bed and smiled shyly. Then her smile vaporized and her eyes widened in surprise. At the same moment, something hammered hard into my kidneys and a terrific pain tore through my body. My legs folded and I crumpled to the floor, landing hard on my side. Through unfocused watering eyes, I saw a figure in a white coat step quickly over me and grab at Hui. As if lying at the end of a long tunnel, I heard the faint echoing sounds of voices yelling and then a sharp scream. I recognized the figure in the coat as one of the men I had passed only a moment before. He wrestled Hui out of the bed as I struggled to stand up, then he spun with her clutched in his arms. A leg lashed out and smashed the sole of a heavy shoe into the side of my skull with such force that I was sent sprawling out the doorway and across the hallway to crash against the far wall. I slid down to a sitting position, one leg folded under me and the other sticking out straight in front as though I was trying to run a hurdles race. The hall spun and lurched wildly from side to side, but I could see the man coming through the door with Hui still held tightly to him, her little body twisting this way and that as she tried desperately to break free of his grip. He turned and started down the hallway toward the entrance. I tried to get up, but fell helplessly back against the wall. *Move damn it.* I fell forward and then crawled after the fleeing man on my elbows and knees, gasping at the knives of pain piercing through my head and kidneys. He was going too fast and I was going far too slow, I realized. Sucking in a hard breath and ignoring the pain, I staggered upright and charged after him as he started passing the duty nurse's desk.

"Hey," she bellowed as the man darted past her. Hui was now screaming at the top of her lungs and struggling wildly to escape his grasp. With surprising dexterity and speed for her size and plumpness, the red-haired nurse shot out from behind the desk and clutched the man's arm, unbalancing him so that he momentarily lost his grip on Hui, who wriggled out from under his arm, almost managing to break free. Just as the man managed to shove the nurse away from him and grab Hui more tightly with one hand by her elbow below the sleeve of the white hospital gown, I cannoned into his back with all the force I could put into my right shoulder. The two of us rocketed past Hui and the nurse. I landed face first in the middle of the foyer while the man in the lab coat rolled in a tight ball across the room to slam into the doors. He jumped to his feet and plunged outside. A second later another figure wearing a lab coat leapt over me and also disappeared out the door. Painfully regaining my feet, I stumbled out in time to see the two men throw themselves into the blue Cadillac, which took off out of the parking lot with a screech of rubber even as Bellows and Lee ran up to me. The car looked familiar. "McCutcheon," I mumbled.

"Elias, what's going on?" Bellows demanded.

I was bent over, hands clutching the sides of my head, the pain ratcheting through my skull so sharply that I felt close to vomiting. "The other one," I gasped. "Danchuk, Kim." I swallowed, croaked. "Check them."

Bellows looked hard at me for a moment. Then he drew a pistol from behind his back and went inside at a run. Lee followed suit. I took another shuddering breath and followed painfully after him. Inside the nurse was cradling a sobbing Hui to her ample bosom. The two of them were sitting on the floor and the woman was making the cooing noises one does when there are no consoling words that a child would understand. I went down the hallway to Kim's room and stepped inside. Bellows was bent over Danchuk, who sat on the floor in a widening pool of blood. His pistol lay loose in his lap, his right hand was clamped over his left forearm and he was staring blankly at the blood gushing between his fingers. Kim was sprawled on the floor next to the bed, blood welling through the bandage covering his wound and groaning weakly. A pillow lay between him and the doorway. A deep slash had gutted it so that the synthetic filling had spilled out on the floor. Lee was hunkered over Kim, his face set in a hard angry, scowl.

Suddenly the room filled with people in various white, blue, and green hospital uniforms and somebody was guiding me out of the room. They led me into Hui's room and sat me down on a chair. I bent over, head in my hands, and let the world spin wildly for a long time until it slowly started to stabilize and I could once again focus on details like the linoleum beneath my feet and the individual words that a nurse was speaking. "Three," I said in answer to her question about how many fingers she was holding up. "Two," I corrected. She told me I'd be okay and then she was gone and Hui was there, looking very small and very worried. When I took her hand in mine and held it she smiled and patted the back of my hand with her other one as if to tell me everything would be okay. I nodded agreement, but knew Hui was wrong.

chapter ten

"Be dead if he hadn't jumped out of bed and swatted the guy with his pillow," Danchuk wheezed through clenched teeth as a doctor finished wrapping his forearm in a white bandage. "Christ, what a joke that looked." It had taken fourteen stitches to close the gash in his arm. Danchuk's skin was deathly pale and his voice was slurred from the effects of painkillers. He was in a hospital bed, his uniform replaced by a ubiquitous white gown. I stood at the back of the room while Bellows hovered beside the bed, listening to the last of the sergeant's description of what had happened. Lee was standing back against the wall, arms folded over his chest, watching Danchuk impassively. Nobody had invited me to be here, but neither had anybody suggested I should not be present.

Danchuk explained that he had been just about to leave the room and take up position in the chair set outside the door until Singh returned from lunch when an

Asian man in a white lab coat had strode purposefully through the door. The man had evinced no sign of surprise at seeing Danchuk. Instead he had stepped toward the sergeant while pulling a long, narrow blade from one of the coat pockets. The best reaction Danchuk could muster in the second of realization he had before the man struck him with the blade was to raise his left arm defensively while trying to draw his pistol with his right hand. The knife had slashed deeply into his raised arm. As his assailant shifted the blade for a second stab that Danchuk knew would gut him, Kim had yelled something like Ching or Cheng and then dived from the bed with a pillow held out in front of him and shoved the man across the room into the wall. The knife wielder had recovered instantly. Crouched, balanced on the balls of his feet, with the blade held in a reverse grip in his right hand he had fixed his eyes on Kim.

Danchuk meanwhile had fallen to the floor with his back slumped against the wall. With great effort he managed to shake off the haze of pain that threatened to cause him to black out and started frantically trying to work the slide on the pistol to chamber a round. But the fingers of his left hand refused to respond correctly. As the man had lunged at Kim, he swung the knife up over his shoulder. Kim danced away quickly, raising the pillow at the last moment to intercept the downward slash of the blade. With a terrific tearing sound the pillow had been slashed from Kim's grasp as the knife plunged to its hilt into the fabric and tore down its length. The pillow struck the floor, stuffing pouring from its guts. In the fleeting moment when his assailant was thrown off balance by the momentum of his own knife wielding, Kim rolled across the bed to its other side.

Danchuk meanwhile had pinned the pistol between his knees and with still fumbling fingers was close to chambering a round. The noise of the slide moving on the gun caused the man to whirl toward Danchuk. His eyes met Danchuk's and the sergeant was struck by the man's calm demeanour as he cooly appraised the situation, obviously deciding the odds were sliding out of his favour. He grinned, shrugged, and dodged out the door, disappearing before Danchuk could raise his gun.

"Singh and Monaghan are out hunting for the Cadillac," Bellows said. "And the Ucluelet detachment has blocked the highway at the inland junction. There's nowhere for them to go. We've got an Emergency Response Team and other assets en route from Port Alberni and Campbell River." He sounded surprisingly confident, I thought. Undoubtedly this was because Tofino, positioned as it is at the terminus of Highway 4 on the west coast side of Vancouver Island, was a natural dead end. Nevertheless, there were still lots of coastal waterways and even old logging tracks that could be used to avoid police barricades if one knew the country.

Of course Bellows had already said that the two would-be assailants and kidnappers were unlikely to know the area. When I had mentioned the man who had been behind the wheel of the Cadillac he just shrugged. Again I pictured the scrawny man in my mind and thought about the familiar look of the Cadillac. "McCutcheon," I said suddenly. Bellows and Danchuk both cast puzzled expressions my way. "The car. It's local. Ian McCutcheon. It's his car."

"I don't know any McCutcheon," Danchuk started to say. I cut him off and began telling Bellows where he lived. "Tell me in the car," he said. Lee followed us out of the room as we hurried outside.

Ian McCutcheon was a loner in his late fifties who lived in a twenty-five-foot mobile home at the end of a dirt track that cut up from the highway into dense bush halfway between Tofino and the western entrance to Pacific Rim National Park. He was a short, balding man, with a heavy gut, who had a penchant for Copenhagen chewing tobacco and dressed perpetually in crisp, clean olive green work pants and matching long-sleeved shirts. About twice a month he drove his Cadillac into Tofino and parked it outside the Co-op grocery store, where he bought several bags of groceries and a box of tobacco plugs. He then drove around the block to the liquor store and purchased several bottles of rye whiskey. On his way out of town he always stopped at the Royal Canadian Legion bar. Here he sat alone in a corner with his back turned to the regulars who frequented the legion at such an early hour — a few old veterans, fewer still of their wives, and the occasional younger workman who preferred the legion to the hotel bar because the beer was cheaper and the wait for the pool table shorter. He would drink two glasses of draft beer and eat a hamburger accompanied by french fries. Once the food was gone and the glass drained a second time, McCutcheon drove home. Every purchase he made throughout the day was paid for in cash, the money peeled off a thick roll of twenty dollar bills that he carried in the front pocket of his pants. He would not appear again in Tofino for precisely two weeks.

I had come to know McCutcheon and his ways several years ago when a stone wall on the property where Merriam and I lived at the time collapsed following an unusually heavy winter rainstorm. The wind and water worked in concert to undermine the old wall and crumble it, one long section falling over on its side. Knowing nothing of stone masonry, I was at a loss as to how to effect repairs. So were all the local contractors I normally would have hired. One finally suggested that old McCutcheon might be able to help and had told me where to find him. As he had no phone, I drove out to his trailer. It transpired that McCutcheon had erected that very same stone wall some twenty years earlier. He agreed to fix it, came and did the work, took his pay, and managed to do all this while uttering hardly a word. Thereafter when I saw McCutcheon at the Co-op, the liquor store, or in the Legion during his twice-monthly expeditions I would offer my regards. He would give me the kind of curt nod one offers as a politeness to a stranger and carry on about his business. Eventually I decided that my attempts at cordiality were an unwelcome imposition and ceased acknowledging him when passing. He gave no indication of noting this change, other than by offering no curt nod. Perhaps for this reason, I had not thought of McCutcheon for a number of years, and the infrequency of his visits to Tofino had led me to almost forget that he owned and drove a Cadillac.

Bellows stopped the Blazer in front of an old wire gate that drooped lopsidedly across the narrow entrance to McCutcheon's property. Behind us, Singh and Monaghan pulled up in a RCMP cruiser. Everyone got out quietly. The trailer was obscured from view by a thick stand of cedars and hemlocks around which the muddy track circled. Anyone at the trailer would not be able to see us either and I doubted they would have heard the vehicles pull up. "Elias, you stay back here," Bellows cautioned. I nodded and, because of the pain that lanced through my aching brain, immediately regretted doing so. A couple of Tylenols dispensed by the plump redheaded nurse had done little to curb my throbbing headache. I knew better than to protest about being left behind. This was police work and everyone would be calmer if the doing of it was unimpeded by the presence of the untrained.

Monaghan and Singh both carried shotguns and wore protective vests. They each had a radio attached to their belt, the mouthpiece fitted into a holder on their left shoulders. Bellows and Lee both shrugged into vests as well. Before putting his on, Bellows pulled off his sports coat. He and Lee drew their pistols, Bellows holding his alongside his right hip. He pushed the gate open and stepped through. Monaghan gave me a nervous smile and winked, then she, Lee, and Singh followed Bellows. The four walked up the road to the tree line. Singh and Lee broke off into the woods while Monaghan and Bellows continued along the road, hugging the edge of the trees for cover and protection as they did so.

After they disappeared from sight, I leaned against the side of the Blazer and, tipping my throbbing head back against the roof, thought about Hui and the violence at the hospital. Bellows and I had discussed it during the drive to McCutcheon's and we were pretty much agreed on what it all meant. That the Asian assailants were Snake Heads was probable. That they had come to kill Kim and to kidnap Hui was apparent. Bellows said it was not unlikely that the Snake Heads would resort to trying to snatch Hui. She was young, pretty, and would be valuable to their prostitution rackets. If they had managed to carry her off, Hui would have soon ended up in some clandestine brothel serving perverts who sought sex with young children in New York, Toronto, or even Vancouver. Thinking of that possible fate for her left me chilled and more determined than ever to see she was properly protected.

More puzzling was the attempt to murder Kim, if that had been the intention of the attack. Perhaps they had sought to kidnap him as well or to break him out of police custody. "We need to talk with him," Bellows had said in the car. "He may hold the key to this whole thing." He looked over at me. "When we're done here, I want Ms. Chan to talk to him again." He gave me an expression that was totally professional and lacking his normal friendly warmth. "But it'll be to a script I write or not at all. Will she do that?"

I shrugged. "You'll have to ask her, Ray. I imagine so, but there are problems." I told him briefly about how upset she was after the short meeting with Kim that morning. Had it only been a few hours since then? So much had happened.

Monaghan suddenly rounded the corner of McCutcheon's driveway and walked quickly toward the cars. "You've got work, Elias," she said with a shaky voice. Her face was a ghostly pale, eyes wide. "There's a man up there who's been gutted by a knife. Looks like he's been there awhile." I took off my hat, ran my fingers through my hair, looked up at the blue sky visible through the high branches of the surrounding trees, and blew out a long breath. Then, as Monaghan got busy hauling a box of crime scene equipment out of the back of the Blazer, I walked up the road toward the trailer.

Ian McCutcheon had died in his stocking feet at his kitchen door. Like his work clothes, which had always been clean and simple, the trailer was tidy and plainly furnished. The old trailer had a small galley-style kitchen that contained an Arborite table and vinyl-backed aluminum chair set positioned below a window that stood next to the narrow main door. Off the kitchen was a square living room with a narrow window cut into every wall. Each window was covered by an old and faded set of red velour drapes that I suspected must have come with the mobile home during the days when such things were sold furnished. The same was true of McCutcheon's other furnishings. Two hideous yellow globe-shaped lamps with gold shades fringed in orange thread were positioned respectively next to either a black leather love seat or the matching easy boy. The floor was covered by a thick gold broadloom, beaten flat by years of wear but still immaculately clean. In the other direction from the kitchen a narrow hall led to a tiny bathroom, an even smaller laundry room, and a bedroom just big enough for a double bed, a chest of drawers, and a nightstand upon which another of the yellow globed lamps stood. Beside it was an Ed McBain novel, a wind-up alarm clock, and a faded photograph of a plump, pretty dark-haired woman. It seemed that the picture had been taken when she was in her late thirties. She wore an untucked red and white plaid shirt over blue jeans and had her hair tied back with a red scarf. She appeared to be standing on the verandah of a small plank-walled cabin. Off to one side of the cabin I could see a view of a lake through a scattered mixed stand of hemlock and cedar. Had McCutcheon been married? I had no idea.

The nightstand contained a single narrow drawer. Inside was a pair of the kind of reading glasses bought in a pharmacy and a thin packet of envelopes addressed to McCutcheon. They were all from a single address in Gold River. I opened one and found it to be a short note from a son I had never known that McCutcheon had. Not that I should have, for like most everyone in Tofino I had barely known the man. The note reported in untidy and hasty writing that he was doing fine after the pulp mill closure but that his unemployment insurance benefits weren't enough to cover his rent and truck payments. He wondered if his father could help with a short-term loan. Bellows jotted down the son's name and address so he could advise him of his father's death.

McCutcheon's bed was neatly made, the shower stall was carefully wiped out so that no trace of moisture remained to cause mildew growth in the grout between tiles. In the little storage room that had been tacked onto the side of the trailer not a tool was left out of the red toolbox to which it was assigned. Everything had its place and everything was duly in it. Except that McCutcheon lay in a wide pool of blood that completely covered the white linoleum in the kitchen. Also the small shed in the yard in which the Cadillac most likely was normally parked stood empty.

"I'd say he's been dead at least twenty-four hours, Elias," Bellows said. We stood over the corpse, our shoes clad in plastic slip-ons and with plastic surgical gloves on our hands. A facemask did little to cut the thick stench of rotting flesh that permeated the room. The blood was dry and hard under our feet. Our shoes left no impression in the thick red crust. Extending from the outside edge of where the blood had run into the hallway a set of bloody footprints marked a path in the linoleum that one of McCutcheon's killers had taken to the bedroom. Inside the bedroom, the footprints traced a circle on the carpet that indicated a cursory search of the room, presumably as part of a search for the keys to McCutcheon's Cadillac. Not wanting to hamper any attempt to determine foot size or other information from these bloody tracks, we were careful to not step on them.

McCutcheon lay on his side with his arms crossed over the wicked wound. It had opened him up so deeply that his intestines had spilled out below hands that had obviously been desperately trying to press them back inside his body. His eyes were open and cloudy, frozen, it seemed, in an expression of terror and hopeless despair.

His face and neck had turned a kind of greenish red. Although the plastic gloves made it difficult to tell, when I bent over and touched his cheek it seemed his body temperature was that of the room itself. McCutcheon's jaw and throat had gone slack, the effects of rigor mortis already passing from the corpse in the normal downward progression from head to toes. All of this presented a good case for believing that McCutcheon had been killed the previous day, but I would leave it to the forensic team already on the way to the trailer to be more precise. I was a community coroner and unequipped either in knowledge or ability to make a more precise analysis of a corpse than this.

"Why kill a man for his car?" I said. "Why come here for this car? For a 1960s Cadillac?"

Bellows shook his head. "You didn't recognize the man behind the wheel?" He stood up and with a feeling of relief I followed him outside into the fresh air. I pulled the mask down so it hung from my neck and sucked in a few deep breaths. We walked over to the doorless shed in which McCutcheon had stored his car and stared at the tire marks worn into the gravel that formed its floor, as if doing so could conjure the Cadillac up for us.

Behind the garage were slates and stones all neatly stacked according to mineral type and size. A small low shed was anchored to the rear wall of the garage. Bellows released the latch on the door and we looked in at a heavy wooden stand set low to the ground at about knee height. Resting on it was a collection of hand chisels, scrapers, and handles. The kinds of tools with which an old-fashioned stone mason worked his trade. In the shed's back corner a granite stone slab leaned against the wall. I walked over and read Ian McCutcheon's name neatly chiselled in simple lettering. Below it a line bearing his date of birth — November 17, 1945 — was followed by a hyphen. The space where date of death would have logically followed was blank. Under that line was the simple inscription, "Gone to join Edith." I thought of the woman in the photograph and knew she was deceased and undoubtedly had been for a long time.

"Ray," I said softly. "A man like McCutcheon. This place he lived. A man just living through the rest of the days of his life like this. I don't see a stranger finding him here. Or coming here. It had to be somebody who knew about him. Someone local."

"Not the killer," Bellows said. I agreed. We knew the killer. The Asian man with the knife in the hospital. I thought about Hui. Hoped that the police had mounted a good guard on the hospital and were watching her well. Bethanie had to get the little girl out of there so we could hide her from these people.

"There's no tracks from another vehicle in the yard," Bellows was saying. "Just some footprints here and in the driveway. Whoever it was can't have just walked up here without having transport to bring them in close. And nothing has turned up at the roadblocks, either. It's like they've just vanished into thin air. In a blue Caddy for God's sake," he said with frustration. I looked down the lane to where some police in coveralls were carrying several large cases into the yard. The forensic team from Nanaimo. At the gate, Monaghan was finishing turning the cruiser around. When I mentioned it, Bellows agreed that there was nothing more for me to do here and I should hitch a ride back with Monaghan.

The doctors had replaced the stitches in his stomach that had torn loose during the desperate struggle with Cheng. Now he was back in the bed, a police officer once again standing outside the door of the room. Was he there to guard him or to protect him? Kim suspected both purposes. He was barely aware of the renewed pain from the knife wound. His brain reeled with confusion. Cheng, how had he come to be here? Why would he pursue Kim, a ship's cook? Why would he risk himself to kill a cook? Kim knew nothing that could harm someone like Cheng. All he had known was what he had seen on the ship, which had been little really until the terrible time of the wrecking and the death of so many of the Chinese people locked away in the hold. There was nothing that he knew from this that the police would not know as well from the other survivors.

It was madness. But perhaps that was all that was needed. Cheng had tried to kill him on the ship and again in the woods after he had made it to shore. Perhaps he merely wanted to finish a job he had started. He had seen that kind of mad attention to detail before. There had been a Khmer Rouge officer who had insisted that each corpse be shot precisely in the forehead before it was thrown into the pits. Even if the head was no longer connected to a body. The bullet still had to be delivered with precision. Perhaps Cheng was like that officer.

Thinking of the officer brought tears to Kim's eyes, reminded him of how badly things had gone with his cousin. He had been so flushed with hope and joy when Vhanna had entered the room wearing the traditional dress of home. Kim knew she had dressed like this as a sign of respect for him. But then she had asked how he had survived and he had not lied. Had not even thought to do so. Could not have. To his horror, he had watched the soft light snap off in her eyes when he confessed to *having been a soldier in the Khmer Rouge. A coldness had blown over her, sweeping away the tenderness that had been there moments earlier in the same way that a storm wind strips the colourful petals from a flower, leaving only the gaunt plant stalk. Kim knew then that she was lost to him. As lost as all the family that had gone into the pits with bullets in their foreheads. He was damned and there would be no redemption. What he had wanted most, he realized, was just for Vhanna to have touched him, to have felt the fingers of a family member against his own. That way he would have known that the continuity of family survived, even though he was lost, known that one person carried on some memory of the others.*

Kim rolled over and pressed his face hard into the pillow, smothering his soft sobs and allowing the fabric to soak up the wetness at his eyes.

chapter eleven

I climbed Vhanna's wall and circumvented her security response net by phoning Jabronski and reporting in on her cell phone so that he didn't come galloping over like the cavalry to save the day. Then I descended the stairs to the beach where she was outlined against a sinking sun that set the blue ocean dazzlingly ablaze and shot golden shafts of light across the pale sand. Vhanna was rhythmically working her way through a long form Tai Chi set. Two sets in one day was highly unusual for Vhanna, who is extremely precise about routine and normally confines herself to one Tai Chi set daily. The deviation suggested to me the depths of her turmoil and her desire to steady her emotions and regain a calm centre in her spirit.

Pivoting her left foot ninety degrees to the right to establish a firm foundation, Vhanna launched herself forward with her right leg, planting it solidly a long step ahead of her while her left arm thrust straight with the palm open as if to push against an invisible opponent's chest. Vhanna then settled back onto her left hip as her right arm rose up in a parrying motion, her left palm braced against the back of her right wrist so that her arms were both extended as far as they would go without unbalancing her. Swaying back onto her left leg, Vhanna's hips turned forty-five degrees to the left as her elbows dropped so that her hands were palm out just in front of her chest. Squaring her hips while pushing forward with her palms shoulder-width apart brought Vhanna to the final, powerful full-length extension that completed the Carry Tiger to Mountain movement and set her up to move gracefully into Whip Out Horizontally.

I settled on the bottom stair, patted a hand on my knee, and chuckled softly as Fergus, who until now had been sitting on his haunches in front of Vhanna looking on with deep concentration, cocked his head to one side and then trotted happily over. He met my eye, stubby tail wagging as much as it could and floppy ears twitching as he approached. When he reached me, Fergus rose up to put his front paws on my knees and thrust his face practically into mine. Several hours had passed since last we met and he was obviously happy to see me. I let him swipe my hand with his tongue before giving him a gentle scratch behind his ears. He leaned into this attention so hard that he almost toppled over on his side in a relaxed swoon.

While I had been concentrating on my good and loyal friend, Vhanna had reached the point in her routine at which she crossed her hands over her chest and then offered a gracious bow toward the red sun as it plunged into the hot purple of the surging waves rolling endlessly toward us. I walked toward her, realizing as I did so that she was still unaware of my presence and remained focused on the set and the meditative quality of it. Not wanting to ask the questions that were needed, I thought briefly of taking Fergus and leaving before she turned.

My eyes grazed down Vhanna's back. She wore a pair of black tights and a grey sports bra that left her lower back and shoulders bare, her long, straight hair forming a dark line down the length of her spine to its base. The tights fit like a second skin and she was barefoot. As I almost reached her shoulder, Vhanna suddenly turned, dropped low and balled her hands into fists. Her body settled back on her hips and into the power centre of her thighs as if any moment she would explode into a defensive assault. I stepped back and raised my hands, offering a "Brave friend, I come in peace" signal. Fergus dithered against my leg, rubbing his flank along my calf and lolling his tongue appreciatively at Vhanna.

"It's you," she said softly and relaxed into a less violent pose that still seemed wary.

Her small, firm breasts were rising and falling under the thin covering of the bra. Her stomach was hard, flat, and naked down to a point several inches below her navel. With the sun throwing darts of light through her hair and around her body she looked pearled by moisture. She swiped a hand through her hair, eyes never leaving mine.

Keeping my voice as flat and free of emotion as possible, I told her everything that had happened since I had left her that morning. I described the attempted kidnapping of Hui, the wounding of Danchuk, the obvious intent to murder Kim, the real killing of McCutcheon, the mystery of the car and the scraggly man who had driven it. Then I told her of the equal mystery of Kim's link to these Asians and of Bellows's insistence that she translate for his interrogation of Kim. I finished with my renewed determination to have Hui placed into the care of Lars and Frieda and how tight the timing was for that to either happen or not because of the decision that she should be transferred to Victoria along with Kim. The transfer had been delayed slightly by Kim's tearing open his stitches when he saved Danchuk's life, but it would soon proceed. And Hui would go too if Bethanie proved unable to work bureaucratic magic.

Vhanna stood there on the sand with her hands resting on her hips while I ran through all this. Her face was deeply masked in the shadows thrown by the setting sun behind her. When I finished my recitation of events she turned toward the water, striding down to where the surf washed across the sand so that it brushed her toes. "The man in the hospital." Vhanna stopped and took a long breath. "Kim, he was." She faltered, then sighed, "He is my cousin. I remember him. He was younger, always at my side when his family came to visit. Like a little puppy. There were three sisters, two brothers, mother, father, grandfather, a couple uncles and several very old aunts. Together they formed the Hoai family. I loved him. I loved them. They were part of the big extended family among which I lived. They were part of the bond that tied all of us to this earth, to our culture, to our home."

I thought of my father, Angus; of my mother, Lila, who had been scandalously young when she married Angus, and who had left us without a word when I was but two weeks old. Thought, too, of a family in Britain that I had never met and who sent cheques but nothing more. I knew nothing about what Vhanna spoke, but I ached for her all the same. Her sense of family was palpable. And they were all dead. All but Kim, who was an enigma.

Understanding at last, I said, "He was Khmer Rouge."

She nodded. "The young boys and girls. It was often the case. They could put on the scarf and take the gun or they could die in the paddies or the mud alongside the road or be pushed into the pits blown open with the explosives and then blasted closed over the corpses." She shuddered, pressed her fists against the side of her forehead. "It wasn't their choice even. Parents pushed them forward, especially the young who were considered as yet untainted, not like the rest of us who were older and thus hardened capitalists. The Khmer Rouge would take them. They believed that they were as soil that could be molded and fed with water to sprout life anew and to grow into their own glorious vision of agrarian utopia where all worked for the common good as dictated by the father Pol Pot." She looked at me, eyes wide and haunted. "Elias, what have I done?"

Vhanna zipped the Miata so quickly through the corners on Tofino's outskirts that I found my right foot futilely stabbing for a brake pedal that the passenger side of the car didn't have. Eyes hidden behind her high-tech sunglasses, wearing a pair of faded blue denims and a white cotton blouse, Vhanna's attention was riveted on her driving. She worked the gears up and down smoothly, accelerating through the last half of the corner so that the car never drifted in the corners despite the speed. Fergus was crowded down at my feet, his body tilting hard against the inside of one leg and eyes fixed on my face anxiously. Neither of us is fond of speed and undoubtedly my own eyes were as wide as his were. I sighed softly under my breath with relief when we passed into the municipal boundary, where a speed zone sign and the town's normal tourist season congestion forced Vhanna to reduce her pace.

The hospital parking lot was crowded with four marked police vehicles and Bellows's unmarked car. A chill of apprehension raised the hairs on my arms. The foyer was clogged cheek to jowl with Mounties, most of whom were talking at the same time. With all the hardware suspended from their waist belts it was hard to squeeze into the space. I spotted Bellows standing next to Danchuk, who was back in uniform but had his left arm in a skin-coloured sling. Seeing us, Bellows held up a hand to quiet Danchuk. Several Mounties, including Corporal Lee, stepped aside and Bellows came through the gap like Moses walking between the parting waters of the Red Sea.

"He's disappeared," Bellows said. He looked hard at Vhanna, as if she might know something about this. I saw the colour in her face drain away. Bellows obviously noted her distress as well for his tone became less challenging. "We've dogs coming. He can't have gone far. Unless, of course, he rendezvoused with the other ones." Kim had escaped, he added, when the Mountie on guard in the hallway between his and Hui's rooms had slipped away for a moment to use the toilet. Somehow in a matter of minutes, Kim had fled his room, paused at an unlocked janitor's closet to switch his gown for a pair of coveralls left on a peg there, and apparently managed to stroll past the duty nurse desk undetected. A search of the hospital had turned up no trace of him. Bellows had no idea where he had fled or where he thought he could run to.

"Elias," he said quietly, "we've already sent Hui in a car to Victoria."

"Listen, Ray," I said, but Bellows cut me off from saying anything further.

"I've got at least four fugitives out there and little enough in the way of resources to hunt them down. I couldn't spare people any longer to guard one child. I called Ms. Hollinger and she was still trying to resolve the temporary custody issue, but it was obviously going to take another twenty-four or forty-eight hours. A decision had to be made."

I swallowed hard, forced myself to stay calm. There was nothing I could do here. Hui was already gone. "Where did you send her?"

"She's gone directly to the Work Point barracks shelter. They'll process her there. Word is that the children will be taken out of there soon and put into foster care homes in the city. Ms. Hollinger might be able to arrange for her to be sent back here then. That part is up to a judge and the Immigration authorities."

Standing by the door, Lee said, "The dog team is here, Ray."

Bellows put a hand on my shoulder. "Look, everything will work out for her. This is Canada. The system will do whatever is right to protect children. Even children who come into the country illegally." He gave a weak smile, as if to acknowledge the lie implicit in his words, and then turned away. "Okay, people, let's go find him."

The Mounties withdrew from the foyer in a mass pack. Outside dusk was giving way rapidly to night. Somewhere out there Kim was on the move or in hiding. Somewhere out there, too, at least three men were lurking and it seemed at least one of them was determined to see Kim dead.

Vhanna slipped her hand into mine as we watched the dogs and their handlers lead the group of Mounties to the end of the parking lot and start descending a rough track. "There's nothing but rocky headlands and rough sections of cobble beach and sandstone shelves down there," Vhanna said. "There's nowhere to go. I don't understand what he's thinking to accomplish by running. He'll just get himself hurt or..." She trailed off and looked with troubled eyes toward the path as the last Mountie disappeared down it. The reflected glow of several flash-light beams bouncing around in the upper branches of the trees growing up from the side of the embankment marked the line of the search party's descent.

I tried to turn my thoughts away from Hui and to focus on Kim. But all I could see in my mind's eye was a frightened little girl who was in the back of some police car being driven through the night with no idea where she was being taken or why. "She'll be terrified. Damn it to hell."

Vhanna hugged me tightly. "We'll call Bethanie. See where she's at with things. We can at least go to Victoria and check on Hui." She shuddered. "They should catch up to Kim pretty quick. He can't have gone far." She looked up at me, the gathering darkness hiding her eyes and face. "Elias, let's go home. There's nothing more we can do tonight."

It was full dark by the time we parked outside my house. The night was moonless and although the sky swarmed with the pinpoint light of stars I could barely see the ground under my feet. I thought of a man nursing a knife wound in his guts while trying to scramble over slick seaside rocks on a night as black as this. Kim would be fortunate if the police tracked him down before he ended up cut off on some rocky point that would soon be flooded by the rising tide.

Once inside I saw the blinking red light of my answering machine. I flicked on a light in the kitchen, went over to the counter where the unit was positioned, and hit the play button. Vhanna meanwhile opened the pantry and pulled out a bag of dog food and shook a generous helping into Fergus's bowl. Not hesitating a moment, he started crunching and swallowing, pausing after a few bites to lap down a generous helping of water from his water dish after Vhanna filled it and put it down beside his food bowl. Watching him eat, I was suddenly reminded that I had eaten nothing since breakfast. My stomach rumbled as the message started to play.

Bethanie's voice asked me to call her at home and left the number. She picked up just after the first ring and quickly gave me a rundown on her efforts to get an order putting Hui into the care of the Jansons. "The problem is the Immigration authorities," she said. "They want to keep everyone off the boats contained in one place. Easier to deal with the hearings that way."

"Will they let us see her?"

"I've talked with them about that. Yes, you can make an appointment. But you'll have to go to Work Point. There's a room set up there or a building or something for that kind of thing. There are lawyers and refugee advocate agencies that are trying to ensure that the migrants are allowed due process under the Immigration Act." That was good to hear. "Elias, the Immigration people have been making inquiries among the other boat people. There's no indication that anyone related to Hui survived the wreck. Immigration has filed her name with the Chinese government to see if any family can be located in Fujian Province. So far there's no word back. If there's family there I imagine Immigration will want to return her." After assuring me that she would continue trying to get the court order in our favour Bethanie rung off.

I hung up and gave Vhanna the gist of the call. She was busy whipping a batch of eggs together for an omelette. I dug tomatoes, green onions, and mushrooms from the refrigerator vegetable keeper and a couple of thin red Thai Dragon peppers that were supposedly one hundred times hotter than jalapeños from a hanging basket where they were drying. While I sliced these up to make a filling, Vhanna melted butter in the frying pan. By the time the eggs were ready to fold over I had the vegetables set and had also grated some white cheddar to throw in. I pulled the cork on a bottle of crisply chilled Italian pinot gris and filled two tall crystal wine glasses to the brim as Vhanna divided the omelette into portions and served them up on a pair of dark blue hand-thrown pottery plates. We sat at the table and ate the omelette and drank the wine in comfortable silence until the food was gone. Then I picked up the half-full bottle and we took our glasses over to the big overstuffed green couch that faced the fireplace. I crumpled some paper into the hearth, added slivered cedar kindling, criss-crossed over this a few larger chunks of dry fir and lit a small fire that was soon crackling and filling the room with a gentle light.

Having finished his repast, Fergus sauntered over to stretch out luxuriously on the oval rug placed in front of the fire for his use. He gave a contented sigh and looked over at us both with the kind of expression that said all was right with the world and everything was in its proper place. If Fergus had his way, we would all live together under this roof.

Vhanna reclined on the couch with her back propped against a large cushion, legs thrust out in front of her, wineglass cradled in one hand so that the stem dangled between her fingers. I slipped a Ray Wylie Hubbard CD into the player. His low Texas drawl filled the room with images of a poet named Rilke, who said that dreams are like dragons guarding our most precious secrets; of rock and roll gypsies out on night roads; of an angel lying on a mattress who spoke of history and death.

I lifted Vhanna's legs and sat down on the couch, placing her calves over my legs, and took a sip of wine.

"Tomorrow I'll arrange an appointment in Victoria so that I can see Hui," I said. "Do you want to come?"

"If you want to get there in one day, I better," she said with a grin.

"The Land Rover's perfectly capable," I replied with mock indignation.

"Maybe with a different driver."

I laughed and toasted her. "It'll be good to have you along."

Her expression became serious. "What do you hope to do?"

Staring at the fire, I considered the question while Hubbard considered a long dirty road with Robert Johnson's path being the only way out. There was not much really that I could do, I realized with frustration and webs of despair spinning through my mind. "I just want her to know that she's not alone. That there are people who care and who want to help." I drained my glass, reached over to the where the bottle rested on a side table and poured some more into it. After refreshing Vhanna's proffered glass, I said, "I want to see for myself that she's somewhere safe."

Vhanna cocked her head to one side and gave me a thoughtful look. "You're really taking responsibility for her, aren't you?"

I dropped my gaze away toward the fire. With more levity than I felt, I offered up the same tired line that I had given Tully.

Vhanna didn't answer my question about an old Chinese proverb. Instead, she lifted my hand, brushed her cheek against it, and gently kissed the inside of my wrist. My hand dusted through her hair as I leaned forward and our mouths met. We kissed for a long time, tongues dancing this way and that across lips and against each other. I slowly undid Vhanna's shirt and, brushing the fabric to one side, bent down to run the tip of my tongue around first one and then the other of her small nipples. Vhanna moaned softly, her hands grasping my shoulders. When I stood up and lifted her in my arms, Vhanna let me carry her up to the bed, her lips nibbling my earlobe as I ascended the stairs to the loft.

chapter twelve

The first hint of dawn light was tracing through the high, uncurtained windows when I awoke and felt that Vhanna was gone from the bed. When I ran my hand over the sheet, a fading warmth told me that she had only recently slipped from between the covers. Fergus's large wicker basket bed in the corner of the bedroom was also empty. I smiled contentedly and lay back with my hands behind my head, staring up at the ceiling while letting my body slowly come awake. Vhanna was still in the house, I knew, because Fergus would only be gone from his bed if he was with her. He is a sound sleeper normally that with the passing years adopts an ever more disciplined approach to being early to bed and late to rise. Combined with regular naps taken during the day, Fergus's hours of wakefulness are probably outnumbered by his hours of rest.

Levering myself out of bed, I gathered up my old robe and pulled it on. Until recently Vhanna had often worn it to keep off the night or morning chill. But a few months ago she arrived with a white terry robe bearing a Marriott Hotel logo that was sized to fit her and hung it without comment in my closet. This was just after she attended an environmental tourism conference in Denver and I surmised that the robe must have been thrown in somehow as part of the conference's package deal with the hotel. I took the arrival of the robe in my house as a promising sign, an indication that Vhanna planned to spend more nights here. This, however, had not yet proven to be the case, although I remained ever hopeful. Vhanna says over-optimism is one of my various downfalls because it sets me up for endless disappointment. I cannot refute that allegation for it does seem that more hopes are dashed than not. Yet I knew that last night had been a time when optimistic expectations had been more than sufficiently fulfilled. And who knew what the early morning might still bring?

I found Vhanna sitting in the kitchen hunkered over the table with a marine chart and a topographic map spread before her. Over the years I have gathered together a complete collection of these maps with regard to Vancouver Island. Fergus looked up from where he lay on the floor on his side next to Vhanna's feet with the miserable expression of a sentry doing night duty. I knew he would rather we were back in the bed and he in his. But Vhanna was peering intently at the maps, a transparent six-inch ruler in one hand and a pencil in the other. Her dark hair flowed starkly down her back over the terry of the white robe. She had taken Angus's old gooseneck lamp from where it sits on my desk, apparently to minimize the amount of light cast through the open cabin in order to avoid waking me. Her eyes fixed on the calculations she was making, she seemed oblivious to my presence as I approached.

Resting my hands on Vhanna's shoulders, I felt her muscles tense and then relax slightly. Still, I could feel hard knots raised by anxiety in the sinew of her shoulders. "Couldn't sleep?" I asked.

She shook her head and jabbed at the marine chart with a finger. "They won't find him, Elias. I realized that suddenly."

Puzzled, I looked down at the map and saw she was concentrating on the section of the 1:40,000 marine chart that includes Tofino and the rest of Clayoquot Sound. Next to it was a topographical chart that detailed the same ground from the landward perspective. Both maps showed the same thing. Dense forest cover and a hard, unforgiving coastline of rocky faces and very narrow beaches all the way from Duffin Cove to MacKenzie Beach where things improved for a short stretch. It looked far from encouraging to me. Vhanna was right; they wouldn't find Kim because most likely he had been washed out to sea on a receding tide. I said as much.

Vhanna shook her head with an angry impatience. "You're not thinking right." She swivelled in the chair, her robe gaping as she did so to expose the upper swell of one breast. Seeing the direction my eyes were following, Vhanna shook her head with some impatience and tugged the robe closed with a sharp movement. "Look," she said, jabbing a finger at the map again, "Kim was Khmer Rouge, right?"

I nodded, baffled as to where this was going.

Her gaze fixed me evenly. There was no uncertainty in her expression. In fact she looked completely calm and assured. "They weren't just genocidal murderers. They spent years fighting a government backed by the might of the United States. When they defeated that government they were soon fighting against a well-armed and well-trained Vietnamese invasion force. Their training probably wasn't much and their arms were poor but they were still soldiers." Again she pointed at the map. "Look at it like a soldier might, not like a civilian."

Despite my immediate reflex to spurn her notion I looked at the map and considered it carefully. I also thought about the ground itself from what I knew of it. "What would he do?" she asked.

"He'd know they were coming after him," I said thoughtfully. "Would they have used dogs in Cambodia?"

She nodded. "More likely trackers, but dogs would have been possible."

"Same thing, either way. He would start taking evasion measures."

"Meaning?" I could see the excitement and repressed energy in her body.

I thought about it. Remembered the courses in evasion during airborne training. "Backtracking. Spoiling the scent if possible by mixing other scents with it. Soils, chemicals, animal scat, various types of vegetation, anything with an odour stronger than your particular distinctive human scent. Crossing paths with other humans so the scent becomes confused and indistinct." I paused, thinking. "The headlands and tide pools could be used to cut off the line of passage he took. If he waded through pools the dogs would have to work to pick up the scent on the other side. Or if he crossed the rocks just before the tide rolled in there would be neither scent nor route to follow. There are a lot of spots there that are impassable in high tide. Jesus," I said, becoming more excited as I thought about it, "if he threw the dogs off, he could slither up into the brush and disappear into the salal and other undergrowth. The Mounties wouldn't begin to start crawling through the bush in search of him. They'll go where you can walk upright and not consider someone being content to take an hour or more to wriggle through fifty feet of dense scrub."

Vhanna nodded. "Elias," she said with a sad smile, "I need to go to MacKenzie Beach and I have to stay there for as long as it takes. Can you come, too? It'll mean delaying going to check on Hui. Hopefully only a day, though." She stood up and looked down at the maps again. Her jaw was set with determination. "I need to bring him in."

We could explain all this to Bellows, I thought, and he could wait there for Kim. But then I realized that Kim would see the man or the posse of police that gathered and withdraw back into the snarl of brush. He could live in that small, enclosed jungle for days, possibly even weeks, in the same manner that Vhanna had existed during her flight across the mountains out of Cambodia into Thailand. There were grubs and berries that could be eaten. Small freshets and seeping springs would provide fresh water. It would take a long time for somebody who was determined to stay free to die in such a small place and no Canadian search party would ever uncover him.

"Okay," I said. Vhanna squeezed my hand and headed up the stairs into the bedroom to change. I stared at the maps a moment more and then followed her.

We sat on a log next to the headland that marked the western end of MacKenzie Beach, trying to look just like two people with no more purpose in the world than to while away the early morning hours watching the surf roll in from Japan and Asia. A heavy morning fog stood offshore and the moisture from it was carried on a dampening breeze. I was shrugged down in my old Filson coat, matching hat plopped on my head, jeans growing moist as the thick cloak of fogged dampness drifted up against the bluffs behind us. Vhanna had on her Gore-Tex jacket and a pair of black rain pants. Both were pearled with beads of water. Inland the fog was burning away in tendrils of fleeing haze but it would be an hour or so yet before the sun and heat from the ground dissipated the fog over the beach.

Overhead several gulls circled and screeched melancholically to each other. The surprisingly shrill, emasculated-sounding chitter of a bald eagle drifted down from the heights of a big Sitka spruce where it had built a nest in the storm-shattered treetop. Some brightly coloured Harlequins were frenetically riding the waves that rolled around and over tide pool riddled rocks just offshore. I focused on these things and purposely ignored the heavily forested headland and the dense woods that stood immediately behind us. The beach further along here was fronted by a row of houses varying in degrees of opulence from a couple remaining rough cabins to great three-storeyed structures that rivalled Vhanna's home on Chesterman's Beach, which was just one big headland to the east of here.

"I wonder if he's out there watching us?" I said.

"If he's not, he will be soon. I can feel him, Elias." Vhanna said this without turning her head toward the headland. Like me, she focused her attention on the lifting fog bank out on the water.

A small seiner fishing boat swirled out of the grey fog into a hole through which sunlight was sparkling off the ocean and we both watched it appreciatively as the vessel chugged up along the coastline toward Tofino. The two booms were pulled upright and the big net was obviously not deployed from its large drum mounted on the boat's stern. A common sight these days when salmon harvest openings were few and far between. I wondered where he was sailing to and from where he had come. Did he sail toward a patch of sea where an opening was expected? Or did he just cruise the coast because that was the only thing he knew and he would do so until the last drop of fuel was gone and there was no money left to buy more?

I unscrewed the top of an old green metal Thermos and poured hot coffee mixed with milk into the lid, took a swallow, and handed it to Vhanna. After a small sip, she passed it back. "Do you think Bellows or anyone will show?" I worried.

"No," she said. "They'll not think it possible he could have come this far. They'll be looking back around the hospital, figuring he might have doubled back. And they'll be looking around in Tofino, too. They don't know wilderness. It's not their turf anymore."

I thought of the Mounties of yesteryear, images of dog sleds, of Sam Steele in the Klondike, and then of Danchuk and even of Bellows. Cops tied to police cruisers. Police officers, like Danchuk, wearing a premature pot belly grown during long hours spent sedentary behind a desk or in a car watching a radar display for speeders, doughnuts at hand. Vhanna was right. They would not believe that Kim could reach here alive and undetected. That he could do so while using no trail at all. Their attention was turned elsewhere. I suspected that Kim, having watched the Mounties guarding him, had reached this same determination before making his escape attempt. He had intuitively known where to run and how to use the ground. Perhaps he had even thought it through as an option when he was first brought to the hospital aboard the helicopter and would have seen the lay of the parking lot and surrounding terrain as they took him inside. He was a soldier in hostile

territory. Escape would have always been a consideration, a potential to be kept in mind.

"I think you're right, Vhanna," I said. "I think he's
out there even now, watching."

The stolen coveralls were heavily caked in mud and torn in several places where they had snagged on thorns or sharp rocks during his long passage through the thick scrub and around the many headlands. At first, when he heard the dogs behind him, Kim had bordered on the edge of panic. A panic that pushed him to run and to scrabble whatever way he could over the rocks and through the brush. He had forced himself to be calm, to think rationally. He knew little of dogs and their ability to search him out. But he suspected they could be thrown off a scent if one proceeded with calculation, particularly in terrain such as this, where the strong salt smell off the ocean combined with the putrid stench of the bull kelp to overwhelm everything else. He had deliberately slowed his pace, calculated each move. He waded through tide pools and backtracked from one to another. Rounding headlands he staggered waist deep in the icy ocean, battered this way and that by the waves rolling in and occasionally plunging over his head into deep pools rendered invisible in the darkness. At times the current threatened to catch him, to drag him out or dash him against the rocks. He escaped each time by clawing frantically at the rocks above and dragging himself free of the water's pull. His hands still dripped blood from the gashes the sharp barnacles had opened. Eventually he was aware that he no longer heard the dogs and that the stabbing beams of his hunters' flashlights were far behind him.

He had moved into the almost impenetrable underbrush above the shoreline then. For the rest of the night and into the early morning he wriggled and slithered like a snake under and over the branches and roots, through the thorns and thickets. Throughout the long, bitterly cold night he had concentrated on keeping the bandage wrapped around his stomach as clean as possible.

When he had decided that should opportunity present itself he would try to escape from the hospital, Kim had had no idea where he would run. True, since they had brought him to the hospital, he had watched the security and tried to make sense of routines that might be of use to him in the event that an escape became necessary. In this manner he had noticed on one occasion a janitor wearing coveralls enter a closet and emerge without them. He had seen that the door was apparently not locked. From the window in his room, Kim had surveyed what he could of the ground around the hospital and noted the fact that the building was set on a ridge overlooking the ocean. He had known that to escape he must find wilderness. In a town, among these people, there would be no hiding for him. He knew nothing of their ways or their language. He would not last a moment.

It amazed him that Cheng was obviously able to function in the open here. His consternation at seeing the man materialize in his hospital room dressed like a doctor and wielding the same vicious blade that had cut him on board the ship had been acute. That Cheng was out there and that he wanted him dead enough to take such measures to attack him in the midst of police had shaken him badly. It had also finalized his decision to run. If Cheng could find him here and get so close so easily, he would not be safe anywhere the authorities decided to hold him.

And Kim realized that the police intended to move him somewhere. Although he did not understand the discussions that swirled around him between the men in uniform and the doctors and nurses who had treated him, he could read the body language. He saw the impatience of the police, particularly the short man that Cheng had cut and who now had his arm in a sling. He sensed the way the police were gaining sway over the wavering resistance being offered up by the doctor when his blood pressure was checked, his heartbeat monitored by the stethoscope, his temperature read by the thermometer stuck under his tongue. When the doctor nodded as he talked and handed some files to the policeman who never wore a uniform and was obviously the chief functionary among them, Kim knew he was to be moved somewhere else.

Once the officer who had insisted on the precise bullets to the skull had told him and the other Khmer Rouge soldiers that if the Vietnamese ever captured them they should immediately attempt to escape. Every time they were passed further toward the rear, he said, the security around them would be heightened and the opportunities for flight back to their lines greatly reduced. To not escape was to be a traitor, he had added.

Kim realized he was about to be moved further toward the rear. There would be much more attentive security than that offered by the single policeman sitting on a chair in the hall. He had hoped they would not move him before nightfall and when the darkness came he had waited for his chance. The moment he heard the policeman scuff the chair back against the wall and stand up, Kim slithered from the bed and listened to his retreating footsteps. He poked his head out to see an empty hallway and fled.

Now he lay deeply buried beneath a pile of rotting leaves that had fallen off the bush arcing over him. Only his eyes showed and he ignored the feeling of the insects crawling on him, ignored their many small stinging bites. He watched the two people sitting on a log on the beach. Standing behind them in a small dirt clearing just back of the beach was an ancient Land Rover, a kind of vehicle which Kim had seen in Cambodia. It was a shame he had never learned to drive. But even if he took the machine where would he drive it to?

It surprised him to see these two here — his cousin and the big man with the hat and close-cropped beard, who had come into the room with her during the disastrous reunion. They appeared to be waiting. He watched the way their heads turned slightly as they surreptitiously tried to scan the tree line where he hid without obviously seeming to do so. After an hour he was certain. They were watching and waiting for him. But to what purpose? He was afraid to reveal himself in order to discover their intent. Would she be here to help the police recapture him? Did she hate him so? Or was she afraid of him? Afraid of having someone like him on the loose in this country? This seemed more likely than her being here to help. That possibility was there, but remote. He did not think he should trust her. And what of the big man? He was an enigma to Kim, a piece in a puzzle that defied comprehension. He had been on the beach the day of the shipwreck and had cared for the little girl who had been put in a room down the hall from his. Why was he with his cousin? What was he in the scheme of things? It seemed that he must be some kind of policeman or government official. Why else was he on the beach that day? Everyone else there had been government people, police or soldiers of some kind. If he was a government person then he must be a threat.

Kim knew he was trapped. Behind him was nothing but a hazardous route back to the hospital and the police there. Ahead of him were Vhanna, the man, an open beach and parking lot that could never be crossed without the two of them seeing him. On his flanks there was the ocean on one side and an unclimbable cliff on the other.

He lay there for another hour, waiting, and testing their patience. They talked in low voices and occasionally one or the other of them or both would stand and *pace a bit. But they did not leave and they continued to covertly eye the trees. There was no question anymore. They waited for him and were certain he would come this way. If they were so certain, would the police he had eluded not also soon arrive to close this avenue of escape? Already he could see other people walking on the sand, emerging from the great houses bordering the beach. Dogs accompanied many of these people. Soon some of them would come to this end of the beach and any opportunity for him to escape from here without being noticed by others besides his cousin and the man would be lost. He had tried to escape, Kim thought, and ultimately failed. It had, he decided, been a fool's mission from the beginning. Alone, there was nowhere safe to which he could run. Cheng or the police would soon find him and that would be the end of it one way or the other. No doubt his cousin would turn him over to the police, too. Regardless, she was his last hope. He must put his fate into her hands. There was, he realized, a form of justice in that.*

chapter thirteen

Something small struck the back of the log just behind where Vhanna was sitting. We both jumped slightly in surprise, looked about, but could see nothing changed. The tree line looked the same, nothing moving. I cast my gaze down the beach to where various people were strolling on the sand or simply basking in the warm morning sun. The earlier fog had moved well out to sea now and the air was warming quickly. Already I had stripped off my heavy coat and Vhanna had undone her jacket. I was beginning to think this a rum idea. If Kim had been going to come out of the woods here he should have done so by now. There were increasingly all too many others on the beach who might take note of his appearance. He would see that, too, if he was out there at all. *Click*. Again we twisted to look toward the line of trees after finding no indication of what had struck the log. Pebbles surrounded it; one more would just blend in. Were we imagining things? Another light crack as something hit the log and this time I saw the pebble bounce off onto the ground. "There," I said, pointing discreetly toward a large bush where a branch shivered.

Vhanna glanced at me and then down the beach toward the various beach wanderers. She pursed her lips thoughtfully. We had not discussed what we were actually going to do when the time came. Poor planning. We could not just saunter over to the trees, gather Kim up, and walk over to the Land Rover without risking being seen. "I want to be able to talk to him first," Vhanna said.

I nodded, had expected as much. "I'm not sure you should be alone with him."

She frowned at me. "He won't hurt me," she said sharply.

I started to protest that she could not be certain of that, but she cut me off. "There isn't time," she hissed. "We have to move now."

She was right, of course. And I realized that it also must be Vhanna who brought him out of the forest. He would not trust me, nor would he even understand anything I said. "Okay," I conceded, "I'll turn the Rover so its back door is up against the brush and then open it. You have him stay out of sight inside the trees as he goes over to where it's parked and crawl inside. You close the door, get in the front, and off we go. Easy as that."

Which proved to be precisely the case.

I passed through the police roadblock on the highway intersection outside Ucluelet after being subjected to merely a perfunctory search of Vhanna's Jeep Cherokee by a harried and rather tired-looking constable. Fergus had maintained a low growl deep in the back of his throat throughout the few minutes the Mountie spent poking and prodding around inside the vehicle. When he finished, we snaked up Highway 4 through the mountains to Port Alberni, set at the end of Alberni Inlet, and then swung onto a main logging road that ran for ninety-five kilometres down the southeast shoreline of the inlet to Bamfield. With a year-round population of less than three hundred people, Bamfield serves as a gateway to Pacific Rim National Park's famous West Coast Trail, is home to a university marine biology station, and fields a softball team renowned for its rowdiness. The little village is divided into two parts by a pleasant harbour. Here fishing charter vessels, commercial fishing trawlers, and many sailboats and other pleasure craft gather during the summer months so the little village is a bustling hub of activity all out of proportion to its modest size. With relief, I saw *Artemis* tied alongside a section of dock just down from the grocery store and small restaurant that are wedged together into a rundown building across the street from the docks.

Artemis is a forty-two-foot former gin boat mounting dual sixteen-cylinder diesel engines built into a white-painted mahogany plank hull. Her decks and cabin are warped out of the finest Asian mahogany with outer walls coated in glistening smooth white poly-resin paint and the trim varnished to a dark plum. Inside the cabin, the walls, cupboards, book racks, and doors are of hardened teak. Brass trimming thick as a wrist reinforces the seals at the windows. Built in the 1920s for a sleazy Vancouver land developer who fobbed himself off as a British lord, *Artemis* had spent most of its seagoing life never venturing beyond the confines of English Bay. With the Vancouver skyline set against the stunning backdrop of looming coastal peaks, Sir Johnathon Talbot found *Artemis* the perfect venue to lull prospective buyers into whatever his current real-estate scam might be with gin and tonics served up by sleek women of questionable virtue. Diamond mines in the Skeena Valley, oil wells gushing black gold near Barkerville, nothing was too preposterous in those days when the stock market had yet to crash and dreams of wealth ran high.

Eventually Sir Talbot's love of gin got the better of him and he died aboard the boat of a heart attack in the 1980s while trying to lure a group of Hong Kong businessmen into investing in a high-rise apartment scheme in the Lower East Side skid row district. *The Angel Queen*, as it was then called, ended up on blocks in a Vancouver shipyard. Between the curse attached to it by Sir Talbot's untimely departure aboard and its unquenchable thirst for fuel during a time of oil shortages and high diesel prices, the ship seemed doomed to rot in place or to be sold for salvage. By circumstance my father had known Sir Talbot and I had come to have passing knowledge of his boat and its story, which I happened to mention to Vhanna one night over a sumptuous dinner of grilled salmon steaks bought fresh off a fishing boat that morning. Next I knew *The Angel Queen* was renamed *Artemis* and had been thoroughly restored. It had also been refitted with every modern navigational, safety, and operational device available. The grand old lady was once again afloat and more opulent than ever.

Leaving Fergus in the Jeep, I walked down to the dock. Seeing me coming, Vhanna jumped off the boat and came over to meet me. She wore a dun-coloured long-sleeved shirt and cream-coloured khaki pants with brown leather sandals. Her hair was combed back into a ponytail and sunglasses were perched on the top of her head. "Come on, I'll buy you a beer," she said and led the way over to a small pub where an outside patio looked out over the harbour. Vhanna picked out a table set off from the others and we both ordered up a pint of icy Lighthouse Brewing Company summer pilsner. I cocked an eyebrow toward Vhanna after the waiter left.

"He's staying below decks. I thought we'd stay here until dark and then move." I nodded agreement. Vhanna took a long draught from her glass and sighed. "On the way down he told me everything. Elias, it's bad." She told me about a young man seeking a cousin in "America" by getting himself aboard a Chinese smuggling ship crewed by Cambodians. Of a terrible voyage with people crammed below decks and a team of killers ensuring crew and passengers were suitably afraid. Of an engine failure on a storm-tossed sea and the disaster that followed as the ship was swept onto the rocks. Of the leader of the gang, named Cheng, who had tried to kill Kim when he attempted to radio for help. She explained that Kim thought the rest of the crew had all perished. He had seen the corpses of the captain and several others floating in the sea or washed up on the shelf. Even as she said it, I knew that the man who had cut Danchuk so badly was this Cheng. Kim had not seen the other man, so did not know whether he was also off the migrant ship.

I thought about all this and wondered at reasons. Hui I understood. They wanted her back. Someone had sent her to America this way and from what I knew of the Snake Heads operations from the few stories I had read she would face a long, possibly lifelong time doing whatever they demanded to pay back the debt incurred in bringing her to the Golden Mountain. As long as there was a chance of getting her back, the Snake Heads would keep trying. "The only thing that makes sense is that Cheng is afraid that Kim could identify him," I said finally, "or that he knows something important about the smuggling operation." We were working on a second pint each, an indulgence for me at this time of day and one almost unheard of for Vhanna.

"Yes," she said. "You realize that he got away completely from the area of the wreck without anyone detecting his existence. If the Mounties know about him, they probably think he died in the wreck and is among the missing corpses."

"Meaning that Cheng can disappear into any Chinese community in North America or even anywhere else to do his work for the Snake Heads without worrying about being caught and deported back to China. Fake identification would be easy enough. But if Kim is able to identify him everything changes."

Vhanna nodded, but she continued to look more troubled than circumstances seemed to warrant. The obvious solution was to bring Kim in from the cold now, sit him down with Ray Bellows and Corporal Lee and lay the whole story out there in plain view. Once Kim described Cheng to the authorities he posed no further risk to the man. The damage would be done.

"Somebody," I said, "let Cheng know that Kim still hadn't given a statement to the police. That's why he took the risks he did. It was crazy to go into the hospital like that and to be willing to kill Danchuk if he needed to get at Kim. Cheng and the Snake Heads had to have somebody inside the police or the hospital helping him."

I told Vhanna about Corporal Lee's attempts to interview Kim and how he had pretended to not understand Mandarin or any other Chinese dialect. He had spoken only Khmer. Until a Khmer translator could be found to take Kim's statement Cheng was in no danger. Coming to the hospital had been a small risk in many ways.

"So who would know that Lee didn't get any information out of Kim?" Vhanna asked.

"Well, Bellows, Lee, Danchuk, and probably other officers like Singh and Monaghan. But none of them are likely sources for a leak to Cheng or his people." I shrugged. "Maybe the Snake Heads have penetrated the headquarters back in Vancouver. Wherever the anti-gang unit operates out of. Seems the only possibility."

Vhanna looked at me levelly. "You were right the first time. I'm not giving Kim up to them until I'm sure his safety can be guaranteed."

I met her gaze, hoping to see some sign of uncertainty or lack of resolve there. But her eyes never wavered and her face remained set. I had a choice. Reaching across the table I rested my hand on top of hers. "Okay," I said. Her eyes softened and her hand closed around mine.

"There are three ways of coming at this," I said from the front passenger seat of the Jeep. It was night and we were bumping along at a speed I thought was probably suicidal down a rough logging road that linked Bamfield via Cowichan Lake to the Trans-Canada Highway on Vancouver Island's east side. From there it would be clear sailing on paved highway into Victoria. If we lived to see the junction. But I knew that Vhanna was actually a very capable driver, as she is in most things requiring coordination and quick reflexes, so I was largely able to focus on the task at hand. Although there was the nagging thought of the risk of our coming around a corner and slamming into a deer, Roosevelt elk, or black bear. I had earlier seen a pair of eyes glowing in the woods and caught the fleeting image of a full-grown black bear standing on his hind legs and raking his front claws down a tree trunk alongside the road.

From his position in the back, Kim stared wide-eyed at the vast, forested world rushing by his window. Fergus sat on the bench seat beside him and I noticed that Kim often reached over to pat Fergus's head and stroke his ears, which was making him an instant friend. Vhanna had bought Kim a blue sweatshirt, a blue short-sleeved polo shirt, a pair of denims, and some black and white running shoes. Thus dressed he looked like any thirty-year-old Asian-Canadian male on a weekend getaway from the city. Adding to the appearance was the small camera case that contained a tiny, expensive video camera and an even more expensive and smaller digital camera.

"There's the possible leak from inside Bellows's unit," I said. "But we can't just call up Bellows and ask him to investigate that and try to follow that lead back to Cheng. So I'm not sure where we go. Then there's the guy who drove the car for them. Somebody who was local had to be helping Cheng. Otherwise they'd never have found McCutcheon, let alone targeted him for stealing his car. Trouble with that route is it's the one most likely being worked by Bellows and Lee."

"And three?" Vhanna said. I could tell by her tone that these two were obvious to her, but she was not yet seeing a third possibility and was rankled by that. More likely she thought I was seeing some avenue of pursuit that was illusory.

In reality this had been something that had been nagging at me since the day the helicopter had landed the Mounties and me on the rock shelf where the ship was breaking up with such disastrous loss of life. "I think the ship was bound for Nootka Sound. It was going to offload everyone somewhere in the sound. Think of how many people that is. They wouldn't have gone right into the port at Gold River or the one at Tahsis. So it had to be somewhere remote. Again some-one who knew the waters, knew the landing spots that would work, knew the logging roads that could be used to reach the main road, had to have helped with the logistics. And somebody had to have some buses, or cube vans, or semi-trailers and trucks to put everyone into for the trip out."

"Roundabout," Vhanna said after a long moment of consideration. "But it's worth a shot."

"We stash Kim," I said, "deal with Hui, and then I've an idea where to start looking."

Vhanna squeezed my thigh by way of agreement and then pushed the Jeep up another notch on the speedometer.

chapter fourteen

Normally when visiting Victoria I stay at the Oak Bay Hotel, both for its charmingly stuffy old England decor and for the glorious views onto Haro Strait from The Snug Lounge, which make it abundantly clear that you are not in the Old World. On a clear day, the volcanic cone of Mount Baker forms a massive backdrop as it rises up to tower over the rest of the Cascade Mountain range on the Washington State mainland. Whale-watching boats roar up the strait toward San Juan Island, where killer whales commonly gather. The hotel is a prime location for relaxing, meeting friends, and sipping imported ales. But Vhanna and I also thought that it would prove a difficult place for Kim to avoid attracting the attention of either staff or clientele.

So instead of a hotel on the shoreline of Oak Bay, we took rooms in the downtown core at Swan's Hotel & Brew Pub. A little more modern and trendy, housed in a restored heritage commercial building, Swan's had the advantage of being just a block away from Fisgard Street — the heart of Victoria's small but thriving Chinatown. Here, we reasoned, Kim would fade into the backdrop. Arriving just before midnight, we managed to secure two rooms positioned side by side on the second floor. The kitchen in the pub downstairs was still open so we pressed through the noisy crowd of thirty-something swingers, all apparently hoping to get lucky but tending to cluster in isolated male or female groups that limited their chances of success. They stood at the various bars or sat at the tables eyeing each other like ten year olds at their first dance in the school gym. Those who tried talking had to do so at the top of their lungs because of the general racket and the booming bass of the stereo system. We made our way into the glass-enclosed patio area where things were quieter and settled at a table, with Kim and Vhanna on one side and me on the other.

Kim's eyes kept darting in apparent confusion back toward the interior of the pub and the short skirts and skimpy tops many of the women wore. He said something to Vhanna and I saw her mouth tighten as she shook her head and responded in a short, sharp sentence that left Kim looking chastened. To my unasked question, she responded, "He wondered if they were all prostitutes, like women dressed like that and in a bar would normally be in Cambodia."

The waiter came and we ordered a pitcher of beer and a seafood platter that, when it arrived, was piled high with mussels and oysters in cracked shells. Kim sipped his ale half-heartedly but led the way working through the seafood. When the plate was empty we sent for another one and, as my thirst was rivalling Kim's appetite, a second pitcher. Later, table swept clean of beer mugs and shellfish debris, we sipped espressos and cognac while carrying on a strange conversation that involved either Kim or I sitting patiently in order to give Vhanna time to translate the last sentence for the other.

On the way into the bar I had snagged a copy of the latest *Victoria Times-Colonist* to see what was currently being said about the crisis of the migrants. "Go Home" the headline blazed in type that filled almost a quarter of the page. Below the headline a photo revealed a group of frightened-looking Chinese in poor clothing being ushered from a bus into a wire-surrounded holding pen that had been set up at the Work Point military base. The accompanying stories didn't require a close read to comprehend. Nothing objective in the reporting and those interviewed unanimously called for the immediate deportation of all the migrants back to China. Several Chinese-Canadians decried these line jumpers who sought to enter Canada without going through the normal immigration procedures. There was little sympathy for those who had died in the shipwreck and none at all for the survivors or the others who had been caught coming off boats that made it safely to shore. An invasion was underway, screamed the main editorial, and the government must respond clearly and decisively or our coastline would be overwhelmed. I was surprised that the words "yellow peril" had failed to be used yet, but suspected that if the boats kept coming it would only be a matter of time before such epithets resounded from the pages.

Vhanna stared at the front-page photo. Her expression was almost fearful. "This is where they sent Hui?" I told her it probably was. She handed the paper to Kim, then leaned over to point at the photo, and said something softly in Khmer. His face tightened. He whispered a reply. Vhanna rested her hand on his shoulder, gave it a reassuring squeeze and said something that brought a hesitant smile to his face. I needed no translation for what had just passed between them. Vhanna was assuring him she would do whatever it took to keep him from being locked up behind that wire fence. I sipped my cognac, drank the last of the double espresso, and repressed my fear that we were embarked on a mission that could only end in tragedy for Kim and possibly for us all.

In the morning, while Vhanna took a leisurely shower, I phoned Dr. Carl Harris in Nanaimo. The regional coroner's voice was soon booming down the line. "McCann, where the hell are you? I've been leaving messages on your machine."

When I used the excuse of being in Victoria on personal matters, I could almost hear Harris's back rising. "I'm waiting on two reports here. One that recounts in general the circumstances of the shipwreck you attended and includes an estimated body count. I don't even expect any kind of recommendations for prevention of such a tragedy in the future or a call for an inquiry into the matter. That's best left to higher authorities than ye or me, but I need that report ASAP. And then there's the matter of," he paused and could be heard shuffling papers, "ah, this McCutcheon fellow. I need a report on the circumstances of his demise as well. You're an on-call community coroner, McCann, and right now you should be in Tofino on call and dealing with these matters, not gallivanting around Victoria."

I explained that the matter here was urgent and that I would be returning to Tofino very shortly and would then write up the reports and courier copies to him by the fastest possible means. He grunted an acknowledgement. "Do it, McCann, or I'll be seriously considering your replacement. It's not as if I haven't already received a complaint about your activities in the Chinese matter from other authorities. Christ, McCann, you know how to stretch the jurisdiction of your responsibilities. Haven't I warned you of this before?"

Although I had no idea what he was talking about, I murmured polite apologies and assurances that I would step on no official toes in prosecuting my duties. "See that you don't, McCann. And expedite those reports." His phone banged down loudly, leaving me listening to dead air.

I dropped the handset back into its cradle and turned in the chair to see a naked Vhanna standing across the room by the bathroom door towelling her hair casually with one hip cocked against the door jam. "Sounded like that didn't go well."

Shaking my head by way of response, I walked across the room and circled my arms around her back, pulling her still damp body against my chest while putting my lips on hers. She continued to casually dry her hair while kissing me back lazily. "We have matters to attend to," she murmured, "and should check on Kim before he gets restless and decides to go out on his own."

"I know. This is just a quick drive by."

She chuckled, darted her tongue into my mouth, and then wriggled out of my grasp to disappear back into the bathroom to finish drying off.

I went to the window and looked down on the street below, only vaguely registering the crowds of tourists and office workers making their way past the novelty shops and other retail stores while a steady stream of traffic flowed down the one-way street. A wiry young man powering one of the city's ubiquitous three-wheeled, two-passenger Kabuki Cabs pedaled by with a couple of overweight and loudly dressed tourists in the back. There was no doubt in my mind that the authority who had been complaining to Harris must have been Danchuk. He had done so in the past and apparently was determined to keep doing so until Harris finally did relieve me of my duties. The justification for this round of complaints escaped me, but I was sure that Danchuk could easily tick off an impressive list of causes for dissatisfaction with my behaviour. What did it matter in the end anyway? It was not as if I wanted this position or needed it. Being Tofino's community coroner was a burden I would be just as happy to be free of. Still, I would do my job and provide the reports as quickly as possible. In the meantime, however, there were other matters of more import than a final accounting on behalf of the dead that would not in any manner change the reality of their deaths.

Vhanna and I took Kim out for breakfast and then returned him to his room with strict instructions to not go out and to leave the "Do Not Disturb" sign in place until we returned. He was to open the door for nobody but Vhanna. Neither of us wanted Kim wandering around unaccompanied when he couldn't speak English and had no identification papers, false or otherwise. Kim offered no argument. Since being reunited with his cousin, and realizing that she was no longer intent on spurning him for his past role as a Khmer Rouge fighter, Kim seemed inordinately complacent, almost carefree. If he had any sense of the seriousness of his situation as an illegal refugee in a strange land whose police were undoubtedly actively looking for him, he gave no indication. Once Vhanna told him that he was to stay put, he nodded and assumed a lotus position on the bed that he had already neatly made on his own. Fergus settled happily on the floor near to the bed, eyes lazily fixed on the dazzling television images. As we left the room, Kim was flipping through television channels with the remote. By the time the door shut it was apparent he had decided to fix on one of the all-sports channels. I could hear an announcer blathering on about a play in some European soccer game.

We retrieved the Jeep from the parking lot and drove over Johnson Street's blue lift bridge. It was a dirty grey day with a hard breeze blowing in cold and damp off Juan de Fuca Strait. From the passenger seat, I guided Vhanna to Esquimalt Canadian Forces Base. We followed a short suburban street that bordered the base and led up to an entry point. Just before we reached the military checkpoint, Vhanna pulled over and we got out and walked along the sidewalk toward a cluster of people gathered in front of a rusty wire fence that was topped by strands of badly rusted barbed wire. The fence enclosed a concrete sports area that backed onto the Work Point barracks gymnasium, a flat-roofed building that was typical of its type and function. The gymnasium had been transformed into a rough barracks for the Chinese migrants who had been rounded up off the four ships. According to the newspaper report, folding cots had been set up on the gymnasium floor. Outside the structure lines of portable outhouses were arrayed with military precision and, presumably, the migrants were able to use the shower facilities with which the gym was equipped.

The more fortunate people standing on the side of the wire opposite the migrants were a mixed bag of curious gawkers, a few media clicking away with their cameras, and protesters. The protesters waved crudely made cardboard signs that told the Chinese in various ways how unwelcome they were in Canada. Picking up on the newspaper headline of the day before, "GO HOME" was the most popular. The sign wavers included young toddlers holding their mothers' hands, a plump First Nations woman who was trying without particular success to get the others to participate in a "Go Home" chant, a man with spiked purple hair and an odd assortment of chains dangling from various pockets and belt loops, and several elderly men and women dressed in the kind of sport clothes they would normally wear on the golf course. All were, however, now united in their cause and laughed and chatted away amiably to each other in the manner of strangers facing a situation of shared adversity.

Inside the fence was a small collection of Chinese who were dressed mostly in the black clothing in which they had arrived in the country. A few wore white shirts. Their expressions were generally forlorn. Several walked alongside the fence, circling the square in the same way that cattle will follow a range fence, pressing to the outer edge of the ground to which they are confined. As they passed the demonstrators, they kept their eyes to the ground, avoiding the catcalls that the First Nations woman and some of the older people offered.

I caught sight of Hui approaching. She was walking just behind two young women, with her head down, and her hands thrust despondently into the pockets of a frayed pair of blue jeans. Not wanting to draw the attention of the demonstrators toward either Hui or ourselves, I squeezed Vhanna's hand and pointed the girl out discreetly. Vhanna paled as she saw Hui's beaten-down posture, the way her step was reduced almost to a shuffle. In the instant that she passed by where we stood, her head turned and she looked directly at me with eyes that were haunted and frightened. Reflexively I raised my hand in a small wave and smiled reassuringly. If she recognized me or if she even saw me, Hui gave no sign. She just kept walking along the fence, following in the footsteps of the two women, head lowered again toward her feet.

"We have to get her out of there," Vhanna said in a hard whisper.

I squeezed her hand again and led the way back to the Jeep.

chapter fifteen

"**Y**ou must understand," said the Immigration officer who had introduced himself as William Logan, "that this request is highly unusual. As unusual as the entire situation we face here." He was a neatly turned out man. Black shoes shined, short grey hair precisely combed, fingernails tidily trimmed, teeth white and polished. His clipped moustache and the stiff way in which he held his body gave him the air of a retired military officer who would never be at home in civilian clothes and so had made a uniform of them.

Vhanna and I sat across from him at a grey gunmetal desk on a pair of hard foldout grey metal chairs. Logan was only slightly more comfortably seated in a metal typing chair that was also uniform grey. The room had served as an office for coaches whose teams were using the gym and was now being used by Logan as his operational base for administering the processing of the Chinese migrants and their various claims for refugee status. Logan appeared greatly out of place in such a room. Its battleship linoleum floor, bank of grey metal gym lockers, steel coat rack on pedestal legs, and faded white walls called for occupation by men in gym shirts with cut-off sleeves, shorts, running shoes, and whistles hung around thick-muscled necks. Logan managed, however, to impose a precise bureaucratic atmosphere upon the room that defied the incongruity of his situation.

"Situation" was his word. He deftly slipped the word into almost every sentence. It was an unfortunate situation, a situation of great delicacy, an unprecedented situation, a situation for which the laws were unprepared, a situation that required the most careful administrative handling so as not to cause confusion or unrealistically raise false expectations for all concerned. I solemnly agreed to his every situation while persisting in reminding him that the situation of an eleven-year-old girl being locked up inside a barracks was by far the most unfortunate of situations. This was particularly so as this child had an alternative place to which she could be situated and cared for until the necessary steps were taken either to make an application for her to be granted refugee status in Canada or to make arrangements for her return to China.

"I am not sure that her situation can be dealt with in isolation from that faced by the others," he said. Logan shuffled a few papers on his desk as if each was representative of one of the people who sat on the other side of the wall on a little cot or wandered lost and confused around the fenced perimeter outside the gymnasium.

His uncertainty was the first positive sign since this awkward interview had begun. "As you have said, sir, this situation is highly unusual," I began. "Unusual situations sometimes require unusual solutions. The fact that this situation has led to the immigrants being kept in custody rather than being released on their own recognizance pending immigration hearings is a case in point. What we are requesting here is that Ms. Huang be released into the care of the Janson family in Tofino rather than being detained here or being transferred into a Ministry of Children and Families group home." I cited the report that Bethanie had filed with him on behalf of the ministry that stated its agreement to the proposal and approved Lars and Frieda as short-term foster parents who were recommended to take custody of Hui pending conclusion of the processing of her immigration file. The report lay on the desk next to Logan's well-cared-for hand.

"There is the language situation," he said with some hesitance.

Lars, I pointed out, knew a little Mandarin. And Vhanna, who had pledged to make herself available as required by the Jansons, spoke the language fluently. Hui also spoke rudimentary English so that she could generally make herself understood. I didn't mention that Lars had picked up his fragmentary Mandarin during a youth spent sailing on Swedish maritime freighters. Instead I reminded Logan that the Jansons had spent years working overseas in Red Cross refugee camps and so were well attuned to the requirements that displaced people, particularly children, might have.

There was the matter of distance between Tofino and Victoria, where the hearings were likely to be convened. The Jansons, myself, and Vhanna were all willing to guarantee in whatever manner was required that we would ensure Hui's presence at any hearing and would cover the costs associated with such travel. This was not a situation in which he had full authority to make such a decision. He could only make a recommendation; an Immigration judge would have to hear the application and rule on whether to place Ms. Huang into the Jansons' care. Understood. When could such an application be made? Logan picked up a cheap, grimy white phone, and looked distastefully at its condition. "Most everything we have to work with here is old surplus equipment that was mothballed when the Princess Patricia's left," he said. "But we do the best we can."

Several calls later and a few notes scribbled onto a notepad, Logan looked up at us with his unreadable expression of compassion and officiousness. "The application by the Jansons for temporary foster parent custody of Ms. Huang can be heard in two days." He passed a sheet of paper with a date, address, and a time of hearing on it across the table to me. "The Jansons will have to be present for the hearing," he said. We agreed they would be present. He stood and offered his hand first to Vhanna and then politely to me. His grip was soft, his flesh cool and dry. "It is to be hoped that this situation can be resolved appropriately," he said. I noted that he offered no definition of what he deemed appropriate.

Logan had agreed to let us see Hui and so from his office we were escorted by a heavy-set uniformed Immigration officer to another room. This one probably served in normal circumstances as a classroom in which teams and their coaches could plan complex strategies for prevailing on the basketball court. We sat for several minutes on stackable metal-framed chairs with splintered plywood seats behind a scuffed collapsible wooden table before the door opened again and Hui was escorted into the room by the Immigration officer. He pointed to a chair set on the opposite side of the table from us. She glanced warily over her shoulder at him before easing herself onto the chair. Hui sat with her head bowed, eyes fixed on the table in front of her, small arms crossed over her stomach. The officer said we could have fifteen minutes and then the room was required for another meeting.

When the door closed I got up from the chair and walked around the table to sit on its edge next to Hui. "Hello, Hui," I said. "How are you?" After a moment, she looked up at me with dark, sober eyes. The hint of a smile touched her face.

"Hello, Eee-rye-ess," she said slowly and carefully as if each word was being meticulously rendered from a Mandarin thought into her awkward English. "I am well. And you?" ·

I agreed that I was well, too. "Hui, how would you like to leave here and stay with some friends of mine?"

Hui stared at me, her lips moving as if she were trying to speak the words and thus understand them. "I don't know how to say that more simply," I said.

"No need," Vhanna said as she leaned against the edge of the table on the opposite side of Hui. She smiled at the girl and spoke to her in what I assumed was Mandarin. Hui's eyes widened in surprise and she grinned. I felt her hand close on top of mine and let her take it as she had on the day of the shipwreck. She looked at me and nodded vigorously. "Yes, Elias," she said. "I like. This bad place." Hui dropped her head and mumbled. "Scared."

Vhanna reached out and stroked her hand through Hui's long, dark hair, while she spoke to her in a gentle, reassuring tone. The little girl looked up at Vhanna and smiled less guardedly than before. A short staccato burst of words followed. Vhanna laughed and nodded her head. "She asked if we will take her to McDonald's. I said we would. See what you're getting yourself into?"

"Surely only a passing fancy," I said. Vhanna gave me a mocking grin and then set about explaining to Hui that we had to leave her for now but that in a couple days we would return and if all went well she would come to live with the Jansons. She then explained a little about the Jansons, including that they had been her foster parents when she was a little girl and would do for Hui what they had done for her. Vhanna had just finished explaining what she had said to Hui when the officer knocked on the door, signalling our time was up. Hui paled noticeably as he came in and gestured for her to follow him. I squeezed her hand and then slowly untwined each unwilling finger from where they clutched tightly to mine. Looking sadly back over her shoulder as she left the room, I sensed that Hui did not trust that we would come back or that she would ever see the Jansons or eat in a McDonald's.

As we left the room and headed out of the gymnasium into the grey day that had now given way to cool drizzle, Vhanna said, "If we fail with this it will be worse than if we had not tried at all, you know."

I shuddered inside my jacket and settled my hat more firmly. "We won't fail her," I said with more bravado than I felt.

chapter sixteen

Watching the cigarette smouldering down between the yellow stains on the insides of Smithy's right index and middle finger I felt a sense of dislocation in time. We were both older, bodies more lived in and deteriorated, but there had been the times when we had sat in grungy, smoke-filled bars like this together in the years before our deployment overseas. Looking around the room, I was not surprised to see several green uniforms. Only now women wore some of them. "Do you ever miss the life?" I asked as I drank the froth off a mug of ale. That had changed, too. Now there was good microbrew beer. Back then there would have been Blue, Old Style, or Old Vienna.

Smithy wore faded jeans, a sun-bleached denim shirt, and an old-fashioned grease monkey's skullcap that looked like it had once been red but was now blackened with oil stains. His cheeks were stubbled and his fingers needed scrubbing with a hard brush. He looked at me and his eyes narrowed. "Those razorbacks fucked me over good, McCann. Don't miss the fucking life one little cunt hair worth." He drained his glass of Canadian and plunked it on the table, gestured for another. I had made it clear that the tab was mine. Smithy had offered no resistance to the idea.

Every military unit has its member gifted with a nimble borrower's hand. When I served in Cyprus that hand belonged to Lance-Corporal Eric "Smithy" Gilmore. Smithy was the man you went to when something needed scrounging from outside the quartermaster store's official supply stream.

Eventually, however, Smithy's talents got the better of him. Not long after our deployment onto the Green Line in Nicosia, Smithy added drugs to the long list of things that he could get you for a fee or a return favour. Just before our rotation home his luck ran out and he was stung by the military police during a buy in a Greek coffeehouse.

I had not seen Smithy for years after his arrest and eventual imprisonment on trafficking charges. When I did meet him, it was while foraging in a wrecking yard outside Victoria for a hard-to-find part for my 1960s-era Land Rover. As I lay under the shattered remains of an identical model, breaking a ruined transmission apart in quest of a special bushing, I became aware that somebody else was working down by the rear differential. Peering through the shadows, I saw a man in stained green overalls who possessed a small, but distinctive, overbite. "Smithy?" I said. An acquaintance was reborn.

It transpired that Smithy was part-owner of the wrecking yard, which also contained a general salvage operation. Smithy was still scrounging and fixing. He has since become my mainstay source for the parts needed to keep my faithful Land Rover operational. His prices are right and I assure myself that the parts are drawn from wrecks that I no longer have to track down on my own. One phone call and usually within a week or two the part arrives in a box at the Tofino bus depot. Who am I to question such efficiency?

When Smithy's second pint arrived I described the information I sought. He pursed his lips, raised his eyes toward the ceiling in what I thought appeared a somewhat contrived attempt to look thoughtful. It occurred to me that I was probably wasting my time here. "These guys are the big league, McCann," he said eventually. Pausing to light another cigarette off the dying end of the current butt, he added, "They want something or someone they just buy it or take it. Ain't nobody going to fuck with them. They want guns, they get them. They want some cube trucks or buses they'll get them and there won't be any problem there for them. They want local knowledge they'll just buy it."

I nodded, convinced this was a waste of time. Smithy was useful for buying Land Rover parts, but as a window on the criminal world of gangs there was nothing here. I was just starting to think about how to extract myself from this situation when Smithy said, "I figure three cube trucks. That'd be the way to do it." I waited, looking interested. "These people been on a ship for what, thirty days or some fucking thing. They been crammed in there like shit in a Johnny Can tank. Apparently stink so bad the cops didn't want to go on board the ones they caught. Had to wear masks. No reason these people wouldn't go along with being jammed into a couple cube trucks. You can run logging roads all the way from Gold River to Port Alberni and then hook onto Highway 14 to Nanaimo and catch the ferry to Horseshoe Bay and it's a clear run into Chinatown where they disappear into swarms of other gooks that all look just like them. Easy shit. All you need is one logger who knows the roads and somebody with a credit card to rent the trucks from any rental agency. Oh, and some soldiers willing to ride inside the trucks with all that stink and sweating crush of people to make sure they stay quiet during the ferry transit part of the operation. One guy could do that. One guy with a knife or gun and a lot of attitude. Maybe they give the people some food and water, maybe have a can they can shit or piss in or maybe just make them go on the floor and let them go without rations until they reach Vancouver." He emptied his glass and signalled the waiter for another. "You knew this, though, McCann. So what are you really looking for and why?"

"I need to find that local you mentioned. The one who knows the logging roads."

He stared at me, held his silence until the beer came and the waiter was out of earshot. "You ain't telling me yet about why."

I thought of lies that might be offered, knew they would be transparent. "I find them or they are going to find someone I care about and hurt her."

He set his glass down, took a thoughtful drag on his cigarette, considered the glowing end of it. "Simple as that?"

I nodded.

"There's someone I might know." He butted the cigarette into the ashtray that was set beneath the sign declaring that the local health authorities had banned smoking in public places and that the bar was a designated non-smoking facility. Neither patrons nor staff paid the sign any heed. He drained his beer in one long, hard gulp and then stood up. "Let's get out of this shit hole."

"Hey, stud, where did you pick up this hot little babe," Smithy crowed as I opened the door to Vhanna's fire-engine red Jeep Cherokee. I told him it belonged to a friend. "The one who might get hurt?" he asked with a surprisingly sober tone.

"No, she's too young to drive," I replied, which drew a puzzled expression from Smithy. I thought of Kim and Vhanna's proximity to him. "Then again," I added, "the person who owns this might also be in danger."

Smithy's jaw tightened, which served to emphasize his overbite more. "How young is the one?" I told him. "Is the owner of this Jeep important to you?" I nodded. "I'm in your corner, pardner," he said. "Need be I can pull in some of our old friends for a little added muscle."

"Thanks, Smithy. But I don't think we want to start a war here," I said as I drove according to his directions back toward downtown.

"Might be what it takes," he said gloomily. Smithy, I realized, had been watching too many action movies and reading too many thrillers. I imagined him calling up some of the old cadre of airborne troops from Cyprus or PPCLI from our Esquimalt station days. Men with bad knees, bad backs, and poor memories with regard to the handling of automatic weapons. Yesterday's soldiers, a disaster in the making. Still, it was a surprisingly generous offer for one so embittered by the service to make to a fellow veteran.

Smithy meanwhile directed me to an industrial area of the city that bordered the waterfront of the Inner Harbour near the Point Ellice Bridge on Bay Street. We parked in front of a nondescript one-storey building housing several warehouse outlets selling specialized contractor supplies like electrical wiring, flooring, and doors. Smithy told me to bring any files I might have that would be useful, so I dug my battered brown leather briefcase from behind the front seat. In it was the information for the preliminary report on the shipwreck and McCutcheon's death. Then Smithy led the way to an unmarked reflective glass door and pushed an inter-com button mounted on the wall next to it. The sign-board area over the door was blank. "Smithy," he said when a voice inquired who it was. The door clicked open. As we passed through, I noted a small surveillance camera mounted up by the eaves that was focused on the entranceway. Whoever was inside not only sought anonymity but also was security minded.

We entered a completely empty room obviously originally designed to be a reception area. Here and there furniture had deeply indented the worn grey carpet. From a bank of electrical outlets and phone or cable television jacks mounted into the far wall, a network of wires spooled across the floor through the open doorway into the next room. "Watch you don't trip over the wires," Smithy whispered, "or he'll bite your fucking head off." We duly tiptoed around the wires and entered the next room.

Sitting at a computer terminal with his back to us was a burly man in a wheelchair. He tapped rapidly on the keyboard, grunted with satisfaction, and then clicked a mouse key. A message bar appeared on the screen and a blue line streaked from left to right across it and then the screen went blank. The man dropped a hand to one wheel and gave it a backward spin that turned the chair sideways so he could face us. I figured him for his late forties. Despite the fact that he was probably about six-foot-two and weighed in at over two hundred pounds he carried not an ounce of fat on his upper body. His torso formed a hard inverted triangle from narrow hips to wide shoulders that looked ready to burst the seams on the brown corduroy sports jacket he wore over a crisp denim shirt. He was a handsome man with close-cropped dark hair, brown eyes, and an easy smile as he extended a big hand toward Smithy, while simultaneously taking my measure. From the waist down his body was a ruin, the legs withered sticks that were held close together and tethered to the chair by a strap.

"Federico, this here is Elias McCann," Smithy said by way of an introduction. "Elias has a problem I think you might be able to help him with."

We shook hands. His grip was firm but absent of any sense of macho strength testing. "Pleasure to meet you, Mr. McCann," Federico said in a soft, cultured voice that held a trace of an Italian accent. "My name is Federico Casanova." He grinned. "I am serious about the last name. It is common enough in Abruzzo Province, which is where my family came from. Now, why don't you tell me about this problem and I'll tell you what I can or cannot do."

As yet nobody had offered any explanation of what the man did that Smithy was convinced would be useful to me, but I decided to just set things out as they were and see what happened. After inviting Federico to use my first name and receiving confirmation that I should do the same for him, I gave the man a brief rundown on the shipwreck and the subsequent events, leaving out the fact that I was part of harbouring Kim from the authorities. When I finished, Federico steepled his hands together under his chin, elbows resting on the arms of his chair and considered things for a moment.

"Did Smithy tell you what I do?" I shook my head and he nodded, as if he had expected that and approved. "Before I ended up in this chair, Elias, I served on the Victoria Police Force. Five years ago during a routine takedown on a grow operation a goofball pulled a gun on us. He got off one shot. Unfortunately it severed my spine. I could have stayed on as a token cripple in an office position, but I didn't want that. So now I'm a free-lance investigator for anyone wanting to find anyone else. I do it all from here." He pointed at the computer. "With this."

My puzzlement must have been clear. "You want to find this man called Cheng. Smithy knows I find people, mainly because I found him, and so he brought you here." I glanced over at Smithy, who was looking kind of sheepishly at the floor. "Trouble is that I don't think this Cheng is the kind of person I can find right now. He's new here and he's here illegally. That means no paper trail has been built yet." He grinned and gestured at the computer before him. "Or perhaps electronic trail is more apt these days.

"You see what I really do is follow the electronic trails that lead me right to the person my client is seek-ing. Most of my clients are skip tracers, companies that have lost funds to embezzlement, and insurance compa-nies who suspect a dead person might not be."

"Sorry to have wasted your time," I said. "You're right, I don't think you can help here." Smithy's face had gone a bit red and he was still focused on the floor, hands stuffed into the front pockets of his pants.

Federico raised a hand in a "hold on" gesture. "You misunderstood me, Mr. McCann. I said that I don't think I can help you find Cheng directly. But there's another way to come at this. Tell me about the man who was murdered." Quickly I briefed him on what I knew about Ian McCutcheon. "Do you have a mailing address?" Federico had started keying information into some form he had called up on the computer. I gave him the address. "We're starting with a simple credit check," he said.

I watched as he sent McCutcheon's details off along some cyber line and a minute or two later we were looking at a complete report on McCutcheon's financial circumstances. "You were right about him being a loner. No credit cards, no overdraft loan protection, no outstanding loans, no unfiled tax reports or overdue taxes for that matter. Very good, but also hell for a credit rating. To get credit you need to show that you've incurred debt and handled it well." He moved the cursor down the screen, checking this and that bit of information. "Hello," he said, "your Mr. McCutcheon was also a miser." Federico tapped quickly away at a calculator and then let out a low whistle. "Your man has, or I should say had, account balances and investments adding up to a total of $553,923.33 at the Canadian Imperial Bank of Commerce in Port Alberni. Best as I can figure, that is, for there might be some other cash lying around there. I don't have any indication as to whether he held any stocks, mutual funds, Canada Savings Bonds, or other investments at institutions other than the bank. I doubt there would have been anything like that, though." He pointed at the screen, gesturing to some low interest-bearing Guaranteed Investment Certificates that were all in small denominations. "These are the kind of investments a bank teller would have sold him if she was moving some money around for him, say, from the savings account to chequing or vice versa. Just trying to get him a slightly better term than his accounts would earn. This isn't the kind of portfolio that goes together with someone trying to maximize their savings' interest-bearing potential." He clicked his mouse and a printer set off to one side hummed and then started printing out the report.

McCutcheon's investment strategy, or rather his lack of one, made sense to me. He was a man with few material needs or desires, a man doing little more than wait-ing to die so he could finally rejoin his obviously beloved Edith. What need did such a man, who already had more than half a million dollars in an account, have of the interest such money would earn? It was a similar conun-drum to that which I faced. But unlike me, McCutcheon was not blessed, or, depending on your perspective, cursed, with a business adviser who would never permit such laxity in the administration of wealth.

While I mused on this subject, Federico ran a routine police check on McCutcheon and learned that he had no criminal record. He tried a couple other government data-bases and insurance client databases but came up with nothing in them at all referring to McCutcheon. "Okay, question is, where did McCutcheon get his money from?" I shrugged. I had no idea. "You say he was a stone mason? Can't see the money coming from his work."

"Maybe he had an inheritance," I offered, "or money from family."

Federico nodded. "Possible. The other options are that he was more than he seemed, meaning he was involved in some kind of criminal racket." He shook his head. "Seems unlikely given the modest way he lived. That leaves his having won a lottery, which is about as likely as you and I being struck right this moment by lightening, or he came into a large insurance pay out."

"Any way to find out?" Smithy asked.

"Sure, but it doesn't really matter, does it? He wasn't murdered for his money, he was murdered for his car."

Even as he said it, I felt an electrical pulse of excite-ment flash through my body. "Maybe not," I said and ignored Federico's puzzled expression. "Maybe he was murdered for money and his car. When we went through the house we found no trace of any cash other than about $30 in small bills stuffed into a kitchen drawer and another twenty in a wallet stuffed into his coat pocket." I explained quickly how McCutcheon had carried a roll of twenties with him when he went into town and always paid for everything with cash. "He was a loner and a miser. I'd bet he kept a healthy nest egg in the trailer that he could draw on when he wanted. McCutcheon wasn't the kind of man to drive regularly over to Port Alberni and there was no indication that he had a client card he could use at an ATM in Tofino."

Federico offered an encouraging nod. "So what if his murderer knew McCutcheon's habits?" he asked.

I was thinking of the scraggly blond man in McCutcheon's car outside the hospital and of a letter in a drawer beside a bed that asked for a small loan. "Jesus, it was probably his son."

chapter seventeen

Like Bellows, I had jotted down the son's name and mailing address from the envelopes in McCutcheon's nightstand. Several minutes after I gave these to Federico we were looking through a credit and criminal record starkly in contrast to that of the father. Daryl McCutcheon had been in and out of debt so often that he had gone into personal bankruptcy twice, had three cars repossessed, several credit cards revoked, and currently owed about $23,000 to various lenders.

On the criminal side he had a record extending right back to his youth that included convictions for several drunk-driving offences, a handful of assaults, three possessions for the purpose of trafficking, and one sexual assault. He was thirty-one years old and had spent six of his fifteen adult years in prison. Most of the other years he was supposed to be reporting to a probation officer. That Daryl McCutcheon had been a disappointment to his father was probably certain. Equally certain in my mind was the fact that McCutcheon's son had led Cheng to his father's trailer so that he could murder the man.

"Murders are always the same," Federico said. "Almost ten times out of ten it's someone close to the victim who is the killer, usually a spouse or family member. Nobody saw this one that way yet because of the stolen car and its use in an attempted murder and kidnapping situation." He pursed his lips thoughtfully. "Although it's odd that your Inspector Bellows wouldn't have run a check on the son just as routine. That should have set off some alarm bells."

It was possible, I realized, that Bellows had already done precisely that. Neither of us was exactly sharing information with the other at this point. We needed to start doing so. Having learned everything I could here, I offered to pay Federico for his time and services. He waved the offer away. "If what we did helps put this McCutcheon guy behind bars that's good enough for me."

As Smithy and I turned to go, Federico said, "There's another thing about criminals, Elias. They generally crawl up from the bottom of the gene pool. What they all have in common is stupidity, cruelty, little or no conscience, a lot of personal grudges against all those they believe failed them and against society in general, and a greedy streak that runs deep as the Grand Canyon. They also usually think they're a lot brighter than they really are. Daryl McCutcheon can lead you to Cheng. And I suspect your Cheng is freelancing here."

"What do you mean?"

"Think about it. The Snake Heads are into major crime. They don't need to be part of a petty crash-and-grab murder. I think Cheng is running loose. McCutcheon was the local guide for the Snake Heads, the guy who showed them where the boat should land. McCutcheon was probably also the nearest contact for

Cheng to seek out if the operation went bad and he and the other Snake Heads on board managed to escape arrest. So Cheng somehow makes it from the shipwreck site to where he can link up with McCutcheon. The first thing Cheng needs is cash without going through the loops and hoops necessary to get it from the Snake Head bureaucracy, but McCuthcheon doesn't have any of his own, so he tells Cheng about his father. You say Cheng was the lead gang member on the ship. That's not a high position. I don't see the Snake Heads resorting to murder to protect his identity. They'd just give him some new papers and shift him off to another soldier job in New York or somewhere. Maybe even send him back to China. After all, the ship wrecked. He didn't actually do a very good job, did he? Cheng cost the Snake Heads money. He could well be on the run from them, too."

"Why grab Hui, then?" I asked, although I already saw an answer.

"Opportunity," Federico said grimly. "She was there and if he grabbed her and got away with it, he could hand her back to the Snake Heads. Maybe ingratiate himself again with them. Make up a bit for his failure."

I nodded. What Federico said made a lot of sense. Would Cheng keep coming, then? Would he keep trying to get at Kim and Hui? I sensed he would. Federico confirmed it. "Remember what I said about criminals. Cheng's typical, which just shows that culture or race doesn't effect anything a hell of a lot here. He's a killer. The way he goes for the same kind of wound with the knife tells me he likes killing, likes to see his victims with their guts open and knowing they're going to die. He'll kill for the sake of the act. That makes him different from the normal Snake Heads, who kill because it's necessary. Doing otherwise draws too much attention your way, attention you don't want or need. Cheng will also think he's smarter than the police and so he'll keep coming until he succeeds. It won't occur to him that he might get caught. He'll imagine himself too smart for that. I'd be very careful, Elias, and I would hide that little girl somewhere safe. Your friend's cousin too." He grinned when he saw my startled expression. "Hey, I wasn't born yesterday. I figure you have this Kim fellow stashed away somewhere or you wouldn't be chasing this so hard. Hui's a target of opportunity; Kim's the real objective for this Cheng. Good luck," he said. And without another word, Federico spun his wheelchair so his back was turned on us and went back to keying away at his computer. Smithy and I quietly let ourselves out.

After dropping Smithy back at the bar so he could retrieve his truck, I hurried to Swan's and met up with Vhanna and Kim. Vhanna had spent the time while I was meeting Smithy and then Federico taking Kim on a guided tour of Victoria's Chinatown and then a long walk with Fergus along the Dallas Road cliffs. This part of their walk culminated in a visit to the Ross Bay Cemetery to see the Japanese graves maintained there. After telling her what I had discovered, she readily agreed with my hastily cobbled together plan. Soon we were checked out of the hotel and racing up the Trans-Canada Highway north over the Malahat Pass. Kim and Fergus were in the back seat, Fergus content in the sure knowledge that we were homeward bound. For his part, Kim had been quite subdued since Vhanna had briefed him about the McCutcheon murder. I sensed he was not looking forward to returning to Tofino and was worried about what might happen to him there. For now our plan was simply for Vhanna to bring him back to Tofino aboard *Artemis* and then hide him away in her house.

Although we avoided discussing the matter in front of Kim, Vhanna and I were agreed that we must soon let the police and Immigration authorities know that he was staying with us. He would undoubtedly be taken into custody, but trying to keep him hidden indefinitely would certainly prove futile. Vhanna agreed with me, although grudgingly, that the longer Kim was on the lam from the official immigration system the poorer his chances for gaining permission to remain in Canada. There was also the very real danger that the police might bring charges against him for being part of the smuggling operation aboard the ship. After all he had been a crew member. For now, however, we had decided to continue harbouring Kim until we got a better sense of how much danger he was in from Cheng and the Snake Heads.

As Vhanna drove, I made notes in a notebook resting on my knee. Once my thoughts were fairly well ordered, I picked up Vhanna's cell phone from its bracket mount on the dashboard and followed her instructions as to how to turn the thing on and make a call. First I phoned the Tofino RCMP detachment and was relieved when the dispatcher answered. "Hi, Nicki, it's Elias. How free are you to talk?"

She let out a throaty chuckle. "Got the whole place to myself, sugar. Everybody's out on the road or sifting stones down on the beach, trying to turn up that missing fellow. Seems he's better at the vanishing act than Houdini. You sound far, far away, Elias."

After telling her I was phoning on a cell phone from somewhere near Shawnigan Lake, I asked her for Ray Bellows's phone number in Vancouver. "His cell number if you have it, Nicki."

"Wait one," she said and I heard her clicking on a computer. "You know, Elias, I probably shouldn't be giving this out to you without his permission and all that yadda yadda stuff." I said nothing and after a moment she grunted. "Don't suppose you're about to tell me what's cooking here."

"I just have to speak with him, Nicki. It's pretty important. I wouldn't ask otherwise."

She smacked what sounded like a chewing gum bubble into the receiver, which was a warning that Nicki wasn't pleased with me. Then she read off the number for Ray's cell phone. "Must be important," she said with a wry laugh, "for Mr. Luddite McCann to be making calls on a cell. Take care of yourself, Sugar." She rang off abruptly, letting me know further that she was not impressed with my taking advantage of our friendship.

Sighing, I checked the number I had scribbled in my notebook and then started going through the routine of firing up the cell once more. Vhanna looked over at me, her eyes hidden by her sunglasses. "Well, sugar," she said in a gently mocking tone, "looks like your credit with Nicki is burning up fast. Better take some flowers around to her next time you go by the station."

"Better idea would be a bottle of Tequila dropped off with her and Lacy at the cabin." For the past six years Nicki has shared a small cabin not far from my own with a slender Haitian woman named Lacy, who works behind the bakery's counter. Rumours abound about the nature of this relationship, but neither woman gives anything away on the matter, and Nicki continues to take on all male comers every Friday night at Rossiter's as the queen of country swing. While Nicki is dominating the dance floor, Lacy is likely to be found at the local coffee shop's philosophy café night discussing whether the 1970s really made a difference or whether world violence could be lessened if men simply discovered and nurtured their hidden feminine sides.

Vhanna laughed. "You do know your women."

"If only that were true," I muttered, as I finished ringing up Bellows.

"Elias, I'm just about to go into a meeting," he said. "Can this wait?" I could hear the distant blare of horns and rumble of traffic over the phone. Bellows must be walking down a Vancouver street.

Without revealing my source of information, I told Bellows my suspicion that Daryl McCutcheon had been an accessory to his father's murder and that the motive was as much robbery as it was to steal the Cadillac. I told him what I hoped he could set up for me and explained that I would be back in Tofino by early evening.

After a moment, Bellows said, "I'll make some calls." There was a long pause, as if he were considering something. "Elias, I was going to leave this until later, but, as I've got you, I'll bring it up now." Again he paused and I sensed he was choosing his words carefully. "It's about Kim Hoai. Is there anything you would like to tell me about him?"

I covered my hand quickly over the cell phone so that Bellows wouldn't hear my audible intake of breath. "No," I said in a voice that was far too wary. "What could there be?"

Bellows' voice was clipped, impatient. "Look, Elias, I strongly suspect that Ms. Chan is harbouring him and that you are a party to this. At this point, I've not ordered any direct action in this regard because we're badly overextended right now. If he's with you then he's out of harm's way. Also Danchuk informed me that the two of you were out of town and I figured you wouldn't be about to leave him in Tofino on his own. So I've given you both a long rope. But piss around with me, boy, and I'll drag you both in and wrap you up tight in charges and paperwork that'll blow any chances of you succeeding in the matter of Ms. Hui Huang. Understand?"

This time I didn't bother trying to conceal my intake of breath. My heart was beating like a drum. "Look, Ray."

"Look, Ray, nothing. Don't abuse our relationship, Elias," he snapped. "Don't admit anything right now, okay? Just assure me that when I call you in a day or two that Ms. Chan and Kim will be available for an interview with me on this matter."

I looked over at Vhanna, who was shooting me puzzled glances while trying to watch the road at the same time. Her eyebrows went up in silent inquiry. I thought to explain the situation to her and seek her agreement, but doing so would only confirm Bellows's suspicions and might sever his patience entirely. I could well imagine our returning to Tofino to find Danchuk and a posse of Mounties waiting at the house to collar Kim and take us all into custody. Danchuk would love that. "Yes, Ray. I assure you that's possible," I said slowly.

"Good move, Elias." The chirping of an audible traffic signal nearly drowned out his voice, as he rang off.

"What was that about?" Vhanna asked as I put the cell phone down. When I told her, Vhanna's mouth thinned into a straight line and she looked at me angrily. "You had no right —"

I cut her off. "I also didn't have a choice. You can see that. Bellows is being reasonable here. A lot more reasonable than he has to be. We can set some terms. Make sure that the situation is secure." I glanced over my shoulder to the back seat. Kim and Fergus were both staring at us with wide, uncertain eyes. Fergus becomes concerned when Vhanna and I raise our voices to each other. Kim apparently felt somewhat similarly. Or perhaps he sensed, even though we were carefully avoiding using his name, the essence of what we argued about.

Vhanna stared straight ahead, driving with methodical and deliberate precision, as she considered the matter. "Okay," she said finally, "but I'll set the terms. Damn, I don't know if we should go back to the house or what."

We tossed ideas back and forth. Vhanna and Kim could hide out aboard *Artemis* up one of the inlets. Or they could go back to Victoria. We debated the ramifications of their not going back to Tofino and being available when Bellows demanded his meeting. "There's nothing to lose if you go back to the house," I said. "Danchuk's none the wiser and Ray has said he won't act. The house is about as secure a place as you could find and there's no way that Cheng or any other Snake Heads could know that Kim is with you."

Not knowing whether the police roadblock would still be up at the Ucluelet junction, we decided that Kim and Vhanna should return on *Artemis* as originally planned. So, after dropping Vhanna and Kim off in Bamfield, I continued on in the Jeep over logging roads to Port Alberni and then took Highway 14 to Tofino. Our caution proved unnecessary as there was no sign of the police roadblock at the Ucluelet junction. Apparently the Mounties had given up on trying to catch either Kim or Cheng that way. Still, Vhanna would have had to retrieve *Artemis* from Bamfield sometime.

Just outside Tofino, I called Father Welch on the cell and asked him to meet me at the dock where Vhanna keeps *Artemis* tied up. A couple of minutes after I parked the Jeep in the dock's parking area, he pulled up in his Volvo sedan. Surprisingly, he was wearing his black shirt and white collar, something he rarely did. "You still look like a bandit, Allan," I said, laughing.

He tugged one end of his moustache and narrowed his eyes threateningly as he scratched Fergus behind the ears. Then he grinned. "Takes one to know one. I was doing the rounds at the seniors' home. Some of them find it more comforting to be visited by a priest in uniform." Welch fired up the Volvo as I slid into the passenger seat beside him and Fergus restlessly rode shotgun in the back seat. It had been a long day and he was justifiably wondering where his next meal might be coming from. "I gather you don't have the money for a cab. Welch's limousine service at your beck and call, sir."

"Sorry, Allan, I wanted to check with you to see how things are going with Bethanie's efforts."

Welch backed out of the parking lot and turned onto the road. "And where, dear sir, am I to carry you in the meantime?" He raised an eyebrow when I told him to take me to the police station. Then he told me that Bethanie had met with the Jansons, that they were now ministry-approved potential foster parents for Hui, and that the application was in the works. As the Immigration official had said in Victoria, a hearing date was confirmed for two days from now. With the ministry stepping in on Hui's behalf to formally ask the court to place her in foster care with Lars and Frieda pending the outcome of immigration hearings the chances of the judge approving the application were much improved. "You could have got this information from Bethanie directly," Father Welch said, as he dropped me in front of the RCMP detachment.

I leaned in through the window and tapped the edge of my hat in silent salute to him. "True, but I don't know her well enough to finagle a ride out of her and ask her to drop Fergus at home and give him a wee bit of dinner." As I walked off, I could hear Welch roaring with laughter.

The detachment door was locked, so I rang the doorbell. Finally someone came and awkwardly undid some latches. "Lot of simple things are hard to do," Danchuk groused as he finally opened the door for me. His left arm was still in the sling, so he had been forced to open the door locks and latches with one hand. "Come into the back, McCann. Corporal Lee has gone back to the hotel for the evening. He just told me Bellows had called and what information I should dig up before you arrived. Then he said he didn't think it was important for him to be here. Don't see why the whole thing couldn't have waited until morning, myself." I wondered if Danchuk was piqued that a corporal from Bellows's unit seemed to have more authority than did a local detachment sergeant such as himself. I also found it curious that Lee was still in town.

Danchuk meanwhile led the way into his small office and plopped down in a chair behind the desk so that it stood between us. "Lee thought that until we resolve the question of Cheng's driver, he should be here to provide an immediate link to the resources of the anti-gang unit." Danchuk shrugged. "Think it's a bunch of crock myself. Nothing in any of this now that the detachment here can't take care of on its own. Finding this guy is just straight police work and no way in heaven that Cheng fellow would hang around here." He snorted derisively. "Guy like him kind of sticks out in the crowd in a town like this."

This was the Danchuk I knew well. A bitter man who feels passed over in the promotion department, consigned by his own prejudices to eternal mediocrity as commander of a detachment in the back of beyond. A man who dislikes having the personal empire into which he has built this detachment disrupted by the presence of others above him or by types of crime that stand outside the humdrum of the small-town norm. It was strangely comforting to see Danchuk returning to type, abandoning the disquietingly reflective tendencies he had evidenced in the days immediately after Cheng inflicted the knife wound upon him.

A white legal-size file folder lay perfectly squared in the centre of a blotter likewise perfectly placed in the middle of the desk. With his good hand, Danchuk flipped the file open and pushed it toward me. "That him?"

I leaned over and studied the mug shots that showed a scrawny blond man with scraggly hair, who stared toward the camera in the face-on shot with vacant eyes and lips twitching towards a sneer. "It's him. The man who was behind the wheel of McCutcheon's car."

Danchuk nodded. "Okay, let's go. Bad enough that I'm going to be late for dinner, but tonight's Donna's bridge night." I decided not to bother delving into the implications of this revelation. Instead I led the way to his Blazer and we drove in silence out to McCutcheon's trailer. Strands of yellow police tape had been strung across the gate to block entry to the site. We got out of the Blazer, ducked under the tape, and walked up the drive. The sun had set an hour earlier and deep lines of shade cast the yard into premature dusk.

At the trailer door, Danchuk inserted a key and opened the lock. Then he pulled on a pair of plastic gloves and handed me a pair. "Gotta say, McCann, I don't approve of this. No way should you be poking around this way. Not part of your duties as a coroner."

I nodded and tried to look suitably respectful of his situation. "Gary, I understand. When I spoke to Ray about this he thought that together we might see something that otherwise might get missed."

Danchuk's little blue eyes bulged forward, threatening to pop out of his soft, round face. "Crap, McCann. You conned Bellows and he went for it." He took a deep breath, obviously fighting to control his temper. "I don't have time for this," he snapped. "Let's get it done."

We walked into the trailer. The thick shellac of dried blood still covered the kitchen floor. "Been through all the drawers already," Danchuk said, but started opening kitchen drawers once more. When I told him that I'd take a look in the bedroom he merely grunted. His animosity toward me hung in the air and threatened to suck away my ability to concentrate. I wanted distance from him. And, in truth, I had no idea where to start with this search or even necessarily what it was I sought, so the bedroom seemed as good a place to begin as any.

The bedroom was as neat as I remembered it. I opened the closet and saw that McCutcheon had owned only a handful of shirts and pants, all work clothes except for one old-fashioned black Sunday suit with wide lapels. Below the clothes were two identical heavy kraft paper shopping bags with strong handles stitched into the tops. Each bag was high enough and wide enough to hold three stacks of paperback books. The stacks themselves were of varying heights. Mostly the titles were police procedurals similar to the Ed McBain on the nightstand. I opened several and saw that each bore the business stamp of a used bookshop in Port Alberni. McCutcheon — ever tidy and thrifty of nature — apparently made bulk second-hand book trades at the store on an infrequent basis. As he finished a book it would presumably go from one bag into the other, for the only book not in one or the other bag in the whole trailer was the Ed McBain on the nightstand. Eventually the finished bag would fill as the unread bag was emptied. When all the books had been read, he probably carried the full bag to Port Alberni and swapped the contents for a new cache of stock. For a little more than a few dollars and the return of the books, McCutcheon was able to finance an obviously insatiable reading habit that helped him while away the days of his solitary existence.

To one side of the shopping bags were two cardboard boxes that were turned on their sides so the contents spilled out. My breath quickened when I saw the boxes. "Gary," I called, "I might have something here."

A moment later the sergeant was at my side. I gestured at the boxes. "Were these like that when the place was first searched?"

Danchuk furrowed his brow and did a credible job of looking like he was thinking hard. "Suppose so," he said finally.

That would have to do. "McCutcheon was too tidy a person to have left them like that himself. If they were like that, then it means someone went through them and didn't put them back the way they were." I snapped on the overhead light so we could see better and then carefully started sorting through the spilled contents of the first box. It contained a number of old Revenue Canada annual tax report envelopes that had been used to store each respective year's tax report and receipt slips. The most recent one showed that McCutcheon reported an annual income before expenses of only $31,000. Looking more carefully I saw that most of that income was from interest payable on investments. Only $8,000 was indicated on the self-employed income line. Under occupation, McCutcheon reported himself as being a stone mason, but it was obvious he was more or less retired. He also reported himself as being single. The tax reports went back five years, which I thought was the legal requirement for keeping such records. Never one to build up clutter, McCutcheon obviously culled one old year's report for each new one generated. A methodical man.

The second box was empty except for a cheap vinyl accordion-style document holder with the name of a major insurance company embossed on it in raised gold letters. I opened the document inside and scanned it. "Jesus," Danchuk said from where he was looking over my shoulder, "he carried $1 million?"

I nodded. "And his son was the beneficiary." The back of the document holder contained several manila pockets and in the last one I found a standard form Last Will and Testament. Not surprisingly, Daryl McCutcheon was again the sole beneficiary to his father's entire estate. There was, however, a codicil setting aside a substantial amount for the maintenance of the cemetery plot of his wife, Edith Mainbridge McCutcheon. This included the weekly placing of flowers on the grave by a local florist. I glanced over at the photo set on the nightstand.

"The bastard killed his father for his estate," Danchuk murmured.

I found myself shaking his head. "I don't think so, Gary. I doubt he thought that far ahead." I looked again in the pockets of the document holder. One pocket was misshapen, as if it had held papers that had been removed. Danchuk grunted and nodded when I showed him the pocket.

"Could have been money," he said. "Or some kind of bonds or treasury bills that he could just cash in."

We were both thinking along the same lines, which surprised me. I set the holder down and went over to the nightstand, opened it and took another closer look inside than I had on the day we found McCutcheon's body. The envelopes containing Daryl McCutcheon's infrequent letters to his father were still there, wrapped in their elastic band. Other than that there was nothing but a single wide elastic band. I held it up for Danchuk to see and explained how McCutcheon had always carried a thick wad of twenty-dollar bills. "There was no money like that found during the initial search," Danchuk said. "Makes sense the son would have taken it. Or this Cheng fellow." Danchuk rubbed the bandage on his left arm as he mentioned Cheng's name.

After a few minutes more searching I agreed with Danchuk that there was nothing more to find, but still I hesitated to leave. Danchuk was out in the kitchen again, rummaging about in drawers there for further clues. I looked down at the photo on the nightstand. On an impulse I picked up the photo and tucked it into the game pocket sewn into the inside of my old Filson coat. There was something about the photograph that bothered me and I doubted that anyone would notice its absence.

We locked up the trailer and walked through the gathering darkness back to the Blazer. Danchuk dropped me at the intersection of the lane that ran down to my cabin and I trudged homeward with my hands shoved deep in my coat pockets. The heat of the day had passed and a cool dampness hung in the air. Out on the water a fog would be rising. I hoped that Vhanna had already brought *Artemis* into dock.

chapter eighteen

Since his wife Camilia died three years ago from breast cancer, the good mayor, Dr. Reginald Tully, has resided in a two-bedroom condominium overlooking the fish processing plant on Tofino's downtown shoreline. An oddity for such structures, this condominium is neither a monstrosity nor a pink stuccoed visual assault of architectural ugliness. Instead it is a three-storey affair built into the slope that runs down from main street toward the waterfront. Retail shops and businesses occupy the ground floor and condominiums the upper two storeys. The grey metal siding and black steel-railed decks lend the structure an industrial air that melds well with the plant opposite and with the fishing boats tied up alongside the adjoining docks. Large windows give Tully and the other occupants superb views of the plant and, more intentionally, I'm sure, of the channels beyond that run between Tofino and the native community of Opitsat on the western arm of Meares Island.

Currently the thick fog lying heavy in the inlet restricted the view to that of the fish plant, itself barely visible in the early dusk brought on by the gathering fog. Only the harsh glare of perimeter floodlights illuminated the processing plant's loading bays. Visible through a set of open doors, men and women dressed in variously coloured rubber bib overalls, gum boots, thick sweaters, and toques stood on rubber mats and aluminum grates designed to relieve the strain inherent in working long hours on hard concrete surfaces. The bare cement floor glistened with pools of water and a steamy haze lifted by the damp, cold air inside the building swirled around the workers, exuded from their mouths and leached off of their clothing in heavy plumes of vapour. Many of them were busy with the task of grading the farmed Atlantic salmon that is about the only fish processed in Tofino these days. Others fed salmon into the specialized Baader machine that automatically and efficiently sliced the fish up into either "head and gut," "dressed head on," or filleted grades according to the current setting. Still others packed either the processed salmon or whole fish into Styrofoam containers filled with ice for shipping.

When it is open, the packing plant provides an employment refuge for many a Tofinoite who finds that the cash flow needed to continue living in this increasingly expensive paradise exceeds available resources. As a result, it is not unusual for someone possessed of a Masters of Business Administration to stand shoulder to shoulder on the processing line with an illiterate who never went beyond a primary-school education. Itinerant artists, drug-fried professional photographers, surf-boarders marking time until the big wave season arrives, aspiring tree sitters awaiting the next Clayoquot clearcut logging dispute, fishermen trying to pull together the money for the next payment on the boat loan, and the other flotsam found in a town standing on the edge of a continent so there is nowhere further west to go can all be found here. Mixed in, of course, with this generally transient work force are the veteran and professional packers, who year after year endure the drudgery, the constant cold and wet, and the cycle of sudden closures followed by openings that demand long swing shifts to fill the orders on schedule.

"Here you go," Tully said from behind my shoulder. I turned away from the window and gratefully accepted the proffered glass containing a healthy dram of Jamieson's Irish. Tully raised a glass that was equally filled and we touched the rims in a silent toast to nothing, then Tully gestured to a seat by the window and invited me to settle there. A Nordic-style affair of black leather, with a high back, low arms, and a swivel base, the chair was surprisingly well suited to taking a body at leisure. All the furniture in the room was Scandinavian, slightly austere and more expensive than the designs seemed to justify.

Dropping into a matching seat set on the opposite side of the big window, Tully sighed appreciatively and sipped from his glass. "Old bones," he said, and rubbed his eyes, as he often did, reaching up under his wire frame glasses to do so. He wore grey dress slacks, a starched white shirt, grey silk tie, and a wine-coloured wool vest, so that he looked exactly what he was — a doctor and politician who has just begun to relax for the evening but has not yet quite adjusted to the idea. The only incongruous part was his feet, which were stuffed into a pair of almost knee-high wool-lined native buckskin slippers with fluffy rabbit fur tassels hanging from the leather laces and intricate beadwork sewn into the leather. "Usually all the mayoralty gifts that come my way during ceremonies either go into cupboards at the office or are handed off to various charities, but these I decided to keep for myself. A gift from the Haida up on the Charlottes." He grinned over his whiskey glass. "Not that they were sewn by them. I remember the craftswoman was actually identified as a Peigan from near Pincher Creek over Crowsnest Pass way. Guess that's why they're so warm, made by a person who knows what winter is really about."

The warmth of the slippers also explained why Tully had neither electric baseboards nor gas fireplace on. Since handing off my Filson coat to Tully at the entrance and politely removing my shoes so as not to stain the pale beige carpet, I had been fending off a chill that not even the warmth of the Jamieson's could defeat. I thought to suggest to Tully that he buy additional pairs for visitors, but that would have sent him on a mission to find suitable warm clothing and there was pressing business at hand.

"Reg," I said, "you've been around here a long time."

Tully laughed. "I was born here. You know that. Only gone for the years it took to finish med school."

"And since that time you've probably treated most of the old-timers in this town."

"There were years until recently when I was the only doctor on the entire Pacific Rim. Young doctors today complain about not being able to get enough patients to finance a viable practice. All they need do is go somewhere way out in the country where the need is plain enough. Nothing concentrates market share in your hands better than the lack of any competition. I had that for decades. Losing it now, but hell, doesn't matter. I'll be retiring soon enough."

I laughed at that. "You'll retire when they carry you out of the hospital feet first. Or out of your mayoralty chambers."

Tully tossed back the scant remains in his glass and got up to fix us another. Ignoring the fact mine was only half gone, he poured us both an equal measure. "Oh, this new develop-or-be-damned contingent that's overrunning the Chamber of Commerce here will likely bounce me out of office come the November election. Fence-sitters like me are becoming a rare and endangered form of politician."

Knowing my disinterest in politics of any kind, it was unlike Tully to discuss such matters with me. Apparently my friend was seriously concerned that his tenure as the pro-business-but-cautious-to-preserve-Tofino's-heritage mayor was in jeopardy. I made a mental note to contribute to his re-election fund and to be careful to avoid having his name linked to mine in any way until after November. The last thing he needed was a reputation for hanging out with reprobates such as myself who were not dedicated to the cause of building prosperity through the erection of new hotels, condominiums, or housing developments wherein could dwell wealthy tourists or rich Vancouverites on the lam from urban blight.

"Anyway," Tully said, "you didn't come here to listen to a politician's woes or just to sample my Irish. So what can I do for you on this gloomy, foggy evening?"

I told him briefly most of what had transpired since Ian McCutcheon's murder, leaving out the probability that Daryl McCutcheon had been a party to his death. "Did you know Ian or Edith?" I asked at the end.

After setting his glass down on a side table next to his chair, Tully gazed up toward the ceiling thoughtfully for a moment. "There were two Ians, Elias. There was the Ian before Edith died and the Ian that existed after. I knew the first, but not the second. I doubt anyone knew the second." After sipping his drink, Tully looked at me through his thick-lensed glasses as if he was measuring me against some criteria of which only he was aware. "You and Ian McCutcheon have something in common," he said softly. "Edith, you see, took her life in much the same manner as did Merriam."

I found myself sitting very still. The palms of my hands felt suddenly clammy. "In Edith's case, she used McCutcheon's .303 rifle to put a bullet into her brain. The same brain beset by a tumour for which no treatment was available at the time. At any rate, none that held a hope of a cure. Like you, McCutcheon came home to find her dead in his living room. Unlike you, Edith left a note explaining that she just couldn't take the pain any longer or the wild mood shifts that the tumour caused. She was thirty-eight at the time. A couple years younger than Ian. Their son, Daryl, had just turned fourteen. Ian McCutcheon was not a complex man or one known for displaying much emotion," Tully said with a small smile that left me feeling that the two of us were again being compared. But I had no idea what conclusions Tully was drawing and realized that I had no wish to know. I was not here for this. I was here to find out more about McCutcheon, with a mind that such knowledge could perhaps lead to his son and from there to a murderer I knew posed a direct threat to the woman I loved. Instead, Tully was drawing me into a web of thought that threatened to distract my attention, pull me into the gloom of analysis of things done and not done that ended in someone taking her own life.

"Lots of people kill themselves," I said more gruffly than intended.

Tully nodded agreement. "Yes, that's true. And there is always the residual effects that suicides have on those who loved them."

Since Merriam took her life, Tully has held a conviction that her suicide deeply scarred me. I believe he thinks that the nature of Merriam's death and the fact that it was I who found her has in many ways altered my personality, rendering me more of a recluse than before and more rootless. Tully is wrong in this. I'm quite sure of that. I was always a recluse and I have been, for as long as he has known me, a remittance man with no need to earn either a living or take an active role in the community in which I live. Tully is too much of a community builder and activist to understand that not all of us care sufficiently about the ongoings of society to partake in it or to try and better it.

"Reg," I said, "there's something I want to show you." Without waiting for a response, I walked over to where my coat hung on the rack by the door and extracted the photo of Edith. "Do you have any idea where this photo might have been taken and when?" I asked as I handed him the picture.

Tully gazed carefully at the photo. "By the look of it, I'd say the photo was probably taken about two years before her death. Just before the symptoms of the tumour began. As to where it was taken, well, I know that Ian had a small cabin up on the edge of Muriel Lake. Background looks about right." He looked up at me, clearly puzzled. "Why does it matter?"

I thought about it for a moment and then told him that Daryl might have been an accessory to his father's murder. I added that Daryl had probably been the driver for the two Asians who had been involved in the hospital attack on Kim and the attempted abduction of Hui. When I finished, Tully's expression was thoughtful and sad. "After Edith's death, Ian just didn't have any heart to give the boy. And he didn't have the ability to help Daryl understand or deal with the loss of his mother. There had always been friction between the two. I think that Edith kept the boy on a pretty even keel. After, well, he just slid off the rails pretty quickly. I haven't seen him in years. Thought he had moved away or was in jail."

"Reg, thanks for the drink and for the information. I better be going."

Tully got up and walked with me to the door. After I shrugged into my coat he put a fatherly hand on my shoulder. "You know, Elias, it's true that you're not that much like Ian McCutcheon. He shut off all his emotions and simply withdrew from the world entirely. Think all he was waiting to do was die and maybe be able to join Edith on the other side. It's different for you. Different circumstances, different person."

I forced a smile and nodded. "It's okay, Reg." As I stepped out of the condominium and closed the door behind me, I knew I lied. *Gone to join Edith*, the inscription had read on McCutcheon's headstone. Words he had carved himself. McCutcheon's love for his wife had obviously been etched as deeply into his heart and as immutably as the letters of that inscription. I knew how such a love felt, but Merriam had not been its recipient. The unwavering depth of McCutcheon's devotion to his wife shamed me even as I knew such a feeling was unwarranted.

chapter nineteen

I stood at the phone in my kitchen, scratching Fergus's ears by way of apology while I talked on the phone to Sergeant Gary Danchuk of the illustrious Royal Canadian Mounted Police. As I explained my theory I realized how narrowly it hung on gossamer threads of logic and desperation. I saw one chance to control events and trap Cheng and Daryl before they acted again. My vision obviously failed to inspire Danchuk.

"You phone me at home with this, as if it can't wait until morning?" Danchuk groused. I could imagine his overset brow furrowing and an angry palm slashing back and forth across his bald patch. Perhaps his endlessly burdened wife would be standing off to one side, listening, her face etched by angry concern at crime and evil once again pervading her home. As far as I knew, the Danchuks mixed with only the evangelistic fringe that skittered around on the frontier edges of Tofino's traditionally liberally inclined society. This small group had established a clubhouse of sorts for themselves in a formerly abandoned Moose Lodge hall on the town's outskirts and marked out their territory by erecting a notice board on which each week appeared some new missive about the forthcoming arrival of Christ or our collective failings as Christians and human beings. Not surprisingly this same group had been bombarding the local paper with letters and commentary decrying the Fujian refugees as immigration line jumpers, drug dealers, prostitutes, and generally evil people. The fact that I could only see Hui's small, stoic, and seemingly eternally hopeful face whenever I read this vitriolic excess, I knew, rendered me much less than a dispassionate observer.

"We can't just let this possibility go unexplored, Gary," I said, hoping to sound conciliatory in tone.

"Darn," Danchuk wheezed hard. "Fine." Another hard sigh, "I'll call Corporal Lee and bring him in on this. Might have to call out the ERT from Port Alberni," he added thoughtfully. His voice turned softly plaintive. "Bother." Then gruffly, he said, "Stick to your phone, McCann. If I call and you're not there…" He hung up without explaining the ramifications.

I cradled the phone and walked across the room into the kitchen, opened the refrigerator door and fished out a bottle of Race Rocks India Pale Ale. After popping the top and draining it into a glass, I stood looking out at the grey fog that hung over the water and snaked through the limbs of the night-shrouded trees. Nothing to do but wait. A sudden dawning of hunger and fatigue wrapped like a shaky blanket over me. Hours and days since I had last slept well. In airborne training we had often been told that only a fool passed up moments of offered rest in a hot zone and I thought it ever more likley that I was such a fool.

Certainly Danchuk would agree. I lifted the phone and dialed Vhanna's number, feeling awkward and hesitant in the aftermath of Tully's comments about McCutcheon and his wife, Edith. Vhanna was my Edith. Had been even in the months just before Merriam took her life. How to live with that? A buzz and then another. Then a phone uncradled.

"Were you asleep?"

"No. We just got in." I could hear the fatigue in Vhanna's voice.

"I won't keep you. I'm supposed to keep the phone line open here anyway." Quickly I told her about what Danchuk and I had found in the trailer and my discussion with Tully, the possibility that Daryl McCutcheon and Cheng were hiding out in the cabin at Muriel Lake.

"Will you be going out there with Danchuk and Lee?"

"I don't know. See if Danchuk agrees to me going, I guess."

"There's no real need for you to go."

This was true. "No," I said, offering nothing more. I could imagine her face tightening the way it does when she must resign herself to my behaving in ways that she considers illogical or even irrational.

"You'll be careful?" She sounded as if she didn't believe such a thing possible.

"Always," I replied lightly.

"Sure," she said with a disbelieving chuckle.

"I should go. Danchuk might be trying to reach me even as we speak."

Her laugh was unforced this time. "Mustn't keep the good sergeant waiting, of course."

"I love you," I said.

A long pause followed, and I sensed that Vhanna was not alone. Kim probably sat nearby. Vhanna's reluctance to express emotions in front of others extended even, apparently, to someone who spoke no English and would not understand. "Be safe." The sound of the phone being set down as gentle as fingers traced across my cheek. I returned my own handset to the cradle. Took a long swallow of beer, felt a chill shiver course through me. Just fatigue, nothing more. I needed food and sleep.

The phone rang. I snatched it up, hopeful. "Damn, McCann, your line was busy. What are you thinking?"

"Sorry, Gary." Surprised to find myself apologizing.

"Lee says we leave first thing in the morning. That's dawn, understand? I don't know why, but he insists that you come too. Monaghan and Singh too. Nobody left here to cover anything. You better be right about this, McCann. We'll pick you up on the side of the road where your lane joins the main road at five o'clock a.m., understand?"

When I agreed that I did he hung up abruptly. My father's antique wind-up brass-faced clock that stood on the mantle over the fireplace showed that it was coming up midnight. I pulled some links of hot Italian sausage, a wedge of pecorino romano cheese, a handful of Roma tomatoes, and a tin of anchovies from the fridge. Then I put a big pot of water on to boil for pasta, started some olive oil heating in a skillet, and set about making a simple spaghetti sauce of diced sausages, tomatoes, and mashed anchovies. When the water was ready I dumped in a big handful of spaghetti noodles, turned the sauce mixture down to simmer, and took the time to quickly lay and set a small fire in the fireplace. After the fire was going, I gave the sauce another stir, pulled the cork on a bottle of Sangiovese red, and slopped some of it into a glass. Once everything was ready I drained the noodles, dumped them onto a plate, spooned on the sauce, and covered it with grated pecorino. Refilling my glass, I carried everything into the living room. I sank into the old chair beside the fireplace and Fergus settled contentedly at my feet as I ate and tried to think of nothing.

Meal done, I washed the dishes and then Fergus and I ascended the stairs together to the loft and, falling into our respective beds, plunged into exhausted sleep.

Awake before the alarm went off at four o'clock a.m., I moved through the darkened house to the shower and turned the knob to cold. Let the icy water sluice away the dull thickness of fatigue, emerged shivering but with a clear head. I pulled on a pair of rugged canvas pants, a denim shirt, and some hard worn chukka boots. Unlocking the gun locker, I looked at the 1942 side-by-side Parker Brothers shotgun there. An antique that I had refitted with modern hard-brazed, laser-sighted barrels several years ago, the gun had saved my life recently when I walked into harm's way. I knew, however, that today there was no possibility of slipping the sturdy weapon into its leather gun case and taking it with me. Instead I would have to rely on the ability of Danchuk and his fellow Mounties to both defend me and bring a killer to justice. I found this thought unsettling. Reluctantly I locked up the gun case, set the kettle to boil, and dumped a few spoonfuls of Kicking Horse fair trade organically and shade-grown dark roast coffee into the Bodum. Good coffee and good news for workers in undeveloped coffee-growing countries. Worth the exorbitant price to know that one could do something good through the simple act of buying and drinking a certain type of coffee. Although it was far too early for my stomach to be much interested in food, I forced down a couple slices of toast and then cleaned up.

As Fergus had not yet awakened, I tried to quietly shake out a bowl of dry food for him. Ever alert to sounds that directly affect his well-being, however, he came slowly, awkward with sleep, down the stairs from the loft to investigate the cause of my descent into insanity. Neither Fergus nor I is much inclined to pre-dawn awakenings. He stared at me blearily, sniffed with disdain at the dry food offering, stumped to the door and glowered back at me expectantly. I opened the door and with businesslike steps Fergus sauntered into the yard to the trees, relieved himself, strode back into the house, gave his coat a hard shake, lapped up a little water from his dish, and then ascended the stairs to regain his bed. At the top of the stairs, he paused to look over his shoulder with an expression that made it eminently clear I was on my own this time around. After spending days waiting in one vehicle or another, Fergus had, having attended to physical needs, evidently decided to spend the day at home. I could hardly blame him. Indeed, what did I hope to achieve by participating in this early morning operation? Why, for that matter, had Corporal Lee insisted that I accompany the Mounties? I would have expected that he, like Danchuk, would not want an amateur present who might potentially put everyone at risk. Still, they were acting on my hunch and perhaps he just wanted me there for no other reason. As it was coming up toward five o'clock, I tugged on my coat and hat, let myself out quietly so as to not reawaken Fergus, and followed the lane to the main road.

chapter twenty

During the night a hard wind had come up out of the southwest and peeled the fog away. Seaward, a half moon stood high on the horizon and glistened brightly, while to the east the profile of the mountains was cast in a rosy hue. A few remaining pinpricks of stars overhead provided confirmation that the weather had cleared and a fine day was promised. The overnight clearing trend had also pushed the temperature down and my breath whipped away in a vaporous cloud on the fresh breeze. I stood in the shadows by the roadside and soon two pairs of headlights approached from the direction of town.

Leading the convoy was an unmarked maroon Blazer that I assumed must be detailed for Lee's use. Following behind was Danchuk's official and much marked RCMP Blazer. The maroon vehicle drew up alongside and the driver's window buzzed down. Corporal Lee leaned out and flashed a toothy smile my way. "Good morning, sir. Would you like a lift?"

Seeing someone sitting in the front passenger seat, I grabbed the handle for the back door and slipped into the vehicle that way. "Nice of you to offer," I said.

Lee laughed and gunned the accelerator. "There's a Thermos of coffee there if you want some. I had the hotel restaurant make up some lunches and snacks. Nothing but the finest for an early morning foray into the bush, I always say." I declined the coffee and offered a morning greeting to Danchuk, who was hunkered in the front with his head down as if he might be dozing. He ignored me. Lee wore civilian clothes under the kind of green quilted vest favoured by hunters. Danchuk was in uniform, including a bright orange jacket. The latter, I figured, might be useful for avoiding being run down by passing traffic when doing speed control on the highway but was a poor choice of colour for an operation in the woods that might call for some covert concealment.

"Gary doesn't think you should be along, Mr. McCann," Lee said amiably. "I, however, see you as part of the team these days. Why, it seems that whenever trouble crops up on this case, you're always right in the thick of it." He glanced over his shoulder at me, and I saw that although his mouth was still smiling, his eyes had transformed into hard flints. "You're like a talisman. Bring you along and something is bound to happen." There was no frippery in his tone now. His attitude was that of a cop dealing with a known felon that could only cause trouble.

Puzzled by the man's demeanour, I turned my attention out the window and we travelled on in stony silence. Behind, Danchuk's Blazer trailed as if hooked to us by an invisible line. It neither came too close nor dropped too far behind; rather the vehicle maintained an almost perfectly steady distance of about two car lengths. Presumably it carried both Monaghan and Singh. I wondered which officer drove. Did it depend on seniority? Which would be more desirable? To be the driver or not? Perhaps gender politics dictated who drove and Singh was at the wheel. Or racial politics were at play and that resulted in Monaghan being in control. Then again it was entirely possible that Danchuk had assigned the driver, carefully considering the potential risk each officer might pose to his precious Blazer. Or maybe he treated it like a reward or as a punishment duty. That seemed likely enough. Perhaps the reason Danchuk seemed in such a funk was the fact that either officer got to drive the Blazer at all. If his arm were not still in a sling, would Danchuk be back there manning the wheel?

This line of thought kept me amused for a few minutes and then, for want of anything else to do, I watched dawn come to Pacific Rim's beaches, bogs, and hillsides as we spirited our way through the national park on a road as yet devoid of other traffic. Out along the shoreline gulls wheeled above white-capped rollers that tumbled up onto the sand and rocks. Far above, a pair of bald eagles, white heads glinting in the growing sunlight, rode a high thermal. With no more than a casual movement of one wing or another they corrected their trajectory as they glided along, eyes scouring the water and ground below for likely prey. It was a good morning to be out on the hunt and I felt a small thrill at the task before us. Since Cheng first struck at the hospital, he had held the initiative. Now we were taking the fight to him. If all went well, we could end this thing today.

Just before the Ucluelet junction, a gravel logging road ran inland. We turned onto this and started what was, in fact, a long dogleg back along the backcountry boundary of the national park toward Tofino Inlet. In essence we were driving almost directly back the way we had come, although we followed a gradual northerly course that would bring us across the base of Kennedy Lake, alongside Kennedy River, and ultimately to our destination of Muriel Lake. The road took us through country that had mostly been logged out years before and then replanted in a haphazard manner over the ensuing decades. In places signs proudly attested to the year of replanting. Most were more than twenty years old, yet the trees were still little more than scrub. It would be more than a century before anything like harvestable timber existed.

The road was broken by an endless series of potholes, wash outs, and small landslides of rock and mud through which we picked a careful course. Where the rains of winter had gouged out deep troughs in the clearcut areas the soil had been scraped clear away to the granite bedrock. In these areas nothing grew and never again would, for there was nothing in which roots could take hold.

Driving one-handed, Lee tried to call Bellows on his cell phone to provide a report on our progress, but we were in one of the all-too frequent west coast pockets where the cell net didn't reach effectively and reception was scanty at best. I reflected that it would be a blessing if there were more such zones around the country so that a person could more easily be out of contact with civilization and the demands of others. Danchuk meanwhile was staring hard at a forestry map, apparently trying to work out where we would turn to get up to Muriel Lake. His brow was furrowed deeply with concentration. I could imagine the deep challenge such map-making posed for him. "Do we know where the cabin is located?" I asked innocently.

Danchuk grunted, as Lee returned the useless cell phone to a pocket of his vest. "Yeah, I got the lot grid numbers pulled last night and had a copy of the property map faxed to the hotel. There's a pocket of cabins off the main road. It's the last one on a track that runs out along a little ridge looking down on the lake. Access to the water by a foot trail." That made sense. I could imagine McCutcheon buying property that would be on the outside edge to ensure greater privacy. It was what I would do, too. An unwelcome similarity.

Rounding the corner, Lee suddenly swung the Blazer over so that it hugged the outside edge of the road and was out of the path of an approaching truck. It was a big crummy, green and covered in dried mud. The windows of the rear section, in which logging teams would ride back and forth to the cut blocks, were caked over so that it was impossible to tell if anyone was inside. I caught a glimpse of two men in the front. The man driving was so small he seemed barely able to peer over the dashboard and his tin hard hat threatened to drop down over his eyes. I didn't get a look at the other man before the long-bed truck was past and we ground on toward our destination.

"There's something I've been wondering, Corporal Lee," I said.

"Call me, Bobby, Mr. McCann," he said. Apparently we were back on good terms. In the rearview mirror I could see that his eyes were no longer flinty. He looked as cheerful as if he were just out on a drive in the country.

"Okay, Bobby," I said and ignored Danchuk's little derisive snort, "I've been thinking about odds. As I understand it we think there might be three of them at the cabin. Cheng, the man who tried to grab Hui, and McCutcheon. Against them there are four of you. But they hold the ground. It seems you maybe should have brought some more people along."

"Notice you don't figure yourself into the equation," Danchuk muttered.

Lee laughed at that. "Mr. McCann is just being sensible, Gary. After all, he's a non-combatant, you might say. We wouldn't want him involved if anything happens. He'd just be in the way." Although his tone was light, it also bore more than a note of condescension that irritated me. But what he said was also true. I was just along for the ride and the more I thought about it the more I was at a loss to understand why Lee had wanted me present. Perhaps that was why I felt a growing sense of unease. But where else could I be that would be more useful? Home with Fergus I would accomplish nothing. At least here I could be part of seeing events through to conclusion. For I was steadfastly certain that McCutcheon and Cheng were in hiding at the Muriel Lake cabin.

"If all three of them are at the cabin," Lee said, "we will take them under observation and call in reinforcements at the time. I was not, however, going to deploy an ERT team all the way up here on what could prove nothing more than a wild hunch. So it made sense to just use the forces immediately available." He looked over his shoulder and gave me a mirthless grin. "Besides I'm sure four well-armed Mounties are more than a match for those three."

"I suppose you're right," I said, although I didn't believe him at all.

We parked the vehicles at the top of the road that ran down toward McCutcheon's cabin. Once again, as they had done at McCutcheon's mobile home, Monaghan and Singh armed themselves with shotguns. Both looked tense and worried, as if they too questioned the decision to go in with so few people. I heard Monaghan say that she had only a sporadic radio link back to Nicki in the Tofino detachment headquarters. Lee seemed unconcerned by this or anything else. He even shrugged off Danchuk's suggestion that he put on a Kevlar vest. The corporal drew his service pistol. Because of his left arm being in a sling, Danchuk had an awkward time of it pulling his pistol and working the slide to chamber a round. When he finished, the four of them, guns at the ready, started down the track leading to the cabin. Nobody had bothered telling me where to wait, so after giving them a good lead I followed at a respectful distance of about twenty yards. I walked close to the side of the road, ready to take cover in the woods if any shooting started.

When the cabin came into sight below them, Lee signalled a halt and gave a few quick instructions to the others. My pulse quickened when I saw McCutcheon's old blue Cadillac standing off to one side of the cabin. No doubt now that Daryl McCutcheon and Cheng were here. I was expecting Lee to call for everyone to back off and take the cabin under surveillance until reinforcements could be brought up, when Monaghan and Singh slipped off in opposite directions. They were obviously being sent to circle around behind the cabin, so that it was surrounded. Monaghan glanced back toward me, apprehension clear in her blue eyes. But she moved out as ordered, like any good soldier will. Danchuk had a radio with the hand mike clipped up by his shoulder. Lee had a portable radio slung on the back of his waist belt. In a few minutes, I heard Monaghan report in that she was ready. Singh followed suit seconds later. Lee brought his radio up to his mouth and said softly, "Acknowledge that. We're going in now."

As calmly as he had proceeded since the beginning, Lee strolled down the road with Danchuk following hesitantly behind. The corporal stepped lightly up on the front porch and stood with his back pressed against the wall next to the door, pistol gripped in both hands and held so the barrel pointed toward the over-hanging roof. Danchuk took up position alongside him, his pistol directed down toward the floor. From my vantage point overlooking the cabin, I could see that his face was very pale and he was breathing rapidly. I didn't blame him. I doubted this was a textbook method for apprehending a group of suspected murderers. Lee seemed to be playing this like a cowboy. Too many times in Cyprus I had seen this kind of cavalier carelessness end in tragedy.

Lee reached out and banged a fist against the door hard. "Police," he called. "Open up." An ominous silence was the only response. I searched the cabin exterior for signs of life. Nothing showed in the small kitchen window. No smoke or heat vapour rose from the chimney. The place seemed deserted. But there was the Cadillac in the yard. I wiped sweat from my palms and longed for the reassuring feel of a rifle in my hands.

Carefully Lee gripped the doorknob, gave it a turn, and then kicked the door with the heel of one boot, spinning inside the cabin behind the opening door in one swift motion. He disappeared inside and Danchuk raced in after him. "Close in, close in," Danchuk was yelling into his radio as he went to signal Monaghan and Singh to break into the back door. I waited and after a minute or two passed with no sounds of gunfire, I walked down to the cabin.

The moment I stepped across the threshold, the smell of blood reached me. The four Mounties were standing in a circle, looking down at something on the floor in the living room. I walked over and stepped in between Monaghan and Singh. Daryl McCutcheon's lifeless eyes stared up at me. He had been neatly gutted. Just like his father. Just like Kim had nearly been on the ship off Nootka Sound. Cheng's handiwork.

The blood pooling around McCutcheon's body was still seeping slowly across the wood floor, spreading outward from the corpse so that we kept shuffling back from it like beachcombers retreating from an incoming tide. Its smell was cloying, as if it still held the heat of life.

"Good thing we brought a coroner," Lee said and winked at me, but once again his eyes were like flints. "Like I said, something always happens when you're along."

"Jesus," Monaghan hissed between her teeth and turned away. She walked over to the big picture windows that looked out over Muriel Lake, which was glinting prettily in the sunshine. Her shoulders were stiff and I could tell she had her arms crossed over her stomach, like she was trying not to be sick.

"Okay, people, let's do this by the book," Lee said. "Monaghan, go back to the vehicles and call up the dispatcher. Get them to roll a forensic team up here soonest. Take a look around, everyone, and see what we can turn up that might tell us where the other two have gone, but be careful about disturbing any evidence."

When I started following Monaghan out the door, Lee called me back. "Guess there's not much question about how McCutcheon died, is there?" If the gore oozing out of the wound in McCutcheon's stomach bothered him at all, Lee showed no signs. He stared down at the dead man, like one might a bug before you crushed it. "Guess Cheng's clearing up the witnesses," he said.

"There's nothing for me to do here," I snapped. Ignoring his mocking expression, I walked quickly out of the cabin into the yard. It was not the sight or smell of McCutcheon's corpse that affected me — it was Lee. His careless manner, both in the approach on the cabin and now with a body found murdered inside, threw me off balance, left me worried.

I stared at the Cadillac and followed the line of tracks its tires had made in the soft ground leading from the driveway to where it was parked. The car had been backed into its current position, rear end almost pushed into the branches of a spruce tree. A car positioned so that it could make a quick getaway, if necessary, by driving straight out. But the Cadillac was still there. Cheng and the other Asian man, assuming he was still with him, had left by another means. I scanned the yard, saw another set of tracks and walked over to them. These were deeper and wider than those left by the Cadillac. The kind of tracks a truck would make. A large truck, I realized. A feeling of dread descended on me.

Striding back to the cabin, I saw Lee and Danchuk huddled in front of the windows talking softly. Singh was rummaging around in the kitchen cupboards, looking more like someone trying to find some tea bags than murder clues. "Gary," I said, "the crummy we passed on the way up here. I think Cheng and his accomplice were in it." I quickly explained about the tracks in the yard. There was also the state of McCutcheon's corpse. The man had been killed very recently. Cheng was on the loose, but he must still be on the road from Muriel Lake to the highway.

Lee and Danchuk quickly made their way outside and I showed them the tracks. "We have to go after them," I said, and added that maybe the Ucluelet detachment could block the road where it met the highway.

"Didn't see any crummy," Danchuk said.

"What's a crummy?" Lee asked with a puzzled grin.

"A big enclosed truck fitted out with benches or seats in the back so that it can carry people. Logging companies use them," Danchuk answered before I could.

Lee shrugged. "Don't remember seeing one either."

He had pulled over to make room for it. Impossible for him not to have seen it. I stopped myself from saying this even as the words formed in my mouth. Instead I spun on my heel and walked up the lane toward the vehicles. "McCann," Danchuk called out, "where the hell are you going?" I ignored him. There was no time. I feared I was already far too late.

Monaghan was standing by the driver's door, radio mike in one hand. She looked frustrated and worried. "I can't get anyone. The signal just keeps breaking up. Damn. I don't like this, Elias."

"I need your help, Anne."

Surprisingly, she didn't blink an eye at the request. "The men in the big truck?" she said softly.

I nodded. "Small man who could barely see over the dashboard. Hard hat drooping down across his eyes. Lee says he didn't see it. Neither did Danchuk, but he wasn't paying much attention to anything."

Monaghan raised her eyebrows. "I was driving. Lee pulled over to make room for the truck. It was the only vehicle we met the whole way up here." She shook her head, like someone trying to wake up from a bad dream. "This whole thing's been crazy. And Lee was never worried. Never in a hurry. Like he knew."

"Anne, you have to raise Nicki and tell her to send someone to Vhanna's. That's where Cheng is going. He knows about Kim." I quickly explained that Kim was hiding there and how I had told Bellows this only the previous afternoon. "He must have told Lee."

She shuddered. "Who told Cheng. Christ, Elias, this is too big for me." Monaghan tried the radio again. No luck getting a link to Nicki. She switched bands and tried for Ucluelet or Port Alberni. Nothing. I looked over my shoulder toward the cabin, invisible around the turn. Lee would be coming soon. Or Danchuk. I could feel time running like water through my hand, spilling away, impossible to hold.

"Will you drive?" I blurted it out. I could think of no way to smooth into the idea. There was no time anyway.

Monaghan's eyes widened. She looked furtively down the road toward the cabin. "I've no orders." She shuddered. "Get in," she whispered.

I ran to the passenger door, wrenched it open and dived in. Monaghan cranked the ignition of Danchuk's Blazer, released the emergency brake as the engine caught, shoved it into drive, and gently, so as not to spin the wheels noisily, drove us out of there.

Monaghan was hell on wheels. She hit the corners like we were in a racing car rather than a clumsy four-wheel-drive box. And somehow we always skidded safely out the other side. Not two minutes after we took off from McCutcheon's Muriel Lake cabin, Danchuk had been on the radio demanding to know what Monaghan thought she was doing. She had taken a deep breath, snapped the radio off, and stepped harder on the gas by way of reply.

As we got closer to the junction with Highway 14 I tried using the cell phone to raise Nicki, but we were still in a communication shadow. I punched in the numbers for Vhanna's cell. No connection. Same result with her normal land line phone. "Damn I hate these things." I shoved the useless thing into its clip on the dashboard.

"Try the radio." Monaghan's voice was shrill. She was as pale as alabaster.

"It'll be okay, Anne."

She grimaced. "Fuck it will. This is not a wise career move, Elias. Fuck, I'll be lucky if I have a career after this stunt. I'm not even sure if what I'm doing isn't some kind of crime. If Lee's not dirty, I'm finished.

Christ, can't believe I'm doing this. On what basis? Jesus. There's nothing that's going to hold up in court." Monaghan brushed her ball cap off her head and ran the fingers of one hand through her short, blonde hair, before gripping the wheel again with both hands to control the Blazer as it skidded into a corner in a shower of gravel. "The radio."

I followed her terse instructions on call signs and channels to give. Nothing but static came back at us. We hit the pavement of Highway 14 and started running toward Tofino with the lights on and the siren cranked right up there to clear a lane through the tourists and commercial vehicles puttering along as if they had all the time in the world. Before us, they scattered to the roadsides or came to nervous halts in the lanes, like so many panicked cattle. Monaghan slalomed past them. "Try the radio again," she said. This time Ucluelet came up loud and clear. Monaghan grabbed the mike from me and gave her call sign. She explained that all Tofino officers were out of position, she was en route to Tofino and needed immediate backup. Monaghan gave the dispatcher Vhanna's address and machine-gun rapid instructions on finding it. Then she cradled the handset and went back to driving at a wildly reckless pace toward Tofino. Normally one to shy away from speed, I forced myself not to urge her to even greater haste. How much of a lead did Cheng have? Did he know where he was going? How long would he spend casing Vhanna's house before striking? Would Vhanna's complex security systems deny him access?

I grabbed the cell phone again. Got a dial tone. Punched in Vhanna's cell number. It rang twice, then she picked up. "Thank God," I whispered.

"What?" she said puzzled. "Elias?"

"Vhanna, listen," I said hurriedly. "Cheng is on the way to your house. He knows Kim is there. You have to get out now."

"Elias," she said uncertainly.

I rushed on, bludgeoning her with the information, forcing her to understand the urgency. "We found McCutcheon dead at the cabin. Lee told Cheng that Kim is hiding at your house. We passed Cheng and the other guy on the way into the cabin. They've got a lead on us. You have to get out of there. Understand?"

A pause as she quickly digested all this. "I see," she said.

"Go to the police office. I don't think Cheng would chance that. We'll be there in a few minutes."

Monaghan touched my arm. "Tell her to leave the driveway gates to her home open so we'll know that she made it out." I nodded, realizing that despite her apprehension over what we were doing Monaghan was thinking clearly.

I told Vhanna what to do. "Can you do that?"

"They close automatically, but I can disable that function from the controls in the Jeep. I'll get Kim now."

"Be careful," I cautioned.

Vhanna hung up. She would be running upstairs. There might be a chance after all. Monaghan swung the Blazer out into the oncoming traffic lane and barrelled up the wrong side of the road past a line of three semi-truck and trailer units dogging along in the wake of a rental motorhome. An oncoming pickup truck saw the approaching flashing lights and heard the siren in time to skitter onto the gravel shoulder and avoid a head-on collision.

The sight of her still amazed him. She was as exotic as the very world in which she dwelt. A world so utterly alien, so impossibly sumptuous that it filled him with a sense of unease. It was all too fragile, like fine crystal in a room full of boys carrying AK-47s with their banana clip magazines and vicious foldout bayonets. He remembered a room like that once. Remembered the butt of his rifle swinging and the sharp splintering of glass that was his reward. He had laughed then. Laughed the wild laugh that was always theirs when they recklessly purged the old ways from the land.

His cousin confused him. She glowed with health, had hard muscles unlike any he had seen on a woman. There was no evidence of the wasting caused by hunger. When he looked at her, Kim could see beneath her adult exterior the young woman-child he vaguely remembered before the coming of the Khmer Rouge. Yet she was not Khmer. This latter realization had come to him as they walked through the streets of what she had called Victoria's Chinatown and then had visited a cemetery that held Japanese graves. Did she think that either would be meaningful to him? He was Khmer. Chinese, Japanese, both were foreigners. As foreign to him as the big Caucasian man with the beard who seemed to be her lover. Kim did not know what he thought of her having a white man for a lover. He did not know what he thought of her having a lover at all. Kim realized he had never considered such things. When he had set out to find his cousin, he had imagined her as someone caught in time, held in limbo, entirely unformed until their lives joined. Then time would start and his life would have meaning and purpose.

Instead here he was in this monstrous house, forbidden to go outside because of the dangers that doing so would pose, able to only venture out on the deck that looked out on an ocean that, no matter its calmness, drew him back into the memory of that terrible day when the ship had gone aground. He would stand on the deck, forcing himself to look at the water, trying to beat down his fears, which he knew were irrational and weakened him. But it was easier ultimately to turn his eyes back toward the house. To look at the twisted, gnarled plants that his cousin grew in the protected corners of the deck area. Bonsai, she had explained. Japanese horticulture, not Khmer.

Kim told himself that he did not disapprove of his cousin. He just did not know her. Did not understand her. Did not understand her world. What was he doing here? He had sought her out, hoping to find the meaning that he believed had been lost along with his family. But he had found only a stranger who bore passing resemblance to him and to a memory from a past that could never be regained.

She was kind to him. Going out of her way to see to his comfort. Fretting over the wound to his stomach, the same injury that did not concern him in the least. There would be a scar. It would join the others.

She had given him sanctuary from those who hunted him. Provided, too, a sanctuary from the police who sought to use him as a tool against the Chinese gangsters. He appreciated that. Too long he had been the tool of others. He did not want that again. But he did not want to remain in this house for eternity, either. And yet Kim had no idea where he would go. He had come so far only to find himself displaced — someone who was nowhere at all.

So he stood on the deck, unable to bring himself to stretch out in the soft chairs that were set about in front of the Bonsai shrubs. He would rather sit on the floor but knew this would cause his cousin concern. She was

*inside somewhere, probably at the desk in the big office
downstairs where she spent hours looking at papers and
making phone calls. Today she wore nylon pants, a
turtleneck shirt, and oddly clunky black leather boots
with tags bearing a Doc Martin logo on the back. All
black. Kim understood corporate logos. Knock-off prod-
ucts were everywhere in Cambodia, selling for prices few
could afford on the streets, impossible sums in the actu-
al stores in Phnom Penh. He did not understand how
what she did in the office related to the pictures of his
cousin that were scattered on the office walls. Pictures of
her in impossibly beautiful places where mountains of ice
soared into the heavens and rivers laden with pink fish
were scooped up by massive, bulge-necked animals that
she said were bears. She stood like an officer in those
photos, despite the pack on her back, and the rough
clothing. In some of the pictures there were other women
similarly dressed, but mostly looking out of place in the
clothing. These she said were clients, but Kim had been
left puzzled by expressions rendered into Khmer or
Mandarin of eco-tourism and eco-adventures, so had no
real sense of her business. He did not understand wanting to spend money to suffer physical hardship, any more
than he could understand this house or this land in
which he now found himself suspended.*

*Kim turned his attention to the plants, tried to
admire their twisted and tormented looking branches.
They reminded him of old women and men he had seen
during the endless war. Large-eyed and wither-skinned.
He wished the dog, Fergus, were here. He understood
Fergus. Had felt a surge of pleasure when the dog had
trusted him enough to rest its head on his lap and drift
into undreaming sleep. That had been during the long
drive through towns that were devoid of people but full
of cars and large buildings around which massive places*

to park cars sprawled. In between these communities had been tame farmland and smaller, easier to understand villages made up of clusters of houses and businesses. Yet most of the businesses had gas pumps standing before them or were restaurants featuring Chinese lettering on their signs. Then they had turned toward the sun and entered a wild country of mountains, trees, and deep gorges running with rivers. It was a land that, despite the sweeping areas that had been cut away and were regrowing, seemed large and endlessly hostile. He had tried to imagine fighting a war in that land and could see whole armies simply swallowed up by it.

He heard a noise behind him and turned from the plant to look into Cheng's hard eyes. Behind him was another man. Thinner than Cheng, with longer hair, and eyes that were trying to hide the inner fear. Kim was not surprised to see the gang leader from the boat standing here before him. Indeed, he would have been more surprised if Cheng had failed to find him. There was a matter unsettled. A matter that had started on a ship when Kim had issued a mayday alert and when he had undogged the hatch to give the people below a chance. Cheng nodded grimly, as if in acknowledgement of the inevitability of this confrontation. Kim saw the narrow knife come out from under his black leather jacket and into his hand, noted the way the man balanced on the balls of his feet. The other man carried a gun, a small black pistol. Kim ignored the man with the gun.

"You have found me," he said to Cheng. It occurred to Kim that perhaps if he let Cheng act swiftly, the two men would leave without going inside and finding his cousin. He did not want her harmed. She had done nothing but try to help him and make it possible for him to survive in this foreign land he now wanted no part of. He had brought this trouble to her doorstep, deposited

it here in an act of ultimate disrespect. No, it was no use, Cheng would not leave without seeking Vhanna out too. He gazed into the man's eyes and saw something he knew well, the soul of a killer who took pleasure in the act. Had he been like that once? He sensed Cheng starting to move, starting the forward motion that would bring the knife into his gut. Kim's hand closed around the stock of the bonsai at his side and in one rapid motion he swung tree and pot into the space between himself and Cheng.

Even as he did so the door behind him flew open and a figure dressed entirely in black shot through it, soared across the open space, and lashed with one foot that cracked Cheng in the cheek. Vhanna descended, as if attached to some hidden line, to the deck flooring, lightly, rising on her toes with a deadly grace that left Kim stunned and confused. She spun to face the man with the gun, even as Cheng bounced hard off the deck railing with a loud grunt, and crumpled to the floor. The other man, eyes wide with a desperate fright, brought the gun up, trying to centre it on Vhanna's chest. Letting out an angry cry, she dropped her right hand in an outward sweep that caught the man's gun hand at the wrist, swept it aside and then drove forward with her left arm in a hard open-handed punch that caught him in the jaw. His head snapped back and the forward momentum of Vhanna's body shoved him up onto the deck railing. As he toppled over an arm shot out and grabbed Vhanna's elbow. In one frantic movement the man clutched tight and his falling weight pulled Vhanna from her feet, dragged her helplessly over the railing. The two fell away, neither making a sound.

Kim lunged to the rail. He could not remember how sheer the cliff was. It fell straight to the beach at least a hundred feet below. But Kim saw only the body of the man, arms and legs wriggling wildly as if to stem his fall, plunge down onto the sand with an audible thump. He looked about frantically and then saw his cousin halfway down the cliff face, dangling from a tangle of brush. She looked up at him and smiled. Although she was very pale, there was not a trace of panic in her expression. He smiled back. Then she rocked her body gently from one side to the other and, like a monkey, swung from one thick cluster of brush to another, reached a seam of broken rock and started working along it toward the stairs that ran from the deck to the beach. She was safe. Kim turned then and saw Cheng struggling up from where Vhanna's kick had sent him sprawling. He still held the knife. Kim rushed him.

chapter twenty-one

We roared down the lane toward Vhanna's house. Parked on the roadside several houses back was the mud-caked crummy. "Jesus," Monaghan said through clenched teeth. She stomped harder on the gas. Earlier, as we came into the built-up area, Monaghan had turned off the siren and lights and assumed a more sedate pace, fearful that the sound of the sirens might spur Cheng to either attack or flee. The gates to Vhanna's main driveway were closed.

"She didn't make it out," Monaghan said with a soft sigh of disappointment.

"Crash the gates," I said.

"What?"

"Crash through the gates. It'll start the alarms. Might scare him off. And we don't have time to piss around trying to get past her security."

Monaghan nodded. "Sorry, Gary," she said, with an almost hysterical laugh. She had been starting to decelerate, preparing to park in front of the house. Now she accelerated and Danchuk's Blazer struck the gates with its bumper. There was a screeching sound as steel ground against steel and then the gates blew open and the Blazer skidded across the brick driveway, almost slamming into the front of the garage. The hood flew up and steam boiled up out of the engine compartment. The sweet stench of engine coolant filled the cab as we jumped out. Bells were ringing wildly and I knew that in Jabronski's office alert lights and warning alarms were indicating a major break-in underway at Vhanna's. He would come. Not that it mattered. Today he would be far too late. It was down to Monaghan and me to sort things out. Or not. I feared we were too late.

We ran for the house. Monaghan had her service pistol drawn, held up in one hand so that it rested against her shoulder. I had argued for her to let me take the shotgun that was mounted on the rack between us, but she had refused. "My way or not at all, Elias. I'm not going to have civilians using Force guns illegally." There was nothing I could say to change her mind. If I had the chance, I would kill Cheng with my bare hands.

"Forget the front door," I shouted, and led the way around to the back. Cheng had not come this way. He would come from the beach, slithering up the cliff some-how in order to avoid the alarms. That was the way through Vhanna's defensive network. It was a way even I had used occasionally to avoid the alarms when Vhanna and I were having one of our all-too-frequent misunderstandings and I sought to reach her directly because it was impossible to discuss love and affairs of the heart over a phone or by letter.

We ran up a short set of stairs, vaulted over a low gate, and charged around the edge of the house to come out onto the main deck. A man wearing a black leather jacket whirled up from where a thin body lay on its side, one arm leaning against the rail, hand dangling limply back on a bent wrist. The jacketed man held a knife, blood slicking the thin steel blade. His eyes were dead and flat. Cheng.

Monaghan's pistol was up, aimed directly at the centre of his body. The barrel wavered, she was panting like someone who had just finished running a marathon. "Drop it," she said in a shaking voice. "Throw the knife down." I could only stand beside her, useless, the shotgun light years away. Cheng lunged to one side and then came at us with the knife reaching out toward Anne's stomach in an exploratory probe. "Stop," she yelled. He came on. Monaghan fired. And kept on firing until the breech clicked empty, smoke curling from around her fingers, expended brass shells rolling across the deck around my feet. I stepped over then and gently closed my hands on her wrist. Her hand gripped the pistol so tightly that the knuckles were almost blue. Her eyes wavered to my face. They were wide and uncomprehending. "He didn't stop," she whispered.

Slowly I unwound her stiff, resisting fingers from around the pistol and freed it from her grip. She stared at the carelessly tossed figure before her, its arms and legs cast wide, the torso leaking blood from several gaping holes. Each breath shuddered through her in a spasm. I slipped the gun into my coat pocket. Walked past the corpse of Cheng. Looked over the railing. Vhanna was there, limping slowly up the stairs toward the deck. Down on the beach, another man sprawled unnaturally, his neck at an impossible angle.

I rolled Kim over on his back. This time Cheng had got it right. There was nothing anyone could do for Vhanna's cousin. He was past caring. Monaghan stood exactly where I had left her, like a courageous war stat-

ue with sorrow-wracked eyes and a determined
demeanour looking down upon the slain. Eyes fixed on
Cheng's body. His blood drained across the deck and
mingled with Kim's. I turned away and descended the
steps toward Vhanna. Despite everything we had not
been too late.

chapter twenty-two

Thirteen days gone by and an auspicious moment despite the unlucky amount of time passed. Vhanna and I walked along a sweeping curve of white sand brushed by a blue ocean that rolled in with long slicks of sound and then sucked back out with a throaty rasp. Overhead, gulls whirled and shrieked at each other like so many playground bullies angling for an advantage. At the edge of the tide line, small shorebirds skittered about, and beside us, Fergus carefully appraised his chances of catching game or simply sending them into terrified flight. I tapped the side of my leg to let him know that such aggressive behaviour would be considered dimly this fine morning.

Much had happened in the aftermath of Cheng's blood-soaked attack on Vhanna's house. Kim, Cheng, and the accomplice had all perished. The fall down the cliff had broken the accomplice's neck and the man remained unidentified, Monaghan's bullets had riddled

Cheng, Kim had died on Cheng's blade. Nothing could undo that terrible sequence of events. Nothing could rid Vhanna's home of their ghosts.

As for Corporal Lee, he was currently suspended, free on bail, and facing multiple charges for various types of conspiracy. Also some charges that Ray Bellows thought unlikely to succeed that named him as an accessory to the murders of Ian McCutcheon, Daryl McCutcheon, and Kim Hoai.

Constable Anne Monaghan had been suspended with pay pending the outcome of an investigation into her conduct, but Bellows said everyone generally agreed that Cheng had only come to justice because of her actions. Even Danchuk, whose Blazer was still undergoing extensive repairs over at the Petro-Canada station, was singing Monaghan's praises. Bellows believed that, in the end, the entire matter of her running off with me without any authority from her commanding officer would be quietly swept aside in light of the results produced.

Eleven days after the shooting I had gone to visit Monaghan. She had been outside her small house, wearing a black halter and denim shorts that rose high on her thighs. Her pale skin, sprayed with brown freckles, reddened in the sun as she pulled weeds out of a bed of scorched-looking lettuce and endive plants. Monaghan had poured an insipid-tasting Lucky Lager for each of us into ice-frosted glasses dragged out of her fridge. We stood in the yard, on the long grass that she never seemed to find the time to mow, and drank beer together.

There was a great silence between us, nothing frivolous to say. So I told her of a Canadian sniper in Cyprus and a day when a Turkish soldier decided to try shooting across the Green Line with his automatic weapon at a small cluster of Greek children that had strayed too close in pursuit of a bouncing soccer ball.

The sniper ended the game with a slug that blew a red mist from the Turkish soldier's head into the air while the children fled in terror back to their parents. Nothing was said to the sniper. His action went entirely unacknowledged. But perhaps the Green Line became a little safer that day in Nicosia. Perhaps not. In the intervening years, nothing seems clearer, the implications of every violent act becomes more opaque.

"It was clear what you did, Anne. It was a righteous shoot." Easy words to say. I didn't have to live with them. Anne had shaken her head, gone back to weeding. I returned to the Land Rover and drove away knowing there was nothing anyone could say to Anne Monaghan that would ease away the uncertainty. Time maybe, but words would not.

Like Monaghan, Vhanna carried on in silence. I had tried to open opportunities for her to express the pain, sorrow, rage, and anger she must feel over the loss of Kim — the family finally found — and the fact that she had killed a man. But she let no emotion through. Vhanna was stoic and calm, like a Buddhist monk sweeping the sand to avoid harming insects with the fall of his step. She offered up nothing and insisted on keeping to herself.

For the first two days after the attack, Vhanna had moved to *Artemis* while Jabronski oversaw the cleaning up of her house. Jabronski had understood. The blood had been carefully cleaned away, not a dry drop or even a fleck of red remaining. Gates repaired. "Kid has to live with the memories," Jabronski had said harshly to me when I came to check on the work, "I'll not let her live with physical signs." He looked at me hard, eyes unblinking. "Makes you want to start carrying a gun in this business. What the hell could I have done for her? I came as fast as I could, but what could I have done?" I patted his shoulder, shared his sense of helplessness. I had stood to one side while Monaghan's pistol barked. I could not imagine what Vhanna had done. Going up against Cheng's knife and the other man's gun with nothing but her body, her feet and hands employing the Tai Chi fighting style that she had practised so religiously and did so even more regularly now. I would have gone in with bare hands to fight for her, but I also knew that in doing so I undoubtedly would have failed. Vhanna had failed, too, in the end. Kim was dead. But she had done all anyone could have and then some. And now she was living back in the house, behaving as if nothing had happened there. The only sign remaining was the small ceramic urn on her fireplace mantle that contained the ashes of her cousin.

"What will you do?" I had asked her when the funeral parlour delivered them to her home.

She looked at me gravely. "Kim was not at home here. There is nowhere here to scatter them that would give him peace."

I looked off from the deck that to me would forever be a place of death toward a sun-soaked sea that seemed at odds with the line of my thoughts. An ocean and sky chiselled out of identical shades of grey slate would have been more apt. "When?"

Vhanna touched my arm. "Soon. It is a matter best dealt with."

"Will you stay long?" I asked, meaning, *Will you try looking again?*

She ignored the question. "You know about the mines. You understand them," she said. Although her tone was soft there was an angry edge lurking there, as if having such knowledge was to carry a form of blame. I had been a soldier. I had set mines in training exercises. More importantly, I had removed them by the hundreds. One mine at a time, probing carefully with fingers and a dull blade to find the fuses so they could be deactivated.

Yes, I understood land mines. I had held a girl in my arms as her life bled away. Bombs, mines, all the same. "Kim would want no legacy, but I am going to give him one that is unnamed." She spoke of a fund to hire and train Khmer to remove mines from the farm fields and rice paddies to bring them back into productivity.

"I could help," I said. "As you say, I understand them." Vhanna brushed my cheek with her fingers and took my hand. Working for a foundation, I thought. Good charitable labour, something a remittance man could engage in without the bother of profit and loss considerations, business taxes, hiring staff, or — God forbid — working for others. Perhaps Tully, realizing the import of this new endeavour, would even let me resign as the community coroner. Much of the past few days had been spent filing the endless reports on the deaths arising out of this tragic affair. My timing in getting the reports completed had barely been sufficient to mollify Dr. Harris. I had no doubt that the previous esteem in which he had held me was much reduced. Not that I much cared. At the moment I was tired of this business of death.

"There they are," Vhanna said. Her eyes regarded me warmly. I squeezed her hand and wished it could always be like this. I began to consider this foundation idea to be a better one all the time.

Down the beach, where a parking lot faced the water — the same spot where Kim had intercepted us that early morning with the toss of stones and Vhanna had taken him into hiding — three figures stepped out onto the sand. A woman with grey hair that lifted on the breeze, a man with the hard bronzed look of a mariner, a small figure with long, straight black hair who walked between them and held a hand of each in her own. The hearing had gone as hoped and Hui Huang was now a temporary ward of the province placed into foster care with Lars and Frieda Janson. Much still remained to be done. There would be more hearings to seek permanent refugee status for Hui, to build a home for her here. Lars and Freida were willing to provide that home and it seemed Hui was also willing for it to be like that.

Vhanna and I walked up to meet them. Fergus trotted ahead, stubby tail wagging in recognition. When he reached the three of them, Fergus squatted on his haunches before Hui and pressed his head against the leg of her new jeans. Even from a distance, I heard her small giggle and her hand lightly brushed Fergus's head. "He normally doesn't care for children," I said softly.

Vhanna chuckled at that. When I looked over she gave me a mocking grin.

"What?" I said.

She squeezed my hand and stood up to kiss me lightly on the cheek. Led me over to the three people and dog. Hui slipped her hands free of her foster parents and walked shyly up to me, eyes lowered slightly, arms gangly at her sides. When we faced each other she reached out and took my right hand in both of hers, held it. Then she looked up at me and her face broke into a wide, innocent smile. She shook my hand, squeezed it tight, and then of her own accord released it.

As if sensing the moment, Fergus broke from our ranks and raced after a flock of shorebirds browsing in foam at the edge of the surf line. His paws threw back a spray of sand with each wild stride, ears flapping urgently in time to each forward lunge of his body. Behind him, Hui ran with an awkward gait through a haze of mist drawn up out of the damp sand by the hot sun. Small birds scattered before dog and child in a flurry of white wings soaring off across the white-frosted deep blue waves toward a dazzlingly blue sky.

About the Author

Hands Like Clouds, the first Elias McCann mystery, was the recipient of the Crime Writers of Canada's Year 2000 Arthur Ellis Award for Best First Novel. In addition to writing fiction, Mark Zuehlke has published many non-fiction works. These include: *Scoundrels, Dreamers & Second Sons: British Remittance Men in Western Canada* (Dundurn, 2001), two books on Canadian participation in the World War II Italian Campaign — *Ortona: Canada's Epic World War II Battle*, and *The Liri Valley: Canada's World War II Breakthrough to Rome* — as well as *The Canadian Military Atlas: The Nation's Battlefields from the French-Indian Wars to Kosovo*, and *The Gallant Cause: Canadians in the Spanish Civil War, 1936–939*. He lives in Victoria.